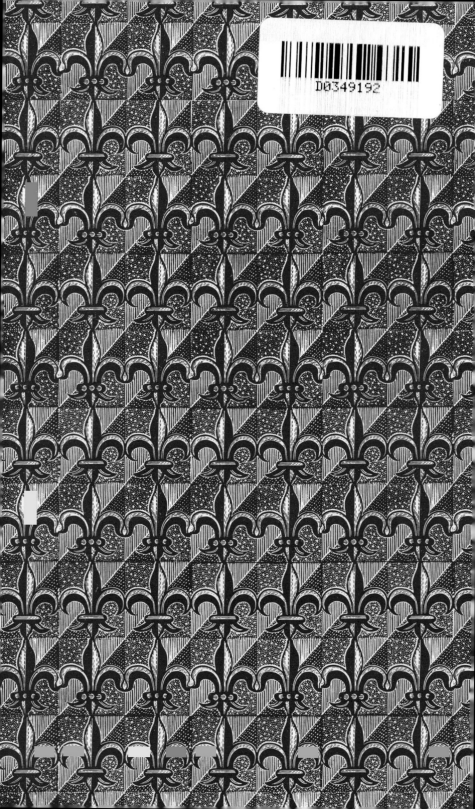

A
GENERATION
OF THE
DARK HEART

By the same author
Mag

A GENERATION OF THE DARK HEART

•

James Sorel-Cameron

•

SINCLAIR-STEVENSON

First published in Great Britain by
Sinclair-Stevenson Limited
7/8 Kendrick Mews
London   SW7 3HG, England

British Library Cataloguing in Publication Data
A CIP catalogue record for this book is available from the British Library.
ISBN: 1 85619 094 3

Typeset by Phoenix Photosetting, Chatham, Kent
Printed and bound in Great Britain by Butler & Tanner Ltd, Frome, Somerset

Contents

> Let us not then pursue. . .
>
> . . . our state
> Of splendid vassalage, but rather seek
> Our own good from ourselves, and from our own
> Live to our selves, though in this vast recess,
> Free, and to none accountable, preferring
> Hard liberty before the easie yoke
> Of servile pomp. Our greatness will appear
> Then most conspicuous, when great things of small,
> Useful of hurtful, prosperous of adverse
> We can create, and in what place so e'er
> Thrive under evil, and work ease out of pain
> Through labor and indurance. This deep world
> Of darkness do we dread?

JOHN MILTON *Paradise Lost*. Book II.

PROLOGUE

A love story.

To begin at the end.

A man and a woman are engaged in the act of love. About them the world is ending in a tempest of violence; perhaps not everyone's world, but their world certainly; the world in which they have their meaning.

He has made this world. He has imposed himself upon it, from a dark beginning until he has brought everything within it into alignment with his own fantasy. He is a madman, who has made everything, everyone, conform to his insanity.

She is a subject of this world, a victim, therefore his victim, therefore the subject of his fantasies.

What is happening between them is not, therefore, an act of love in the literal sense, for he has imposed it upon her, not just at the moment he physically possesses her, but in the whole circumstance of her being with him, of her being who she is; she has no active part in it at all: neither, strictly, is it a rape, for she has been the subject of this man's fantasy for so long that she has no real independence of it, no will nor individuality to oppose him. It is the exercise of a monstrous egotism upon a blank receptacle of that egotism. It is the most dismal of human engagements imaginable: the act of love reduced not merely to a casual, violent release of over-charged masculinity, but to a final flourishing justification for a generation of cruelty and murder, of masculine power enshrined as a final truth, of a life-long love-affair with death.

Within her, as she receives him, however, she finds a last final strength to resist him. She does so by love, by accepting, in spite of everything, what he does to her as an act of love, and by communicating this to him.

The moment he becomes her lover, he is destroyed.

Her name is Rachel.

A love story.

GERMINATION

A QUIET CHILDHOOD

I will tell you everything, Rachel, so that you may know me as I am, as I have always been. Don't be afraid.

High summer. Across the low bowl of farmlands and small towns across the south, purple clouds gathered, dense and moving before a heavy wind, shifting and piling their weight. In still spaces at the bottom of the night, the lightning broke over the landscape, exposing it in long moments of blue nudity; and behind the lightning came long growls of thunder, rising from the limits of audibility to vibrate in every opening. The storm massed, but the rain did not break. The dusty earth waited.

His father would remember this hour vividly, even when he had forgotten everything else. He stood looking out at the massing storm. He seemed able to draw no conclusions from it. It was merely the hour of his attendance upon his wife's long turning down the spiral of parturition. He was a man generally given to conclusions, but the weather that night expressed with factual bluntness his waiting, his wife's waiting, their endurance, the endurance that he sensed, against all his wishfulness, to be at the heart of his life, of all life, here made explicit. His solitude and his insignificance before the shocks and repression of the storm seemed inevitable.

In the depth of the night, they came and told him that he had a new son, that all was well. He went in to his wife, kissed her heavy face, held the scrap of new life in its blanket. It lay still and tiny, strange. A rise of emotion took him briefly. It's the beginning of something, he said to himself, at least that. He did not think of the little thing as a person, just as a beginning; as if a line was drawn somewhere on a blank sheet of paper, a title-page, the opening of a new account.

As he went home through the storm-dark, large spots of rain fell like tears.

They named him Richard. Various diminutives and variations were, in his infancy, tried upon him – Rich, Richie, Dickie: none adhered to him; nor even perhaps Richard. Somehow they did not seem to have got his name right.

His mother watched his infancy, noted the differences from his elder brother and sister: his self-absorption, his strange quietness. She thought at times that he was going to be tremendously intelligent, at times that he was slow, handicapped in some way. She tended him scrupulously, but he seemed to need little of the attention that Paul and Susan had needed at his age. She noted how her husband, Kenneth, seemed more interested in Richard than he had been in either of the others, would take him often on his knee, would sit on the floor and arrange toys for him. It was his lack of demands for attention, she thought, that Kenneth rewarded; the passivity that allowed the father to build fantasies upon him. She watched this and began to distrust it, begun to distrust the quiet, solid child who submitted to his father's dandling with a growing watchfulness.

In due time she took Richard down to school. He proved neither stupid nor brilliant. He was a solitary little boy, the teacher said, happiest when working and playing on his own. She once told his mother that she thought there was a lot hidden away in that little head of his, if only we knew how to get at it; but by then, Gwen Tollman was only glad to be able to believe that her son was normal, was growing up into a normal boy: what more could you want? Various interests and hobbies were offered to him, supported by seasonal presents, but nothing seemed to catch his interest. He would explore his new toys with curiosity, but he never seemed to make them a part of himself.

He passed into senior school without visible trauma. By that time, Paul was sixteen and Susan fourteen, and they were both showing signs of awkward adolescence, giving little Richard a shadow in the attention of his family in which he was quite content to sit. Whilst she, their mother, struggled to try to make Paul, who was clever, take his education seriously, and whilst she registered her considerable anger at the love-bites on Susan's neck, Richard would sit apart watching television, or go up to his room to read a comic.

Sometimes, if the rows grew dangerous, Kenneth would go up and sit with Richard, would talk to him, look at his comics, play board games with him. Then Gwen began to grow resentful, longed for some of her husband's quietude to be shared with her, for her own resources seemed at times to be pathetically limited. And as they spent more time together, Kenneth grew to have a marked preferential affection for his youngest child; and as this happened, Gwen began to grow jealous of Richard; and the jealousy quickly, and for no logical reason, grew into a fear of him. She could never catch this fear clearly enough to take hold of it and explain it to herself; but she found herself nervous under the shadow of this strange still child, whose strangeness and stillness seemed to be accruing a power that she did not like.

The senior school was large. Its organisation and efficiency were continually under the pressures of cynical, overstretched staff and ill-disciplined, ill-motivated pupils. In the corridors and out in the yard, and in the classrooms of the weaker teachers, lurked a depressing anarchy, of motiveless aggression and of its inverse, which was an instinctive boredom with all that the school, and the system of which it was a part, was trying to effect. It was a dull place at best: at worst a place of hidden viciousness and terror.

He passed five years at this establishment without it making any apparent mark upon him. He did not join in with the sporting or cultural activities, such as they were, his academic progress was unremarkable, and few of the staff recognised him as anything other than a quiet face amongst many others. He fulfilled what was required of him, although none of it seemed to adhere to him. Few of them could remember his face a year after he had left. He slipped through the system without touching it in any serious way.

Amongst his contemporaries, however, Richard Tollman was not the blank space that his teachers assumed him to be. He made no friends, established no loyalties, no camaraderies; but he managed, nevertheless, always to be there, somehow. At the darkest edges of the school, he stood like a shadow.

He did not himself smoke, but he was there, this dark-haired, dumpy boy, almost from his first day in the school, on the edge of the gang of smokers who crammed into the damp littered spaces between blind walls. At first they suspected him, told him to go away. He went, but was there the next day. They threatened him with violence, and he looked at them as if their threats had nothing to do with him. If they told him to go away, he went; but he always came back, the next day, the next week, stood there, watching them. They grew used to him, grew interested in him. They offered him cigarettes, but he always refused. They posted him as look-out, although his attention always wandered back to them. They tried to send him out to buy their cigarettes, to hide them if an inspection was threatened, but he would have nothing to do with that. He never joined in with their conversations, although he always seemed to listen in. They tolerated him.

Later he began to go out with the petty thieves and vandals, but he never joined them. If pressed seriously to prove himself, he would leave. When he was older, he went with the drinkers and the sniffers; or rather, he would turn up where they were and sit or stand about. Those of them who were more aware distrusted him, imagined him one day leading the authorities into their midst. But he only ever wanted to watch, to listen, to mark their degradations and their pleasures. He ran with them from the snatching at shop counters, trampled with them across flower beds. He crouched down and peered as they pulled the clothes off befuddled girls and achieved their first blundering copulations. He watched them

11

spinning off into their intoxications. He watched them gasp and vomit, watched them shit in clammy bus shelters. He watched them batter themselves at walls and windows, trying to spoil the world as they were spoiled.

Some of them, individually, tried to take him into their confidence, but this too led him to retreat. His distances and his motives remained immaculate. The watching was all. It absorbed him completely, satisfied him more than they ever were satisfied. They were striving always to prove themselves against an inimical world: he never for a moment imagined that he had anything to prove.

He might have watched in secret, but he never did. He wanted them to be aware of him. Whoever he watched knew that he was being watched. Sometimes he was driven away. Sometimes, increasingly, they permitted his watching, began to perform for him, do things they would not have done without the shadow of his attendance. He was careful to show neither disgust nor, more importantly, approval at what they showed him. He watched with his head tilted, his lips tight, his breathing even. Sometimes they waited for him and, if he did not appear, the evening's degradations were aborted and they went limply home. He had become the focus of their lives beyond the tattered boundaries of their upbringings. Although he hardly ever spoke to them, although they hardly knew who he was, he had become their leader.

His interest was sharpest when there was fighting. He would watch scrupulously when the arguments and insults slipped over the edge, when the obscenities were backed with a shove, when fists clenched and jabbed, when bodies locked and fingers clawed at hair and skin, when the soft weights of bellies and genitals were screwed about the stab of a metal bootcap, when cheeks were opened with rings, when the little knives flicked at eyeballs.

One sour winter's day, a black boy was kicked down, catching the back of his head on a metal door edge. His head split and he died there on the playground writhing and arching his spine, grabbing with his hands as the strength left them, his eyes going wider and wider as if they would burst out of his head. Everybody fled, apart from Richard Tollman who stayed and watched him die, only moving away when the teachers came to sort it out, to try and find out what had happened. He was deeply moved by this experience. He had seen, at last, the reality of life stripped down and struggling, reduced to its essential, pure and beautiful, total and final. He acquired a great truth that day.

He was short and dark-haired. He was solidly built, but the bulk might have been fat. He grew little in his five years at the school, adolescence merely confirming his features, setting them in him. He had never really looked like a child should look and, as he approached manhood, he never acquired any definite masculinity.

At home, he watched television for hours on end, but never minded if his mother came in and turned the set off, sent him away to do the something useful she always spoke of but never specified. To Gwen Tollman, when she cleaned his room, it seemed like the room of a lodger. It made her almost glad of the mess of Paul's room and Susan's room, in spite of the disgusting evidences which she occasionally unearthed there.

Paul, at the age of sixteen, announced that he had had enough of education. He was a serious disappointment to everyone but himself. His father found him a job in the warehouse of the firm at which he worked, but Paul was a poor employee, hung on for the wage packet but did as little as he could get away with to earn it. At least once a week he got drunk, fell through the front door in the early hours and, if they were lucky, vomited accurately. Gwen decided when he was eighteen that he ought to leave home, if that was how he wanted to lead his life; but he showed no inclination to leave, was quite happy with his life. Even when he lost his job he was not seriously concerned. He loafed about the house more, played loud music and smoked, had unpleasant friends round, grew flabby and stupid.

Richard was the only one who could provoke him out of his lethargy, and then only into violence. For some reason, Paul came to hate his brother with a venom directly proportional to its irrationality. In the long family rows of which he was often the centre, when the pressure came hard upon him, it was Richard he turned upon, Richard who never said a word, who sat there and got on with his life as if it was all happening somewhere else. Somehow Paul felt it was all Richard's fault. Whenever any corner of self-disgust caught Paul, it was Richard who came to mind, Richard who seemed to be accusing him, Richard who was in some way storing it all up to use against him, Richard who was driving him down below the surface of his life from where he could only fight his way out. He once went into Richard's room and attacked him, knelt over him and punched him, forced open his mouth and dribbled spit into it. Their parents were out, so Richard had no protection from this. Only when he had made him cry, which took a long, long time, did Paul release him, going then into his own room and breaking things, before going and stealing some money from their parents' room and leaving to get drunk.

He had, of course, faked the tears. Paul's violence had stimulated him strangely. He did not resent it, any more than he would have resented an illness. He felt that he had come near to something strong when Paul had been hurting and humiliating him. He found, on reflection, that he despised Paul for not being up to the logic of his strength.

Gwen Tollman asked Paul why he hated his brother so much. Paul gave no coherent answer, grew surly at the question, and that frightened Gwen, for she too could give no coherent answer to why she disliked her youngest child. Paul once said he thought Richard was going to be queer, and Gwen jumped inside at this possibility, felt a terrible guilt for she believed the mythology which asserted that homosexuals were most likely moulded in their relationships with their mothers. She tried to talk to Richard, explained the mechanics of sex to him, tried to offer him affection, but was defeated as always by his watching, his silent assessment of her.

'Do you like girls?' she had asked. He was fourteen at the time.

'They're all right,' he had said, as if asked if he liked some sort of food.

'Do you like boys more than girls?'

'I suppose so.'

'Why?'

'Boys do things,' he said.

'What sort of things, Richard?'

'I don't know . . . fight, things like that.'

She had to leave shortly, to go into her bedroom and cry.

At about this time, Richard began to go out in the evenings, to stay out late. Gwen watched minutely but could find no evidence of any of the vices she anticipated. She asked where he had been.

'Hanging about . . . with some friends . . . up at the park . . .'

When she confined him to the house, he stayed in, never once defied her.

A week later he would ask, 'Can I go out again yet?'

'Where to?'

'With some friends. Up at the park.'

Gwen dreaded the police arriving, some secret being exposed, her son at the centre of something frightful and shameful; and, although the fear was never realised, it would not go away; it grew, rather, in the mounting silence.

By the time she was fifteen, Susan Tollman was well known. Without beauty or grace, she compensated by her availability. Gwen watched her daughter wound up with sex like an alarm clock. By the time she was seventeen, her mother had given up trying to make her aware of what she was becoming, feeling that if Susan ever came to a sense of her degradation, she would fall apart. If only she had been able to talk to the girl; but Susan lied and lied and lied, when there were used condoms under her bed, when she came back in the early hours of the morning, tipped out of some filthy car, when she was discovered by a neighbour against a shed door with her jeans round her ankles and a boy shunting himself at her, it was always, always, 'We weren't doing anything, just kissing, just having a bit of a cuddle. What's wrong with that?' The lies were cynical: she could not have seriously thought they would be believed. She lied merely to push her mother away from her. If only there had been some regular boyfriend, if only there had been some sign of an involvement, but she was just a receptacle, her mother knew, for exploitation and, soon enough, for contempt; and Susan was finally too stupid to be aware of herself as other than a bundle of pleasures to be gratified.

Richard must surely have seen and known what went on; the quiet watching boy who you didn't know was in the house until you had been back an hour and were convinced that you were on your own. Gwen might have confronted him about it, but, not only did she feel that she would have got nothing from him, she also shrank back from the possibilities of Richard's knowledge of what his sister got up to, a knowledge that however detached it might appear, like all his knowledge, had the smell of complicity to it.

She was right, of course. He had appeared one afternoon at Susan's bedroom door and had stood watching his sister dumped on her bed under one of Paul's drinking companions. It was an image of blunt ugliness. He saw his sister's flabby heaving and imagined her having some sort of sick fit. He watched the squeezing of the man's pallid buttocks and imagined ramming something sharp and fanged between them.

Susan became aware of him slowly, a change in the temperature, a realisation that made the shoving of the man within her an irrelevance. She shook him, hit him until he stopped. He glanced back, swore, leapt up and stumbled about, his cock like a bloated leech, trying to cover himself, to effect some sort of escape. Richard stood and watched and Susan watched back, sitting up, not even bothering to cover herself: it was too late for that. She was very afraid of him suddenly. Somehow his appearance was worse than her mother or father's would have been.

'Richard?' she said. 'Please, Richard. I'll give you ten

pounds. I'll give you anything you want. You can stay and watch if you want to. Please, Richard, please.'

He frowned, wondering what it was that she was pleading for; and indeed, as she thought about it, she didn't know herself. Pleading was merely her first, instinctive reaction. Eventually Richard moved away, and they heard him going downstairs, turning on the television. The man finished his dressing and left with hardly another word. Susan had gone quiet, had huddled herself up and was no longer interested in him anyway. After he had gone she struggled to pluck up the courage to go down and face her brother; but she did not find it and, in time, their mother returned from work and the opportunity was lost.

Thereafter, whenever Susan brought someone back to her room, she checked carefully to find out if Richard was in the house or not. If he was there, she would say, 'Des and I are going to go into my room for a bit now, Richard. You won't come in, will you?' And he never did, but she felt it necessary to say this to him, almost as if she was asking his permission. And in her love-making, she was always aware of him, downstairs, through the wall, listening. And it always made her afraid to think of him there, and the fear, she found, was an exciting fear: she preferred him to be there. At moments she cried out louder and louder, hoping that he would come again to her door.

One afternoon when he was fifteen and she eighteen, working then at the till of a local store, she came back home alone and found him there. She drifted about the house restlessly, came into his bedroom and sat on the end of his bed, tried to raise conversation with him. Eventually, she asked him if he'd like to come into her bedroom for a bit.

'What for?' he asked.

'Oh, just to talk, you know. I've got some new music that you should listen to.'

After a long moment's thought, he rose and followed her through. She put on the music, lit a cigarette, asked if he minded if she got changed. He watched as she took off her overall, as she took off her bra, plumped and lifted her breasts as if examining them. She asked him if he had a girlfriend yet. She asked him if he had ever done it with a girl. She asked him if he had ever wanted to do it. His negatives were clear and cold.

'You ought to find some girl who'd do it with you, Richard,' she said. 'You're a bit good-looking, you know.'

He regarded her nakedness clearly, then began to laugh a little, just a little. She asked him what was wrong.

'You want me to do it with you, don't you, Susan?'

She smiled at him, scratched idly inside her knickers.

'You don't want to do it with me, do you, Richard?'

'No,' he said, 'I don't.'

Then she grew angry, grabbed the clothes she had just shed and pulled them back over her. She told him to get out, to fuck off, to go away and wank himself off. He didn't go at once, watched her anger until it broke into tears, then went back into his own room and closed the door.

He had, once or twice, masturbated. Waking with an erection, he had filled his mind with images of killing, and toiled a little discharge out into a tissue. He did not enjoy it, was motivated by curiosity only. The moment the spasm became unstoppable, he loathed it, loathed the shuddering pulse that he had no control over, loathed the aching vacancy that followed. It was like squeezing pus from an infection. Susan's offer he had found funny.

★   ★   ★

19

Within six months Susan had become pregnant, had pretended it wasn't happening long enough to lose the option of an abortion, and was now desperately trying to find someone to marry her, or let her live with him, or anything to get her out of that house once and for all. She would go under any circumstances. Paul's drinking was becoming serious enough to rule out any hope of employment. Richard was about to leave school with not the remotest idea of what he wanted to do with his life, without the remotest aspiration to activate his life in any direction. Gwen Tollman fought and fought to try to regain some sort of dignity to her home, grew progressively shrill and aggressive; and then her spectator husband broke down, sitting about, unable to go to work, not shaving, not even getting out of bed some mornings.

Kenneth's breakdown was so predictable as to be banal. He had become increasingly withdrawn as the family turmoils escalated. Whenever Gwen made the slightest attempt to involve him, he shrank further and further back. The angrier she grew, the tighter he withdrew; until one day the withdrawal was no longer strategic, but pathological. His only communication up to then had been with Richard, if it could be called communication. He went up and sat with his youngest son, no longer talking to him or playing games, just sitting up there and sighing, whilst Richard watched him.

Once, as he began to lose his grip finally, he had said to her, 'Richard is the only one who understands anything in this house.'

'What does he understand, Kenneth?'

'He understands everything. He's going to be a great man one day. Out of all this, a great man will come, do you realise that?'

She turned to her younger son who sat mute at the

table, eating neatly and precisely as he always ate. 'Well, Richard? D'you hear what your father says about you?'

'Yes,' was all she got, a response that didn't even disturb his eating.

Gwen went into the kitchen and broke the most valuable thing she could find to break, waited for someone to come through to the sound of the smashing, but no one came.

Richard, meanwhile, was considering how he might put his father out of his misery, telling himself that he would be doing everyone a favour. The nobility of the motives he felt soon became lost in the intimate details of how he might achieve this. There would be too much blood, he considered: it wasn't worth it.

The day Kenneth Tollman went into hospital, Gwen came home with a sense of relief, feeling better than she had felt in months. With her husband out of the way, she felt she could face her other problems squarely. She did not notice anything strange about the house for some hours. She noticed that the money was missing, but assumed that Paul had found out her latest hiding-place. Then she began to grow suspicious. She searched the house. Kenneth's camera was gone. The desk in the sitting room had been carefully plundered of bank books. She went up to Richard's room and noticed that many of his clothes were gone. Her holdall had gone.

When Susan and Paul came home for supper, which they did most evenings before setting out on their various entertainments, she told them, 'Richard's gone. He's taken everything of value and packed his bag and gone.'

They looked at her, and at each other.

'Thank God for that,' Paul said. 'I hope the little cunt stays away for good.'

21

Susan began to snuffle.

'What are you blubbering about, you silly bitch?' Paul said.

'I . . . I'm just . . . just glad he's gone, that's all.'

Gwen Tollman looked at them both. She had not known what to do about Richard's flight. She had been numbed by it. But, feeding off the reactions of Paul and Susan, she too felt a relief so great that it dwarfed everything else around her. She too began to cry. Susan came and hugged her, and Paul sat staring into his plate with his head in his hands, hissing through his teeth.

I wonder often what I would have done with your privilege, Rachel, how I would have grown in the nurture of power and wealth. I do not think it would have made much difference. We are what we are and, if we are strong, where we come from does not matter.

My childhood was uneventful and, I suppose, contented. I certainly have nothing with which to reproach my parents, nor even my brother and sister. If, at times, they tried to hurt me I understood, even then, that they had many hurts of their own, and it is the nature of family life that such hurts are exercised on those within easiest reach.

By my brother and sister, I was given a profound and intimate education in human weakness for which, in retrospect, I am grateful. Neither of them ever grew up, ever had any awareness of themselves as part of anything beyond themselves. They defined themselves as objects capable of receiving pleasure and set forth with a single-minded urgency for self-gratification. In this, they were overwhelmingly ordinary, I suppose.

My awareness grew under their examples. I knew that I was different when I knew that I would never, could never, take delight in any merely physical gratification. Truly, there was never anything that I seemed to want, because I knew that to want something would be in some way to be given it; and to be given it would be to put myself under obligation, to give other people access to me; and I never imagined anything that I could want that would have been worth such vulnerability.

As soon as I had any definite idea of myself, I knew that I had to be immaculate, that to survive in the world, in any world, first of all I had to keep myself impregnable. I had to be sure that whatever happened externally, within me I would remain untouched. It was not fear. It was never fear. I knew, as soon as I knew anything, that it was strength. If it had been fear, I would never have been able to do anything with it.

You know what happened to them, Rachel. It happened to thousands, to millions. It does not touch me. Once I left them, I was nothing to do with them any more.

SOME SIGHTINGS OF HIM IN THE CITY

He went to a city and lost himself within it.

In a house, no more now than a nest of hardboard-walled boxes, he found a lodging for a season, set up his clear private space up under the roof-slope.

Next to him, two boys, younger than he was, one black, one white, lovers, pedalled a successful entertainment for the more reckless gutter-crawlers in a room with no furniture, mattresses wall-to-wall, lurid drapes, mirrors, garments discarded for effect and for ready use. They would go out once or twice a week to the centre of the city, amongst the pubs and restaurants, the dance-halls and opera houses. They were pretty and they sustained a line in vulnerability that was particularly appealing to a certain type, the type they fed upon. They could cry and cower, and their visitors, falling into fantasies of strength and corruption, were fleeced with scrupulous thoroughness, pushed out shriven and trembling into the night. They were professional in all things, and coped ruthlessly with the violence they not infrequently invoked in their trade. They were expert in exotic fighting skills. They could switch in a second from quivering naked waifs, dripping with degradation, to bolt-hard thugs who could stun with the stab of a hand, who would drag some fat victim down the long stair-cases, through a zigzag of alleys to a derelict site, to leave him amongst the rubble. They did not kill their victims, or not intentionally, just dumped them. In time, one of them would surely return primed for revenge. They made considerable amounts of money, but never spent it on anything more than vanities. They lived in a world where nothing had value beyond its immediate use, where the pursuit of life was abandoned to the addiction of shocks and sensations. They had in this a cold purity. They were beyond the claim of anything.

They had noted the squat youth in the next box when he arrived, but neglected him soon enough. His quietness, the way he seemed to move in a gathering shadow, led them to disregard him at first. But the house had a sort of community; it held a shuddering mass of terrors and terminal ecstasies which generated a com-munity, if only of mutual paranoia. Thus the quiet youth became, in time, distinct. The silence of his room, the absolute solitude of it, became palpable. It did not take them long to suspect that they were watched from this silence, and thus its emptiness became a part of what they did, a part that they quickly determined to confront and expose.

They went down to the street and stood in a doorway to make their plan. They waited until he had gone out, hours they waited; then they went up to his room and broke their way in. The emptiness of the room – bed, chair, clothes, no books, no papers – confirmed their suspicions. They confirmed also the spy hole through the partition wall. They posted themselves, one in his room, one in an empty box on the floor below, and waited, waited hours for his return.

He came up the stairs quickly and soundlessly, but they were ready. He knew at once that he had been invaded. He turned, but heard the fast pursuit behind him. He slipped into his room and into a stranglehold that was half an inch, half an ounce away from snapping his spine, with the other close upon him, the pretty face pushed into his, the breath sweet, the eyes glittering, the tongue active upon his sweating face, the hands meanwhile opening his trousers, pressing his testicles together like ripe fruit.

'Who are you?' they asked him. 'Who are you?' But they did not want an answer at once, did not give him enough throat to make one. The question was rhetorical: by crushing him, they sought to squeeze the answer from him physically, as if his humanity stretched to bursting would make him real to them. When the pressure of the pain made him sag, they released him. One stood against the door, one sat on his bed, and they watched him squirm and coil and retch, curious, exchanging glances, puzzled; for they had not found him out.

They brought him water and revived him. And when he was revived, he closed up again, shuffled into his silence. They hit him from time to time with their careful expertise and, although they could generate any amount of physical response, they could do no more than this.

'Shall I fuck him?' one asked.

'If you want to,' the other replied. But wanting was not the motive for this interrogation. They grew increasingly uncomfortable with the situation, wanted it resolved. The longer they watched, the longer they struggled at him, the less they seemed to reach him and the more difficult the situation became. They had thought that they knew people, that their cynicism and violence could reduce anyone to their terms. They began to become nervous.

'Just tell us who you are and we'll leave you alone,' they said at last, repeated it, tended him and pleaded with him. At last he came to the surface from which their violence had driven him. They apologised for hurting him. 'Just tell us who you are. Just tell us.'

He lifted his face and seemed to look over them, through them. 'I am nothing,' he said, 'nothing at all. You could kill me if you wanted and it wouldn't mean anything.'

This frightened them. They went to hurt him again, but held back, made reflective for the first time that either of them could recall, their instincts brought into the open, made explicit, squirming. They were unhappy. They looked at each other. They held hands, both knowing that they would have to finish him; but it would have to be a cold act, and neither, at this moment, had the stomach for that. They held hands to give each other courage.

He had been moving restlessly since they had first released him, and therefore they neglected his movements, not noticing how they had become personal. Then there was a glint, a spray of liquid. Then there was nothing but the white pain of the bleach in their eyes. Then there were the bars of pain where he struck their heads with something heavy and metallic. Then there was nothing.

It had been his fault, of course. He had watched in secret, had come to admire them, to take pleasure in their way of sex which seemed strong to him, an assertion rather than

27

submission of themselves, their cocks like flexed muscles. They administered pain with clear precision, and received it like vigorous massage. He had no desire to join with them in anything they did, nor did he feel any overt stimulation in his watching. He admired them like athletes. He ought to have known that his watching would bring him into danger; and, when it did, he was angry only with himself.

He had expected to die at their hands, and, although he had trembled, his flesh unsteady against the immaculacy of theirs, he had not been afraid of death. And it was the lack of this fear in him that had given him the power to defeat them. He felt himself possessed of a strength they did not have. Their strength was all on the surface: his was within.

He had seen them falter, seen their emotions bewildered, and, when he sprayed the bleach into their faces, he felt that he had done the right thing, that he had made them cry. Standing over them and striking them down had been a statement of himself upon them. He struck them one by one, a blow at a time, the jar of the metal singing in his palms. Once they were still, he did not wait a second, ran down the racks of stairs and out into the night, feeling that he had run from the indulgence of some immense pleasure that might, had he taken it any further, have involved him seriously.

Another time, he took casual work in Mr Gazzali's warehouse.

Mr Gazzali had no wife but many children, many cousins, nephews and brothers. He owned an import business, five large stores, seven tobacconists' and news-agents', three laundries, three restaurants, and a cinema. Each branch of his business was run by a family; and each family was a part of his big family, by birth or by adoption. Mr Gazzali was short and fat, white-whiskered, bald-crowned; the image of benevolence. He would drive round to his properties, visiting them all at least once a month, always arriving unexpectedly. He would totter out of his large car sweating and smiling, with the nephew who always came with him sitting on the back seat coming out also, leaing against the side of the car sulkily whilst Mr Gazzali would be greeted with all the respect due to him. He would bring something for someone in the family; but never gifts for all at any one visit. He would bring, sometimes, sweetmeats for the children, bright silken wraps for the women, a carton of scented cigarettes for the men. He would sit in the house behind the shop, would glance over the books which were opened before him like holy texts; but he would spend most of his time asking after the family here, keeping this family in touch with its various cousins at all their various removes. He would always take the man aside at one point and ask if there had been any 'troubles' since his last visit, by which he meant racial troubles. If there had been any, he would write carefully in a leather notebook every detail, every word or gesture, every fear. 'I am deeply sorry,' he would say, taking personal responsibility for everything. 'It will not happen again.' They blessed him with their gratitude, under which he beamed. They offered him refreshment, which he always refused.

The benevolence of Mr Gazzali was genuine and boundless; but it was only possible in those days by means of the power which he had amassed over the years, and which he exercised without the slightest scruple or restraint where he felt it necessary. The laws of the land and those who operated them were so compromised and ineffectual, what could Mr Gazzali do but be his own law? He had believed, as a young man starting out on his success, that time would blend the communities, that the initial suspicions of culture and colour would be dissolved. This idealism withered as he grew older and, as the indigenous culture atrophied and crumbled into criminality at level after level, he accepted the impossibility of his ideal, chided himself for his sentimentality and set himself to protect his own with a force that was easily the equal of anything ranged against him. His family was drawn together fiercely about its own traditions and loyalities, shutting out the society beyond it which, as the years passed, disgusted and appalled him progressively.

And they all knew soon enough to leave the Gazzali family alone; that to rob one of his shops, to frighten one of his nieces on her way home from school, to daub slogans, to throw excrement, any provocation led to rapid retribution, on a scale that usually began with a smashed nose and went up in drastic stages from there. There was the sudden appearance of dark figures, in the urinal, in the car park, at the back door late at night, figures who moved swiftly and were running off before the pain registered. Even the most anonymous and casual provocations were patiently and silently traced to their source and repaid. The efficiency was almost demonic.

In his retail outlets, Mr Gazzali employed only family, but in the fetching and hauling of the warehouse he was obliged to offer work to others. In the warehouse, the nephews lounged and supervised, many of them aggressive young men glad of any opportunity to exercise their share of Mr Gazzali's power, but by no means as discriminating as their uncle in marking its objects. The outsiders in the warehouse worked cowed by the threat of this power, although the old man was often about the place and was strict with his nephews. It was not a bad place to work. The pay was fair and reliable, and there were occasional bonuses in the form of damaged goods. No-one pilfered. No-one idled. No community or organisation grew in this workplace. Dismissal was arbitrary and instant. The workers were treated with no respect whatsoever. They were kept sweet enough, but were never let into the offices, never given more than lifting and stacking and counting to do. They worked and rested and ate in the same large barn through which their employer's nephews roamed in packs.

He came to work in Mr Gazzali's warehouse in the middle of a heatwave, when most of those who could at least survive without working left their jobs to lounge about in the shade, to drink from the standpipes, to sleep out the long static hours. Mr Gazzali was irritated by this, but accepted that if he would treat his workers like dross, then dross they would become. He was resigned to going short-staffed for the duration of the weather. The appearance of the stubby youth, with his long hair and scrawny beard, amongst those few of his workers who were too frightened to take time off was therefore notable.

Mr Gazzali noted him closely and saw that he was not the drug addict he had first thought him to be, that he worked well, that he kept himself aloof, that he was intelligent, observant and wary. This made Mr Gazzali wary in turn, but he would not dismiss the youth at once, for he fancied that he had some purpose here, and Mr Gazzali needed to know what it was. He sent out to have him traced, and it appeared, for all Mr Gazzali's enquiries, that he was just another drifter, living alone in a basement room in a derelict building, with no friends or connections, no word of where he had come from. He

31

briefed one of his most reliable nephews to watch this newcomer constantly about the warehouse, and he asked frequently for reports, but there was never anything to report. When the season improves and they begin to flock in out of the rain, Mr Gazzali thought, then we will rid ourselves of this stranger.

But when the time came, Mr Gazzali did not dismiss him. He had become intrigued by him. He found that he looked forward to seeing the youth when he passed through the warehouse, seeing him walking down the rows of crates with a clipboard, seeing him eat his food squatting against the wall, seeing him in the lines that unloaded the lorries. He knew so much about this young man, all there was to know, although that all was really nothing. He began to see in him an image of the loneliness of the city, of all the dispossessed amongst whom he made his business, a discarded object of the society that had once been so great, so powerful that it ruled the world, now reduced to broken and meaningless fragments; for to be without the power of the family was, Mr Gazzali knew, to be meaningless. He longed to be able to draw this boy in somehow, although the political implications of this amongst his nephews ruled out such a sentimental notion.

He himself hated Mr Gazzali with a cold passion that was new to him. At night in his basement he considered it. It was not racial, or not merely racial. The more he saw of the city, the more he understood that those with any power within it sustained their power by corruption and hypocrisy. Gazzali was the embodiment of this. When Gazzali approached him, he felt the corruption enter his throat like a virus. He waited and watched and began to plan. At times he felt that his loathing must in some way be visible, for Gazzali often approached him, bade him good day. He would draw himself up, dart his eyes about, set his teeth and feel the ache in the hands he did not dare to clench.

'Good day, sir,' he would say, placing the words carefully down like a move in a game.

Mr Gazzali eventually discussed him with the nephew he had briefed to watch him.

'How can such a young man,' Mr Gazzali speculated, 'who must have the fire of youth in him somewhere, live with so little? How is it possible to live so alone? He intrigues me. He is like a puzzle that you can see all the parts of clearly, that is so simple, and yet you cannot see the solution.'

The nephew was well enough in his uncle's confidence to smile sardonically at these effusions. 'Perhaps he has some crime behind him, uncle, or perhaps he imagines some crime that he has committed. I think that he is possessed, in hiding from his terrors. Just another madman.'

The possibility of this caught Mr Gazzali up short. Yes, that must be it, he concluded, rousing to the practicalities at once. The young man was dismissed first thing next morning, though not without a decent severance gift.

Mr Gazzali saw him once more, the night the warehouse burnt down. There had been a wedding that night; one of his favourite nephews had taken a bride. A new business was to be opened for them, a garage, a new colony in Mr Gazzali's empire. There had been lavish preparation and lavish celebration. The warehouse had been watched by a team of the younger nephews, who were disaffected at being excluded from this great family function. They brought in drink and girls, indulgences strictly forbidden by Mr Gazzali; they sought, not so much to indulge, as to assert their defiance of him. And whilst they fornicated and became drunk, cursing Mr Gazzali with adolescent bravado, there was an explosion in the refrigeration plant that brought down a wall, that somehow sent a spark into the petrol tanks, that sent a bolt of amassing fire through the body of the warehouse. And whilst the foolish nephews blundered about, more keen to conceal the evidence of their disgrace than to respond to the escalating disaster, the fire battened upon the vitals of Mr Gazzali's empire.

The wedding feast rushed out to witness the destruction. The women wailed and tore their clothes. The men rushed at the fire with the courage of their fury, but were driven back scorching, went to sit in the darkness and weep. Mr Gazzali watched stony-faced as the heart of his empire was consumed. A large crowd of white faces gathered at the periphery of the family, an outer circle come to witness the downfall of Mr Gazzali. He turned to face them, and saw their white souls lit up in the glare of his destruction. He called his closest nephews about him, raking the faces for a sign of triumph there, a sign of guilt. He knew some of them must be responsible. His first instinct was for war. But it was a war that he could not win. He could only find out the perpetrators and have them dealt with. It was a long, tedious and unpleasant task that would take much of his ageing strength, but it must be done if anything was to be contained here. Then amongst the crowd he saw the stocky youth with long hair, his image swimming in the fireglow with unnatural clarity across a space adrift with motes of ash. Mr Gazzali stepped forward but stopped, caught his eye and stared hard into that implacable face, quite unable to understand what he saw there. It was not fear, nor triumph: it was not sadness, and it was not mockery. It was like looking at a wall, a wall across the road finally blocking everything.

The damage was enormous but not, materially, fatal to Mr Gazzali: its effect upon him personally, however, was fatal. Led away at last from the dying fire, he felt that he had lost, that the forces ranged against him which he had fought so long and so successfully had finally found out his heart and had, at a stroke, pierced it. He knew now that his power, which had before seemed absolute, was finite, like life itself. Even the greatest emperor must face the dark one day, the same dark that came for the most abject of his subjects. This was a commonplace that he had mouthed often without really believing it: now it came for him with all its cold irony.

The nephews could not comprehend his sudden resignation, brought him the names of many possible culprits, begged for his permission to exact retribution. But he knew as he heard them that their judgements were obscured by their anger or by their need to ingratiate themselves with him, that the names they brought him had been snatched at random. He refused his permission, asked only that the silent youth be found, and searched long and hard for an answer. They searched and searched for days, for months, but he had vanished. And the more they searched, the more the old man became convinced that he and he alone had brought about the fire, that he and he alone must be brought to account for it. In time they knew that their respected uncle had lost touch with reality, that the young man had never really existed, at least not in the way that Mr Gazzali now imagined him. They knew that the empire in which they had all been so strong was coming down; they began to ignore the old man and began the squabbling over who would inherit which parts of it.

At another time, he became ill. He was lodging then in a derelict school, and, when he felt the illness accumulating within him, he retired to his lodging, gathered a few possessions about him, buried himself in blankets and sacks and let the sickness have its will of him. He became very ill indeed, wracked with aches and fevers, his eyelids heavy as if bruised, his joints swelling, his throat and lungs dry as clinkers. He came very close to death at that time, gasping and choking with the weight of his sickness closing tighter and tighter about him. He would almost certainly have died had he not been found there and tended back to health.

A nomadic gang of thieves took up residence in the school shortly after he did. All of them had begun as petty thieves, but were now banded together, grown strong and therefore ambitious. They operated in a pack with forethought and strategy, broke open respectable business premises, raided houses in the residential areas, surrounded rich cars in laybys and service stations, robbing the occupants and driving away. Thus they had become known, marked and wanted. The law now left petty criminals alone unless their crimes were committed too publicly; there were too many of them to be pursued, and the police had long since lost any credibility amongst the poor that might have assisted them in their pursuits. Anyway, professional vigilante bands usually deterred the smaller criminals from incursions into places where the police mattered and where they were expected to be efficient. This gang challenged all these complacencies. They called themselves the Enterprise. They numbered at this time about twenty, men and women living in a community that was growing strong, with loyalty and mutual trust and with an honesty of purpose that had begun to give a political dimension to their activities.

After a successful summer, they retired to the derelict school to winter out on their plunder, to lie low for a few months whilst the pursuit died down. Their last excursion had cost the lives of three of their number, including a woman known as the Virgin who was considered to have been their leader, although there were really no leaders. With her death, and the publicity that had surrounded it, the authorities might well find it convenient to believe that the gang had disintegrated. They determined to foster this illusion for a while, plan their next moves, gather recruits.

The school had been large; over a thousand pupils had once studied here. It was a sprawling site with many buildings, but the core of it was a high brick institution, over a hundred years old, with high classrooms and long corridors. They had used this school before, but had not been near it for over a year, so their first job was to search it thoroughly, mostly to see if the authorities had traced them here.

They found no evidence of the authorities, but they did find him in a high room in the old building, a writhing heap of sacking that stank and groaned. One of the women in the group was known as the Doctor because she had, at one time, trained for that profession. She was brought to the sick man whilst the others kept their distance, afraid of infection. She examined him and told them that although what he had might carry infection, she had drugs enough, that his collapse was due to his lack of food and warmth as much as to the sickness. They would risk it. They settled into their quarters, spread about the school buildings, posting watches and arranging the communal affairs of their organisation. The Doctor, and a man called Halt who was her lover, set up in the room next to the sick man and tended him back to health.

The Doctor had not held out much hope for him, but she had tried out her skills, glad again to be working with real disease, rather than with the wounds, fractures and dysenteries which were her stock-in-trade. She expected her new patient to succumb in spite of her, expected merely to ease him with her opiates. But once the medicines began to work within him, he seemed to batten on to their power and show a resilience and determination that began, eventually, to bring him through.

He was a model patient: never complaining, always submitting to her treatment, never embarrassed or discomforted by whatever she did to him; but this pliancy was balanced by a complete denial of anything else. He told her nothing of himself, asked nothing about them, showed no emotion at all, not even gratitude. She did not resent this, understood it indeed: it was not an age for glib confidences; but she watched him curiously and became, after a while, intrigued by him, as had all the others who had made any sustained observations of him. He could recognise this by now, and he shut himself down, weak as he was, under it, knowing that this was only a temporary defence.

'Some of our friends would like to meet you,' the Doctor said to him one evening.

'I'll be fit enough to move out of here soon,' he said.

'Well, it's not quite as simple as that,' the Doctor explained, watching him retract and draw into his self-awareness around him.

'Fine,' he said, 'fine.'

They had caught a police informer, a girl of about eighteen. She was an addict and no serious spy, just

someone who drifted about amongst the dispossessed
and met with the police once a week to swap the nightmares of her withdrawals for a supply of her need that
would keep her going just long enough. The Doctor
brought him down into the old boiler room of the
building where they were interrogating this girl. They
had given her a shot and she sat naked and filthy on the
bare concrete, her knees clasped in her arms, her head
rolling about and her eyes rolling about too, but to a
different rhythm.

'Is the Sergeant here?' she was saying. 'He's a good
man, but I know what you're thinking. You're thinking
he's my boyfriend. He's not, honestly. He's not like that.
He won't take advantage of me.' She was uncannily
well-spoken, an accent from another world, from a rich
girl's school. They stood about her and watched her,
large and silent, considering her, dark shapes around the
edges of the room, the only light from a powerful lamp
that ran off a generator which chugged and filled the
room with diesel fumes.

'Where d'you go to meet the Sergeant, Felicity?' a man
said kindly, but some distance from her.

'D'you promise not to tell?' the girl said.

'I promise. Cross my heart.'

'Well . . . d'you know the car park on Stanley Street?'

'Oh yes.'

'Well, I'm to go there, every Tuesday, at six o'clock
sharp. You mustn't be late. Oh no. He brings his car, and
it's warm in there. He brings me a burger, a big burger,
and I get the relish all over his seat, but he doesn't mind at
all. And he gives me my . . . my little bag of light.'

'All right,' the man said, but not to the girl.

Someone stepped behind her, a tall black man stripped
to the waist, a body thick with muscle. He knelt down by

39

her and put his hand on her shoulder. She sighed and leant her head back on to his touch, began to uncurl her body against his legs. With his other hand he reached round her neck and, with a sudden twist, broke it. She flopped at once as if the strings that held her had been dropped.

The Doctor stepped over, felt for the pulse and said, 'Yes.'

He had not taken his eyes off this spectacle for a second, but the eyes about the room were upon him. He looked round and recognised what was in play here, that he was under scrutiny, on trial; that he was a part of this death by his witnessing of it. He felt it was an imposition upon him.

'What do you suggest we do next?' someone said.

He did not realise for a while that this question was addressed to him. When he did realise, he took a quiet breath, shrugged, smiled, said, 'Go and kill the Sergeant, I suppose.'

'Did you know her?'

'Her? No.'

'We were under the impression that she knew you.'

'I've never seen her before.'

'Go and look. Closely. Look closely and make sure you don't know her.'

He stepped over at once into the light where the dead girl lay sprawled, her eyes and mouth open, her limbs askew, the white flesh garish. He knelt down by her and looked clearly into the face, glanced down the body. It was repulsive, a length of human refuse.

'She could be anybody,' he said.

'Close her eyes.'

He closed them with the tips of his fingers, wiped them on his shirt, looked up and around them.

'Will you come and kill a policeman with us, then, Sickman?'

40

He did not take his eyes off them for a second, faced them with a smile twisting the edges of his mouth. 'All right,' he said.

'Have you killed anyone before?' the Doctor asked him.

'I don't know,' he said.

'You must know.'

'Not like this,' he said.

'Like what then?'

'I've never stayed around to check.'

They liked him then, although none of them entirely trusted him. The black man, whose name was Screw, was told to watch him and to lose him the moment he became unreliable.

The Doctor thought this harsh: 'Bring him in on something easier,' she said.

'No,' they told her, 'let's put him straight into the fire, give him nowhere to hide'.

Later that night, the Doctor came into the Sickman's room. He was standing at the window, looking out into the icy night. He looked over his shoulder at her as she appeared, but did not turn to face her.

'Are you going to be all right tomorrow?' she asked.

'I expect so,' he said. He turned himself round at last, leant on the window sill and studied her.

She came forward into his regard but, coming close enough to see his eyes, she stopped. She remembered his comment about the girl – 'She could be anybody' – and she saw that he was looking at her in that way too. She left him, feeling hurt, realising that she had wanted something from him, something personal that he would not give her; and in her wanting and in his denial she felt vulnerable, pitiable, squalid.

★   ★   ★

The Sergeant sat behind the wheel of his car, waiting for Felicity's face to appear at his window. He had her burger waiting for her, and her little packet of poison. He was looking at his watch when one of the derelict cars about fifty yards away began to move. When he looked up, the car was being pushed very fast towards him by four or five stooped, dark figures. He started his engine, but they had the car across his as he shot out. The impact of the crash jolted him forwards. He saw that one of the men pushing the car was down. He reversed quickly, but the crash had jammed the steering and his car skewed and rammed into the rear wall of the car park. He turned on his radio, but someone was on the roof of his car, shearing off the aeriel. He took out his pistol and fired through the roof, the noise of the shot deafening him, the smoke of the cordite choking. When he regained his senses, he thought they had gone. He looked round but could see no one but the figure on the ground, who was trying to lift himself, his body a broken lump. His engine was still running. He jerked at the steering wheel, but it was solid in his hand. Then he heard something at the side of the car. He looked in the wing mirror and saw two figures stooped at the petrol cap. He took a deep breath, checked his pistol, leant back and began to lower the door window ready to swing round and shoot. The window was no more than an inch down when a bullet starred the glass. There was no sound of a shot, just the dull smash of its impact.

He realised then that he was going to die, and as the realisation hit him he felt himself dissolve, felt all the power go from his muscles. He wanted to have the strength to raise his pistol and do it himself, but he did not have the strength. He looked into the mirror and saw they had broken into his petrol tank, were lighting a bundle of rags. One of the figures there crawled along the side of the car and peered in. The face was not cruel, just curious. As he trembled and gibbered, he was under the scrutiny of a strange watching that filled him with a disgust for himself and for what he had become at this moment. The figure was suddenly pulled away and he watched them running into the darkness, the darkness that momentarily seemed to close around him before the petrol tank exploded and there was a roar of light and furious heat in which he was obliterated.

The Sickman was thereafter accepted as a member of the Enterprise, although he had never asked to belong. The killing of the Sergeant drew them out of their hibernation. They moved from the school into an empty office block, from there to a discarded hospital. They plundered as they went, but only for food and fuel. There was talk of moving out into the country, and there were long arguments over this. Those of a political inclination felt they should stay in the city and take the action to where it would really matter, not lose themselves in the woods; another faction disapproved of this, said it opened them to informers, made them weak, said that only by being closed and strong, unattached to anything, would they have any chance of survival.

The Sickman could be relied upon to put himself into the heart of any action, sauntering out into open streets to attract any potential ambush, moving quickly and cleanly when necessary, and with a patience the lack of which had spoiled so many of their operations. Screw taught him to handle a gun, and to use his feet and head in a fight. He was an excellent pupil. 'He's a natural,' Screw said. 'He's not physical, not aggressive, but all that gets in the way sooner or later. He fights without ever getting himself involved. He's lethal.' They tried to draw him into their discussions and, although he would offer his opinion if asked directly, he never seemed to take any personal interest in what they decided. His opinions were always, only, absolutely practical.

The Doctor became increasingly interested in him; the emotions that his denial of her had generated were proving deep-seated, needing resolution, and, although he remained as implacable as ever, she could not leave him alone. She felt as if he could explain something to her, something about herself which lay in the shadows within which he seemed to live. Whenever they moved camp, she was careful to set up quarters near his. She spent time with him on their many days of inactivity, told him about some of their earlier escapades, about her own life, her husband and child, her travels abroad in the days when such things were possible, when the world was whole and its troubles local.

'I'm one of the politicals,' she told him. 'I want us to go out and fight for things to change, for a world in which we would not be able to exist as we do. If we are successful, then we'll be destroyed. Do you understand what I'm saying?'

'I think so,' he said, watching her.

'And you, what do you want?'

'I don't want anything.'

'What's your real name? I can't call you Sickman.'

'I've had a lot of names. Names don't mean anything. I have no name because I'm no-one.'

'How long have you been like that?'

'Oh, for as long as I can remember.'

'Did you never have a home? A family?'

'Probably, once. I don't bother thinking about any of that.'

'Was there something that made you like this?'

'Nothing particular. It just seemed the best way to be in these times. I think I was always like it, but in these times it's the best way to be. Nothing and no-one. I like being like this. I'm glad to be alive in these times, Doctor.'

'Don't you ever want peace? Freedom?'

'Isn't this freedom? I'm free.'

'Have you no ambitions?'

'No.'

'I think you could lead us if you wanted to.' He stopped at this. It was the first thing she had said that had caught his interest.

'I thought you had no leaders,' he said.

'No-one wants to lead us. You could lead us, though. In a year, if we survive that long, you could take control here. You'd be a good leader.'

'I'm no political, Doctor.'

'I know,' she said.

'My first decision would probably be to get rid of you.'

'I know that too,' she said. 'I never said I wanted you to lead us. In fact, the prospect frightens me. But I think you could do it. If you wanted to.'

He smiled at her, shrugged, but did not give her a response. In a while she could stand his watching, his waiting no longer, and she left him to return to her lover.

After her departure, he felt a moment of strange regret. He turned as if to follow her and, as he did so, he stopped. Suddenly he became aware of the danger he was in. He had liked this woman; she had an integrity and courage to which he responded. He had correspondingly begun actively to despise the moron whom she allowed to fuck her. When she had come in to see him, he had felt sometimes that she wanted him to step over to her, to touch her, to search for her pleasure with careful, curious fingers. He had imagined doing this without revulsion. Now, as she had spoken about leadership, about the future, he knew that he had been walking blindly into a fog, and that if he was to survive he would have to clear that fog. The prospect of it shook him, animated him as if, at last, he was clear of the clinging of his sickness.

They planned to break out in March, to turn over a police barracks that was, as all the barracks were, full of supplies and arms and hard cash, fat, corrupt and complacent. It was to be a very big job and reconnaissance was begun seriously, maps studied, points of incursion selected, scrupulous time schedules drawn up. The magnitude and danger of the project caught them up and drew them together. The day came: the morning broke and they met to shake hands, to embrace, to stare into each other's faces with set lips. They moved out under their separate covers to take up their positions. There was to be no further communication between them until the assault.

There was no assault. At every staging post, so carefully selected, armed police waited with precise orders. They were shot down one by one. Those who surrendered were taken into some alley and dispatched. The Doctor, waiting in a subway with Halt, heard the boots come down the stairway, was alerted at once and turned to her lover to conceal them both with an embrace, pressed herself against him, felt him trembling and trembled against him. They were pulled apart. She glanced at the visors, the black muzzles. She knew what was coming and she felt, at last, a great relief lifting her. She leant back against the wall and breathed deeply. Halt was calling to her from a long way away, but she no

46

longer wanted him. She heard an officer say 'Yes', and she too was saying 'Yes' as the bullets entered her tired head.

They had vans waiting for the bodies, drove them to the barracks, stripped and hosed them down and laid them out on a concrete floor. There were twenty-seven of them. The Minister arrived and walked down the row of corpses, pausing curiously by each one.

'All of them?' he asked.

'Yes, sir,' he was assured. 'We even got the three they left behind at their base.'

'Splendid. Splendid work. Well done indeed. And the informer? Which one is he?' There was a silence. He looked round.

'That one, I think, sir,' said the Commissioner, indicating with his swagger stick. He turned to the officer in charge for confirmation. 'Inspector?'

'Er, I think we may have missed him out, actually, sir. I don't think he was where he said he would be. His information was otherwise perfect in every particular.'

The Minister looked at the Commissioner. 'Is that going to be a problem, Michael?'

Some weeks later he visited the subway where the Doctor had died. It was deserted, and he had time to explore the pocks in the wall, note the shadowy stains, to reconstruct the scene clearly in his imagination. He felt neither sadness nor satisfaction: it seemed logical, inevitable. It was, as he had wanted it to be, a clarification. And now that he was clear, he could move forward; and now, with the perspective of these, his first significant dead, behind him, he began to conceive of directions, purposes. He must be quickly busy.

★   ★   ★

Oh Rachel, I loved my years in the city. It was my time of absolute freedom. There was blind chaos, and I blended into it. It was my element. I was nothing, absolutely nothing; and being nothing, I could be anything, do anything, become anything and then cease to be at will. I was reduced to essentials, stripped down and vital. I was as I had always dreamed of being.

I can now recall little of those years specifically; everything swirls and blends together, faces and buildings, the terrors and the triumphs; moments of pure loneliness, when everything else seemed to have gone down around me forever; moments when the action was so crowded that I lost myself completely in the switching and slashing of survival, when I became pure instinct. I learnt there the moment to watch and the moment to strike out; I learnt the subtleties of loyalty and exploitation; I learnt how in betrayal can be realised the greatest loyalty of all, the loyalty to yourself. I learnt how to use violence with the minutest integrity.

I came close to death on many occasions in those years. There were at least three occasions that I can unpick from the debris, when I abandoned myself to the certainty of obliteration. Physically I was afraid: I clearly felt the panic fastening itself to my muscles. But I can recall also the clarity of those moments, the way that I seemed able to see myself in these extremities from outside, to feel the final assertions of myself before the oblivion. And there was an ecstasy in that, in the acceptance of finally becoming nothing. After it was over, after I had escaped, when the thrashing of my consciousness had begun to calm, I felt a peace, a longing, a deep sensual awareness of what had almost been. In an ideal world, everyone would have the chance to greet death consciously, to approach that moment with clarity. The purpose of human life is perhaps only the preparation for that moment of the final liberation.

My dominant memory, if I had to distil all those years into one image, is the memory of burning: the tiny struggle for the fire to catch, the intimation of the first threads of smoke, the little crackles of life, the leap of flame in the moment of certainty, the beautiful, surprising logic of conflagration; and then the power of it, the suck of the air into the swelling body of the fire, the roaring and roaring that brought explosion and destruction, that brought worlds down around it, that ate and ate, buckling metal and bursting walls, bursting clusters of lives like bubbles of spit. I was drawn to fires, always drawn, always urged by the lunatic within me to go closer and closer, to feel the sweat and scald of the heat tightening my skin, tempted almost to offer myself to it, to become one with it. It seemed to represent my most profound understanding of the true nature of life. When I was ill, feverish, I had hallucinations of fire. I became myself a great devouring furnace. Hell, Rachel, would have no terrors for me.

It brings me great consolation to know, as now I do, that at those times when I came again and again to the extremity of life, there existed another world, the inverse of the world I belonged to; and that in that world, in security, sheltered by wealth and family, you were at the other extremity of life. Where was I on the day you were born, Rachel? I hope I was at some vital juncture, breaking out, forged to you from the first, becoming as you became, making my way towards you as you began your journey to me.

HE BECOMES EDUCATED

Leaving the city, he offered himself for a position in the state information service, the largest single employer apart from the security forces. He had to submit to a basic intelligence test and a short interview to assess his political sympathy. The recruits were not paid well, but in these times, increasingly, a bed and regular food was enough of an inducement. He passed the test and the interview with ease and took up his position, and the lodging that went with it, in a commandeered university building close by a provincial capital in the east of the country.

At the interview, only the very first question had bothered him.

'What is your full name?'

He looked uncertain and his interviewer, a woman in her fifties, had shot up her eyes to regard him, her pen paused, her mind coming out of the routine, alerted, beginning to formulate other questions, new questions.

'Mark Michael First,' he had said.

The woman sighed, wrote, let the routine take her over.

In those minutes, he had acquired not only a name but an identity. He had not planned this name; it came to him in an inspiration that alarmed him initially, made him feel suddenly exposed; but which, as he thought about it, filled him with pleasure. He was First now, completely new, completely himself, primed and ready to move outwards.

His lodging was on the top floor of a student residential block. The student cot had been replaced with bunk beds, the bookcases with metal lockers. There was no-one in the room when he arrived, so he packed his few clothes into one of the lockers, chose the top bunk and lay on it to wait for his supper hour, a sense of strong neutrality upon him. The world was trembling about him, and he was on the point of driving into it, locking himself and bringing it into a recognition of him that would be substantial.

He had not been waiting half an hour when the door opened and his room-mate appeared, an untidy man of about his own age with an enormous rucksack, wearing baggy trousers and a jacket that had once been of good quality, a filthy shirt and a tie which was undone. The new arrival and he looked at each other.

'Anthony Standing,' the other said, wiping a lank of hair out of his eyes and extending a hand.

'Mark First.' He took the hand without shifting his position on the bunk, gripping it fiercely as if to pull its owner towards him.

Standing laughed nervously, surveyed the room, tried a locker door, found it occupied and opened the other locker. He knelt before it and began to unload his rucksack. His clothes were in plastic bags and he had a sizable pile of books. When he was unloaded, he stood up again to see his room-mate's eyes upon him.

'Trainee operating?' he asked.

The head on the top bunk nodded.

'It's weird to be back at university. I don't somehow expect it'll be as jolly this time round. What d'you reckon?'

'I wasn't at university.'

'Ah well. What time's food?'

'Six-thirty.'

Standing followed him down to the dining hall. There were long queues. Loudspeakers conveyed information – lists of numbers and rooms, barely audible.

'Does any of that refer to us?' Standing asked.

'Do you know your number?'

Standing burrowed for a scrap of paper, showed it to him.

'We've a meeting at eight in the central common room.'

'I shall have to keep close to you, Mark. I was never very good at all this institutional stuff.'

They collected their trays and found a seat. He watched as Standing's attention wandered round the women, following them as they moved, apprising them.

'Not much youth and beauty,' Standing said, 'but then not much prim virginity either, by the look of them.'

They ate – scalding soup with meat and vegetables in it, spiced quite fiercely, mopped up with slabs of dark bread.

'Bloody ethnic food,' Standing said. 'Still, it's better than the ration queues. What did you do before this?'

'I've been drifting about for a few years.'

'I was a teacher. Of English Language and Literature. It's a splendid job, teaching, all those clean bright minds; and clean bright bodies too. That was my downfall.'

They went to their meeting, in which scores of trainee

52

operators were harangued by various speakers who tried to instil some spirit into the bewilderment; but the public address systems were faulty and failed to establish anything over the abiding confusion. They tried the bar, which was packed and impossible. They wandered about the busy concourses, where other new arrivals clustered around noticeboards, entered loud political discussions, or just stood around in solitary knots, lost in it all.

Standing was restless, looking around as if for someone he knew. First watched him continuously, kept by him, followed him. Standing was a little restricted by this, by his room-mate's silence, and by his obvious focus of attention which was Standing himself, only and ever it seemed; but after a while he seemed to have submitted to it, found that they were walking together, or that First, rather than following Standing, had come to be leading him, or at least taking the decisions on where they should wander next.

They wandered back to the residence. Up in the room, lying on their bunks, Standing began to unfold his life, on the briefest of promptings. He had come from a good family, gone to a good school, a good university, done well, taken a job in a rich girls' school and lasted less than a year.

'I had a room with a little shower room off it. They used to come and play in the shower with me. It seemed almost innocent, not serious in the slightest. First one, Patricia, who burst into tears one afternoon over some poetry she had written, whom I comforted, at first in all honesty, then before I knew where we were going we had arrived. I worried what I had let myself in for, but the next free afternoon, she came back, brought a friend, Jennifer. Then I knew it was all just a game. Then others used to come. They all knew about it. Mr Standing's shower room. They all wanted to come and play. Please, sir, could I go and take a shower? A shower? Of course, Annabel. Anything you want, just give me a shout. Please, Mr Standing. I don't seem able to get this shower to work properly. Well, Emma, I'd better come in and see what's wrong. Make sure you're decent now. It was a dream, a fantasy world. They were the great days of my life. I shall never see days like that again.'

'Did you go to prison?'

'Oh no. They were all over age. I was that careful, at least. Dismissed with all possible ignominy.'

'I think prison would be interesting.'

'Rather you than me.' But Standing was silent after this, considering the words that had come from the bunk above him, wondering what they implied. He began to wonder about this strange companion whom chance had set there above him, but not yet too seriously. Standing was a man who got on with everyone.

They attended the training sessions. They were working in the same block, learning the codings and procedures, learning how to find their ways through the vast system. They were not taught anything that, after a month, was of any intrinsic interest. They did not deal with people, only with factory and farm quotas and outputs, distribution schedules, transport potentials; a complex world with which they had no contact and which, Standing said, probably didn't even exist. 'They make it all up. It's a great fictional system to prove that they're doing something, solving all the problems.' Both of them coped easily with the demands made upon them. First learned quickly and assiduously. Standing too learned quickly, but then grew bored and tried to find ways to break into the intricacies of the system, behind the masses of data.

54

His attempted interferences were soon spotted and he was warned off, reminded of the ration queues in the world beyond.

'There must be something we can do, Mark,' he said in the safety of their room.

'What do you want to do?' First asked him.

'I don't know. Screw the system up in some way. Catch it in its own contradictions.'

'What would be the point of that?'

'Oh, just something to do, I suppose. I'm very bored here, Mark, Aren't you?'

'I don't think I've ever been bored.'

'You mean you'd be happy to play out their little fictions forever? I don't believe you.'

'They may be fiction,' First said, 'but they're how the world is run, Anthony, and I want to learn about that.'

So Standing began to explain how the system worked, as far as he understood it. He was a fluent teacher, and he had a fluent pupil, although the problem, as they apprised it, did seem to be beyond them for the moment.

Standing was always restless, always needing to be with people. Their work shifts were long and tiring, the tedium dulled their minds and made their limbs ache; but in the evenings they were always in the bar, Standing always the centre of attention. Many of those on their shift and in their residence came to regard him as something of a character; not a leader so much as someone to whom they could all relate. He knew them all and chatted freely; he articulated their mutual dissatisfactions clearly and entertainingly. Those who were serious about the work and the system it sought to serve, usually the duller ones, kept clear of Standing and his clique, watched with disapproval as he induced hoots of laughter at one of the supervisors, or at the latest pomposity from the government exhorting them to this or that self-denial in the cause of national salvation. Standing was clever and cynical, and stood for the absurdity of everything.

He was never in the bar without his taciturn and watchful room-mate. The others assumed him initially to be some sort of dull admirer of Standing's – a shy boy who wanted to be accounted one of the men. If they watched closely enough, however, this impression was belied. It was rather the other way round; Standing seemed to defer to First, always seemed to look at him with smiles, perhaps of complicity, perhaps asking for some sort of approval. His friend returned his gaze clearly but, as far as anyone could see, without expression. Their relationship, whatever it was, was never explained in public, but it was there like a wall, a background to everything. Standing's relations with the others were bright and superficial: with First, he seemed to share an understanding that at times made the others uncomfortable. None of them got anywhere near First. Those who tried to draw him in quickly retracted under his curious, silent digestion of them.

Anthony Standing was not a reflective man, and could not have said clearly what he felt for Mark First. In some way, however, he had been colonised by his room-mate. Perhaps it was that blankness of his past, his lack of shadow, that made him powerful. Standing had been curious about his past and had begun to probe, but with no success. First's past was kept sealed tight; and the tighter it was sealed the more intriguing it became. Standing became convinced that he was living with a man who had seen horrors, who had probably participated in horrors, and who was quite possibly dangerous. He was rather stimulated by this.

Perhaps, though, the attraction of Mark First was his capacity to absorb all that Standing could teach him, the perfect pupil, who could barely read but who questioned Standing closely on the way everything worked. The information systems were only the beginning. Standing was no serious intellectual, but he knew his way around the library that was kept open, the only extant function of the original institution, and he went and found books to fill in gaps in his knowledge that had been exposed by his companion. He found that he was reading, not, as he had always read before, literature to feed his melancholy imagination, but political, economic and sociological theory to feed the voracious mind of his room-mate. Standing felt at times like a cock-sparrow feeding a cuckoo-chick, but then, he reminded himself sardonically, the cock-sparrow fattens the monster with all its little heart. First seemed to have found a use for him that he was glad to be put to. In the dark companionship of their room, his brain had never been busier.

First's questioning was thorough and always theoretical. He did not seem interested in what Standing understood as friendship, shared no confidences, no gossip, expressed no opinions that could in any way have been said to have been personal. The one thing that interested him was power. It was an interest of limitless intensity. He sought in all his inquiries of Standing to understand how the power of politics and economics worked, how men controlled other men, why men submitted to the control of others, how inequalities of power were established, how they were sustained, and how defeated.

It began to interest Standing too. As he explained things, he began to sense that, under all the complexity and contradiction, under all the theories, was something single, simple, dramatically simple. He came near to asking First what he was after, but he never had the courage to do this; he felt that if he did, he would lose the confidence that he thought he was establishing with this strange man, a close confidence that was growing in importance in his life. It was never an equal closeness, for First never gave anything away; perhaps this was its power. Standing rather felt himself drawn into a strange active shadow.

His sociability was a foil to this solitary intimacy. He needed to be out and about with people, unbracing himself in convivial company, getting a little drunk – only a little, for the bar retailed only weak beer. He needed at these times to have First with him because he felt that otherwise he would be completely swallowed up by him, digested and neutralised; he needed the affirmation of the crowd to remind himself of who he was, who he had always thought that he was; and he needed First in attendance here so that he might see him as he felt he really was, still fundamentally independent of anything First sought to make him; although, as the weeks passed, he felt less and less secure of this, felt that First's presence with him in his sociable hours extended his knowledge of him, and consequently his power over him. As this occurred to him, he found that he did not, after all, resent it; he found that he was beginning to perform for First in all things, to become in a strange way the active part of First's personality.

Their company in the bar was exclusively male, and this began to bother Standing. He had, ever since his early adolescence, needed to be with women. He had that ability to attract women, to draw them to him sexually.

He was lucky in this, and knew himself to be so. He assumed all men aspired to this power. In Mark First he had met someone for whom all that appeared to be of no importance at all. In their early days he had suggested that they set out to find some female company, but this had been met with a complete blank, a lack of response so solid as to be restrictive.

It had occurred to him that First was homosexual; but that didn't really work either. First was modest in his habits, but never obsessively so. Standing watched him dressing and undressing, saw a body chubby and undeveloped, scarred in interesting places; but First revealed his nakedness without any twitch of self-awareness, as if his body was of no interest at all. Standing was not so assured of his own physicality, particularly as he often found First watching him as he changed, his eyes narrowed, curious to see everything there was to see. Standing at times wondered if there was anything particular First wanted to see him do. Such thoughts brought a tense sweat to his flesh.

Standing tried to probe First with a degree of sexual banter, but he showed no interest in Standing's amorous anecdotes, never laughed at any of his jokes; laughed at very little in fact, and when he did laugh it was a private affair, a quiet and internal mutter of amusement, never something that might be shared.

First brought a growing restriction to Standing's sexuality, but it did not abolish it. He wanted often to go out in search of a woman, saw several of their acquaintance achieving this and was envious. But First's presence blocked every sexual move he considered. They appeared to have become inseparable, and First would hardly want to come and watch that; but then again, he might want to come and watch, and that was a further

59

complexity. There were social evenings, dances of a sort, to which they went but sat out amongst their clique and mocked. Standing began to imagine a streak of sexual puritanism in First, began to feel, as his own desires began to tug at him more forcefully, that this might be a source of difference between them; and so he entered the longest spell of celibacy that he had ever endured. It began at last to make him restless, and he sensed First's awareness of this, his curiosity in it.

He decided eventually to tackle his companion directly on this. It was summer, and there was to be a dance and barbecue down in the meadows – a present from the authorities, celebrating some significant date in the national calendar, in appreciation of all their devoted work.

As they wandered down amongst the crowds, Standing turned to his friend and said, 'I think, Mark, that I'm going to try and find myself a woman tonight.' First was silent. 'You don't mind?'

'Why should I mind?'

'Why don't you find yourself a woman too, Mark?'

This was answered with one of his strange laughs, and no more was said about it.

The night was warm and soft. The glow from the bonfires intensified as the shadows gathered. They found themselves amongst a group of their clique, keeping as always out of the main centres of jollity, the singers and guitarists, the groups of dancers swaying to slow rhythms. Standing was quiet, and their group grew moody without his impetus. In his quietness, he felt First watching him more closely than ever.

Eventually he rose and said he was going for a piss. He wandered into the darkness of a clump of bushes and, as he relieved himself, looked to see if First was following him. He could not see him, but he knew that this did not necessarily mean that he was alone. He did not return to the group, but made his way round in the darkness towards one of the groups of dancers. Here there were women, many of them unattached to men, sitting and drinking and laughing, decked for the occasion with ribbons and scarves, bright colours over their working clothes. He sat down by a group of them and begged something to drink. They regarded him with amusement, offered him a bottle, which he found to his surprise contained a rough sweet spirit, more potent than anything he had tasted in months. He chatted with them, found them easygoing, full of laughter, without the political seriousness he had dreaded. They are just like us, he thought, and wondered why there were no women in their clique. How good it would be, he thought, to have the intoxication of women among us. And then he thought of First and a shiver went through him. He looked about him, peered into the darkness, but could see nothing.

'Come on then, whatever-your-name-is,' one of the women said. 'Come and dance.' She stood, took his hand and pulled him to his feet. They moved away from the cheers and whistles of the others, and began to jig about a couple of feet apart to an old song full of the sweet energy of a world gone by. He watched his companion and saw she was young; not pretty, but tall, shapely, alert, with a lot of hair let loose across her shoulders. He smiled and shrugged at her as he moved, as he matched his movements to her movements. He saw her laugh, look back at her friends and then back at him, smiling at him, lifting up her arms, the invitation of which he did not at once accept. He felt his old charm moving in him, felt its power here, loved again the way it made him feel, the

61

way it always made him feel. His heartbeat grew strong and his limbs loose. He danced himself within reach of her, came in very close without touching her, until he could feel her breath upon his face. He put his arms around her and closed his body against hers abruptly. She laughed and leant back, the rhythm of the dance confined now to the movement of their hips and shoulders.

They rejoined the others for a while, but sat together, his arm around her shoulder, her hand on his leg. The bottle came past them again, or perhaps it was another bottle. The fires were dying down, the crowds thinning. He and the woman were making an exclusive warmth between them, shuffling against one another. Some of her friends got up to leave. Goodnights were exchanged. They lay down together and kissed, opened each other's clothes and, in the darkness, explored each other's private warmth. After a while she sat up. He too sat up and saw that they were alone, apart from shadows that were probably other couples dotted across the meadow, none near enough for them to distinguish.

'What's wrong?' he asked.

'I felt we were being watched,' she said.

'We probably are,' he said, 'our names and numbers taken down. Does it bother you?'

'What *is* your name?' she asked.

'Anthony Standing. And yours?'

Chris Dooley.' She lay back down and sighed.

'It doesn't matter who we are, does it?' He leant over her.

'No, I suppose it doesn't.'

He began to smooth his hand over her, to edge the trousers off her buttocks.

'Is it good that it doesn't matter who we are?' she said, lifting herself to assist him.

62

'Oh yes. It's freedom and equality.'

'I think it's sad,' she said exploring the length of his cock with her fingertips.

He was out of practice, but found her as keen as he was. She locked her legs round him, and they were quickly finished, after which they became functional, dressing, dusting each other down and wandering back hand in hand, to part with a small kiss at the door of her building. He found himself wondering if he would be back before First, whom he assumed must have witnessed his whole performance. He realised, with a sudden alarm, that he had begun to imagine him to have frankly supernatural powers of observation and movement.

He had not watched Standing taking his pleasure in the meadow; that did not interest him. Standing's appetite was, however, a problem. It was a blur upon his friend, a flaw within him. He wanted Standing to find everything he needed in the relationship between them; but that had been wishful. He had watched Standing fret and finally go off to satisfy his appetite. He had not wanted to stop him, would have encouraged him if he had known how to. He needed to see the effect of that satisfaction, whether it would put a distance between them. He dreaded that. He needed Standing, wanted him with a ferocity that brought the violence into his mouth again. So much was coming to the surface in him now, flooding him with energy that would burst within him if he did not have some way of releasing it; and Standing was the focus of it, the beginning. If he lost Standing, then he would be set back months. He would have to start again with someone else; and he did not want anyone else. He wanted Standing. Standing was his brother, the only man who had ever meant anything to him. He lay awake fully dressed, waiting for his return, waiting whilst he was cuckolded by some scrawny slag. He imagined Standing bringing her back, imagined having to share their intimacy with her. A bolt of anger rose hard within him.

When Standing returned, he noted First's wakefulness. It made him feel guilty, but he said nothing, pulled off his clothes and, with a grunt, got under his blankets.

'Find what you were looking for, Anthony?' the voice came at last.

'Oh yes. Very pleasant. Very pleasant indeed.' Then, after a while, he added, 'We should draw some women into our set, you know, Mark.'

'Did you have someone particular in mind?'

'Oh, no.'

'You have established no new loyalties tonight, then?'

'Oh, no.'

There was then silence, and Standing began to slip into sleep, into the warm oblivion his fulfilment required, when the voice came again from above him, bringing him abruptly back.

'I don't agree with you about women, Anthony. They bring in the emotional factor. Not that they are really any more emotional than men, but if you bring men and women together, emotions are generated. And emotions are an obstruction.'

'An obstruction of what?'

Another pause, then, 'Of everything. I think there must always be separation between men and women.'

'Aren't there ever emotions between men and men?'

'Yes, sometimes. But they are easier to isolate and suppress.'

'To what end, Mark?'

'I thought you knew to what end. To gain control.'

'To gain control? Of what?'

'To gain control, firstly, of yourself, and, from yourself, of the others. That's what everyone wants in the end. Emotions are a way of avoiding the issue, an admission of your inability to take control. They are weakness, human frailty.'

'It is possible to avoid them?'

Oh yes.'

The certainty was physical. Standing tightened beneath it, waited for the voice to come again. It did not, and he felt obliged to speak himself.

'To gain control, Mark,' he said.

'Yes. It's simple, Anthony, easy. All human beings are equally useless, without any value or significance at all, but this is a very frightening thing for people to accept, so they make societies, make rules by which they all try to live, and by which they give themselves values; political, social, emotional values. But it's all a lie. No one has any value or rights, or any beliefs that mean anything in the end. All you have to do is to recognise this, know it and use it. To know it is to be free, absolutely free of everything and everyone; to use it is to have control, strength, power, to bind others to you, everyone, everything. You start from nothing, you accept nothing and then . . . and then you can have everything.'

'That's what you want, is it? Everything?'

'Don't you?'

'It . . . it never really seemed a viable proposition.'

'It is. Well? Are you with me, Anthony?'

'Of course. You know I am.'

'I just wanted to hear you say it.'

Standing felt himself grow suddenly warm, felt himself included in something in a way that he had never been included in anything before. Its beauty was, of course, its darkness, its essential, liberating nihilism. Suddenly, First was right. Everything was possible, Everything.

'I'm sorry about this evening, Mark,' he said at last, weakly.

'Don't be sorry. If you need to go and copulate, go and copulate, so long as you are strong when you do it, and remain strong. I think you understand that.'

Later, Standing said, 'What are we going to do?'

'For the moment, we are going to wait and watch and learn as much as we can. Your sexual skills might be very useful.'

You never knew Anthony Standing, Rachel. He was the other half of me, without which I might never have been possible. When he had gone, I rose and set my face towards the end. He was my first true brother, and the only one I ever truly loved.

I thought it would be hard to remember and reconstruct him as he was then, but it is not hard. His qualities were always there, plainly visible. He had a great softness which was never weakness, never sentimentality. It manifested itself in his gregariousness, in his sensuality. He loved to be amongst people, engaged with them, moving himself in relation to them, in friendship, in conflict, in the act of love. He was, when I met him, almost bewildered by the ease with which he could draw people to him, cashed in on it socially, sexually, but it was never merely a means to any end. His ability to enthuse others, to lead them and seduce them, to direct them always to where he was moving, this was the end in itself, this was the delight.

His character had a natural tendency to trivia and

cynicism, but that was only the nature of the world in which he operated. If I had not been there, he might have grown old in his fecklessness, become sad and dissolute. I gave him the still point about which all his turning had force.

It became obvious that he would bear my public face, be my outreach. Through him, I could keep my distance and yet engage with the world. I waited and watched as he began to give himself to me, as he began to reinvent himself in relation to me. I gave nothing away, but I let nothing slip. It was a love affair of the purity and depth that I had only dreamed might be possible, a slow, strong interlocking of minds.

Although I think you would have been too young, it pleases me to imagine you as one of the schoolgirls who brought him into disgrace when he was a teacher. I imagine you naked together, like young animals, touching and delighting each other in true innocence of being. It is a warm fantasy of the old world: the two great loves of my life together in a world in which I did not yet exist. In my mind now, after it is all over, you are together like that. I bless you both.

INCUBATION

THE BROTHERS

They noticed a change come over Anthony Standing towards the end of that summer. Something seemed to have gone hard within him, to have crystallised. It was paradoxical: the easygoing, shifting cynicism in which he had most easily dressed himself was played down, and this made him superficially more dour and serious, less attractive as a drinking companion; there was, however, something else, the gleam of something inside him that caught those who stayed with him long enough: an enthusiasm, a possibility of something that, although it was never specified, was intriguing and dangerous, was lifting him and driving him from just below the surface. The result of this change was to make his company considerably more exciting for those who could still stomach it. As the weeks passed he seemed to grow larger and louder, to need more and more space. It began to become actively dangerous to be with him.

He felt that he was becoming, externally at least, a creature of a type he had formerly regarded with contempt, the beer-bully, the loud-boy; but perhaps that contempt had been based upon his cowardice, or perhaps upon a sense of his superiority, social and intellectual, that had been spurious. Now he had a genuine superiority, based not upon his father's dignity, nor upon the reading he had absorbed in the long hours of his idleness; his superiority now was a physical energy that swelled within him day by day, a mental priapism that would not let him rest, that yearned to be discharged.

And so he drank until the world buzzed in his head and his movements were monumental lurches oblivious to obstruction. He argued loudly, instinctively, wheeling against any contradiction with sudden and cruel intensity. He turned to fight on a moment, rising and kicking the chair away, concentrating on the space before him and upon his protagonist, seeing if he would rise too, or just turn and slink away. They turned and slunk away too often. There was such weakness everywhere that it disgusted him as he challenged and revealed it. His heart jumped when one would not slink, when one stood and made himself ready. He loved to fight, to grapple with another straining torso, to drive his fists against something hard but human, more human than ever as he struck it and brought it out, feeling the recoil of his blow, the shuddering of the damage. He was not a skilful fighter, coming in always too close, too keen to make contact, impatient of the preliminary positionings, the strategic advantages. Often he was knocked down, rising before the swell of pain blocked his anger, ready for it, the iron band of hurt about his ribs, the swilling of blood in his mouth. The blows he took were a part of it, the counterbalances of his energy, the price he had to pay for the reality of his aggression; without them it would have been too easy; they made him strong. He would rise laughing, shaking himself clear, setting his feet, head down, bull-like.

Often he was knocked down, but he was never defeated, for he never fought alone. There was a group of them now, the old clique stripped of its passengers, who rose with him, set their shoulders against his and rolled into the fighting with him. They were bonded by their action, spent their time together, grew drunk together and not only with the beer, with the immediacy of their living. They huddled together and talked and, although he never mentioned First to them, Standing shared with them the vision First had given him, watching it light them as it had lit him, feeling it wind him up again as he shared it. They began to address one another as 'Brother', at first ironically, but soon with a seriousness, accepting it proudly as a badge of belonging, excluding those who were not of their set, admitting others whom they felt might belong, who distinguished themselves. From five they became ten, from ten, twenty.

They began to generate resentments amongst the others on the campus, but they fed on these resentments, became communally proud of them, bonded further. The women particularly set themselves against them, or most of the women. They were glad of this, defined themselves against everything a certain type of woman represented: the fostering of weakness, of neurosis, of pathetic little individualities for which endless excuses had to be made. Standing was truly glad to be free from such cloyments towards which, in his days of universal sexual sympathy, he had always had to make propitiations, gentlemanly deferrals which, from his present perspective, seemed hypocrisies.

He and his brothers were not without female company, but it came now on their terms; for there were women who were not immune to the masculinity Standing and his friends embodied, who courted cynically the sour disapproval of their peers. They had, these women, a hardened recklessness which matched the spirit of the Brothers. They would drift close, usually in pairs, sit down, accept drink, accept the attentions that were offered them, touched by giggles of apprehension or holding a thin line of sardonic distance. The propositioning they shortly received was devoid of niceties; there was no attempt at seduction. If they accepted the offer to walk out with one of the Brothers, they knew where they were being taken. None of them was ever coerced, Standing made sure of that: they knew, at least theoretically, to what they were submitting. Sexual congress with one of the Brothers was perfunctory and fierce, a bout of physical exercise, a sport with no obligations offered or accepted. It seemed, perhaps, to these women, the exercise of a kind of freedom, meaningless beyond itself, human relations reduced to elementals. Standing and his Brothers knew it to be thus, and wanted no commerce with women who believed otherwise.

Standing, at this time, ceased to have Mark First in constant attendance. First was still around, often still in the bar, often seen walking with Standing alone and talking to him; but they were not the double act that they had been. More often, First was alone, sitting in the library, eating alone with a book propped in front of him. He was as immaculately unapproachable as ever. Unless you knew who he was, you would not have noticed him, a small stocky man with pallid skin, his head cropped clearly, exaggerating his prominent eyes and nose. It would have been very difficult to assess his age: he might have been twenty, he might have been thirty-five.

He had been selected for promotion, was now a senior operator, supervising others, and becoming greatly disliked by those under his authority. He was absolutely precise and demanded absolute precision from others. He made no allowances for anything, penetrated every covered-up inaccuracy. He seemed to treat those under him merely as extensions of their work. The long room where he worked was silent below the rattle of machines and the slither of papers. Even breathing was done quietly. He would appear suddenly at your shoulder; and even when he wasn't looking over you, you always felt him there, watching somehow. The women hated him more than the men, although they could detect no overt prejudice in him. The general opinion of him was that, underneath all his rigidity, he was monumentally stupid, without the imagination to be anything other than he was.

Behind his back they mocked him, passed round caricatures of him that depicted him usually as some sort of sexual deviant. The most popular of these showed him naked with a bloody knife in one hand and his testicles in another, saying, 'They just take up unnecessary space.' This was copied and circulated and, one day, after he had turned upon a woman, dressed her down publicly for her incompetence in language clinically impervious to the bitter weeping to which he reduced her, someone placed a copy of the caricature on his desk. When he had done with the woman, had allowed her to withdraw her misery to the lavatory, had not allowed anyone to go with her, he stepped back to his desk and was confronted with this image of his self-mutilation. He did not react, glanced at it briefly, then placed it to one side and continued with his work. It lay open on his desk all day, stuck in the throat of everyone there.

In the evening, one of the women lingered and approached him, a tall woman who almost alone did not join in with the communal mockery of him.

'Mr First,' she said. 'I would like to apologise.'

'For what, Muriel?'

'For that obscene drawing.'

'You were not responsible for it, surely?'

'Passively responsible, as we all were.'

'Would you tell me who was actively responsible?'

'That . . . that would not be proper, I think.'

'Very well.' And he shuffled his papers together, stood to leave, ushering her out before him so that he could lock the room; then turning away, going briskly and leaving her diminished. She had wanted to tell him, had become disgusted with the entire malevolent atmosphere of the room, nurtured a secret admiration for their senior operator, for his precision and his certainty, for the strength she knew lay below the exercise of his authority. She would have told him everything at the slightest opening, at a smile, at a hand upon her shoulder, the faintest melting towards her. She was stupid even to have imagined that such a thing might have happened.

He had noted the woman's interest in him. It entertained him briefly amongst the hostility of his subordinates; but he preferred the hostility, breathed easier in acid. Muriel Jarrow. She was just another woman who caught him up in her fantasies, and, thinking about her, thinking what he might do with her attraction, he became bored. He did not need her. He had Anthony, and any other intimacy would be a disloyalty.

The caricature was a delight. He had to stop himself smiling at it amongst the cretins he supervised. He showed it to Anthony that night when he came back from his evening with the Brothers.

'We'll deal with this, Mark. Fisherson'll tell us who was responsible.'

'No, no, Anthony. I don't want to be identified. The time will come. They will know where my balls are soon enough. Tell me about your evening, that is far more interesting.'

So, as usual, Standing listed who had been there, what had been said, who had fought, who had fornicated. First lay silent under the unfolding of this chronicle and Standing, on his lower bunk, could only hear the breathing above him, and only then when the excitements of his narrative did not overwhelm him.

He loved to tell First his exploits, was always aware as he did them that he would later have to account for everything in minute detail. This was part of the thrill. The retelling, the reliving of the incidents, became ritual, an offering of the day to the controlling spirit. Blow by blow, given and received, he reimagined his fights, clause by clause his arguments, the sliding delight of his copulations. One day, the voice would come from above and say 'Yes . . . yes', but it never came, but the wanting it to come, the waiting for it was everything. Once it had all been said, Standing would fall into sleep, secure in the knowledge that the burden he had delivered was being digested and valued by the silent man above him who never slept.

The campus had initially been fairly open, a place of work with its security tight only in the most secret places. Now, however, people were beginning to drift in from outside in substantial numbers, to join the supper queues, to scrounge drinks in the bars, to take a little slice off the bounty that seemed to be available to the workers here. At first, such people were obvious by their ragged clothes and shifty movements. They were soon challenged and sent off. As the months passed and the whole place grew shabbier, as the sense of its wider purposes gave place to drudgery and a spreading despondency, the outsiders managed to evade detection fairly regularly; their shabbiness was beginning to be reflected amongst the workers. They grew, when challenged, more aggressive, shouting obscene paranoias at those who removed them, fought and broke things.

Then some of the outsiders began to come in with more sinister intent, committing robberies on the residential terraces, breaking into rooms and even assaulting people who had stayed out too late. With nightfall, fear began to swell in every darkness. The numbers of the campus security teams were supplemented, but they were never where they were needed. It was widely rumoured that they were corrupt, that they tipped off the marauders, took their cut.

Then one of Standing's Brothers was assaulted late one night by a gang of youths as he sloped back from his woman to his residence. His nose was broken and his clothes stripped off him. Standing and his group went into corners and muttered, and then, a week after the assault, a gang of the marauders were caught and beaten up systematically and severely, two of them crippled, one blinded, all of them stripped naked and defiled. The oldest of them was nineteen. They were not necessarily the group who had committed the original assault, but the point was made emphatically; the incursions effectively stopped.

The authorities were outraged by this retaliation. Standing and his gang were interviewed, but all had smug alibis. No-one seriously doubted that they had done it. They strutted about the place after this with an augmented arrogance, drawing a general disapprobation in which they glowed.

★　　★　　★

Fifteen, including Standing, had perpetrated the revenge. It had been carefully planned. The youths were just drifting about in the early hours of the morning, looking for some action. They were overpowered individually by men in black masks who worked throughout in total silence. They were dragged down to an empty garage and punished one by one, beaten about the heads and bodies with clubs, left in a blubbering and bloody heap on the floor. Paraffin and urine was sprayed over them.

In the days that followed, the revengers, one by one, were taken aside by Standing and were introduced to Mark First. He clasped their hands, congratulated them, told them that they had proved themselves, that there would be other, larger tasks. Their greatest achievement, he told them, was the discipline with which they had acted. This they must perfect.

'Above all,' he said at last, peering closely into their faces, 'think about death. When you feel angry or frustrated, imagine what it would be like to kill your way out of that emotion. When you touch a woman, imagine what it would be like to kill her. Imagine it, but do not do it. Harden yourself to it, but do not give way to it. Then imagine what it would be like to die. As you lie in bed at night, imagine there being no waking up. Imagine the burst of pain that becomes so large that you cannot stop it from swallowing you completely. Imagine it. Become familiar with death, and you will become strong. Very strong indeed. Very soon such strength will be needed.'

They were disturbed by this. Each went away with this powerful incitement like a mark upon them. To none of them did it occur to challenge First's right to say this. Standing had always given the impression that there was something or someone just behind him, an urgency to which he was always answerable, a power of which he was only the executive. Thus, when First made himself known to them, they understood at once. Standing had chosen his men well.

Later, from a distance, some of them wondered about First. He was quite unlike they were. They could hardly imagine him bar-fighting or fucking. But when they remembered his words, his face upon them, the tight clutch of his hand, they felt an excitement that justified him. When, afterwards, they saw him moving quietly about on his own, they recognised something in him that they would never before have imagined. If any of them had ever wondered where all this Brotherhood was going to lead, they ceased to have doubts now.

They began to have secret meetings. Standing would pass the word and they would congregate at dead of night in some empty shed or old tutorial room with the blackouts down, never in the same place twice. Standing would say secretly to each of them, 'First would like a word tonight, in garage twelve, at the usual time.' They would lie awake, tight with anticipation, waiting for the moment to slip from their rooms, dodge through the darkness to the appointed place, moving tensed for violence, alert for marauders, for the security men, for casual night-ramblers. They learnt to be invisible. The rule was that, if they were seen, they were to return to their rooms, to miss the meeting; this none of them wanted, for it implied their unwillingness to participate, suggested disloyalty. First treated non-attendance seriously; for whatever reasons, security, lack of nerve, oversleeping, the opprobrium was the same.

First would always be there when they arrived, usually with Standing, but not always; and even if he was there, Standing would never speak, would keep to the background. There was a paraffin lamp alight which threw soft shadows around: First always seemed to be the centre of the shadows, as if he himself was generating them. He greeted them with an embrace, a clasp of his hard body against theirs that seemed to test them as much as greet them. He sometimes spoke to them of their personal behaviours. He seemed to know everything. He spoke to them of their purposes, of what they were doing and who they were, of what they were becoming together under his direction.

'Remember,' he would say. 'If it is necessary for us to be brutal, then we will be brutal. But do not indulge your brutality. You have not been selected for brutality, but for integrity. Your integrity is your strength. Violence is trivial and self-defeating if it comes from the emotions. If it is a function of your inner strength of soul, then it is real strength, through and through. I have told you all to prepare for death. You think that is because I want you to be strong. This is true, but it is not all. We need to be perfected in our strength and our resolve. In doing this, we will become purged of our weakness, our human frailty; and in this, we will become purged of our individuality. We will be truly free. Free of others and free of ourselves. Human individuality is a stupid, losing struggle against reality. In renouncing our individuality, in knowing that we do not matter, not in the slightest, then we reach out for reality, wire ourselves into the brutal reality of the universe.'

At another time, he told them, 'Be under no illusions. I ask everything from you, and I will give you everything in return. I ask for your loyalty. I ask for the submission of yourself to my command, absolutely. I ask that nothing you do, nothing you achieve or become, shall belong to you any more, but to me, only to me. You understand this. You have already pledged yourselves to this, and to go back on it now will be the end of you. You are me. You do not have anything that I do not own. You are parts of my body, and if you become corrupt, you will be hacked from me, a dead limb. You are nothing apart from what I require you to be. But in return for this loss of yourselves, I will give you the world. It will all belong to you, to us, to our absolute certainty, our absolute unity. The world that now exists is coming to an end. You know that. You see it everywhere, feel the rumblings of its collapse coming closer and closer. When it ends, soon, my brothers, soon, then there will only be us. The old world will fall around us and reveal us like a sculpture coming out of the stone; and those who do not belong to us will recognise that we are the only future, we are the truth. They will welcome us in the certainty that we offer, in the safety of our absolute strength. They will hate us at first, as they writhe from their old corruptions. They will always fear us, but that is what we want, that will only feed our strength. In the end, they will come to respect us and to love us, to know our beauty and perfection. We are the athletes of power, the gods that they have always longed for but never been able to see. They will see us and, in the final hour, they will worship us. We are the world. Nothing is beyond us. Nothing. Nothing.'

The promises he made them entered their blood, drove it through them, making their muscles hard, their lungs burn with air like acid, their cocks swell, brought a fizzing into the base of their skulls. They would have died for him and killed for him on sudden impulses that rushed through them when he turned himself upon them. They felt no warmth for him, and certainly received none from him, but he emanated an intoxication that caught their hearts in a grip that was personal, intimate, inexpressible. He turned them into something that was incredible. They felt the possibility of becoming perfect machines.

Sometimes he would leave Standing asleep in his repletion, would go out into the night alone. He would exercise his old street skills of silence and invisibility, become part of the darkness. He needed little sleep. He was charged with too much and could not keep his mind still enough for sleep. He envied Standing his freedom to release his energy, sometimes dreamed of slitting a throat in the darkness, of finding a woman or a black to unloose himself upon, but he resisted this. He must be beyond such personal indulgences.

As he moved through the night, he imagined the sleeping world around him, imagined the fear and loneliness that were bunched behind every dark window. They needed him, they all needed him, and his time was coming. He moved like a spirit amongst them, imagined himself entering their dreams, making them writhe and turn and sweat, grow hard under the presence of his spirit. He would fulfil his promise.

He passed by the windows of the Brothers, and from them he felt a corresponding heat. They were little pockets of fire in the desolation. He had a solidarity with them that was immaculate; they were coming together about him, massing about his core, piling their energies into his purpose. The sense of power he felt at these times beat a pulse in his heart and in his loins that gave him a certainty so absolute that, at times, he did not feel big enough to contain it.

He crept back to Standing, stood and watched him sleeping, and loved him then until the tears came into his eyes.

★   ★   ★

We had no direct hand in the collapse of the state. We protected ourselves and waited for our moment, no more. That the collapse came at the moment we were ready for it demonstrated clearly that our cause was ripe. We were no opportunists; not for us the mere filling of a vacuum. Quietly and carefully we prepared ourselves for our moment; and we prepared not physically, but mentally. To have physical power without the beliefs with which to wield that power is to stand briefly atop a shifting dune; the beliefs turn the sand to rock and then you can step out easily, then the power comes meekly into your hands. Power is a function of belief.

It is useless now, I know, Rachel, to offer justifications for what we were and what we did. There is no need for justification. We were, we are: that is enough.

Anthony in those days was the moving force, and I was his spirit. I was invisible, living a quiet life on the edge of things where I could watch and judge, take decisions from a distance. No-one knew who I was; at first, no-one at all. There were times, later, when I wished it could have always been thus, but I had my responsibilities.

As he selected our brothers after he had tested them, he brought them to me to be bound formally to our cause; I gave them my identity as the secret badge of their belonging. As I looked into the eyes of each of them, as I felt them see me, recognise me, a bolt of power went through me. They became me, and through them I grew and grew. Each was like a new organ of my body. Oh, I needed to keep myself removed and quiet, to absorb all this new strength that came flooding into me and to feel it as it flowed out of me. To move too soon, to stand out and to accept the trappings of my position too soon might well have been too much for me. There were considerable pyschological risks that I faced during those days and, whilst I would not for a moment equate them with the risks that Anthony and the others took, they were nevertheless capable of destroying me.

INNER AND OUTER CIRCLES

A hot night brought the senior Brothers together in a small room without windows, behind a locked door, in a closed darkness. They sat silent, contained each within his own bulk, waiting within an intense blackness that swelled about them and inside them. The surfaces of their flesh and of their awareness were monumental, straining against the silence. They struggled to contain their breathing, as if it were a symptom of their frailty. They were aware of one another as replications of themselves. Each felt the same physically and emotionally, held in a rigid unity. They waited through minutes and hours that had no meaning.

At last, a split-second after they had all been expecting it, a key entered the lock of the door, the wards turned with a quick biting. The door opened, and the circle was briefly invaded by a grey gloom, by a swirl of dank air from outside, rousing for a moment the rankness within. The door closed again, and for a few moments the silence and the darkness were allowed to re-establish themselves.

First struck a match, and a flash of painful light

brought the four men, each stooped similarly on his chair, each a weight of black humanity, each sweat-sodden and hard-mouthed, into a glaring instant of reality. Then the match went out and, after another pause, another resettlement of the darkness, First stepped securely across and took his place in the circle.

'Tell me,' he said.

'The army have taken over a town in the north, have started shooting the civil administration.'

'A concerted plan?'

'We think not. It sounds like an opportunist.'

'Who is he?'

'A man called Cheverton, a Colonel, Special Forces.'

'What do the files say about him?'

'No recorded political loyalties. An individualist. I think he's making it up as he goes along, riding the circumstances. This makes him very dangerous to them.'

'What have they done?'

'Nothing direct. Probes have gone out to the regional commands, but no direct orders. They seem afraid of forcing the other commanders into a choice too early. They don't know what they're up against yet. They're stalling, hoping it'll resolve itself, run out of steam.'

'Will it? Are they right?'

'Hard to tell. If they are right, they'll be lucky this time.'

'And if they're wrong?'

'If they're wrong, then . . . chaos.'

First was silent then. The concentration swelled back amongst them. Ideas, possibilities, scraps of further information rose to each of their minds, but they waited, submissive. Some minutes later, First began to speak again.

'It is time, therefore, for us to submerge. No more

meetings, no more attempts to assert ourselves over anything. We must blend in as much as we can. If the army comes here, they will have to find their way to us. The longer it takes, the better. When they find us, we will be ready for them.'

Then again the silence. Then First rose, went to the door and let himself out into the night. At the prescribed intervals, without speaking further, the others let themselves out, Standing last of all. The five minutes of solitude he spent there filled him with an impatience that he strove with all his discipline to master. He wanted to run out shouting. He wanted to find someone to fight. He wanted to go to a woman. He wanted to go to First. The last of these wants was the only practical one, and when he had stayed his time out, he set out to fulfil it.

He found First back at their room, not as he had expected, lying on his back on his bed, calm and detached, but standing by the window gazing out over the grey blocks of the campus, his arms outstretched, his palms flat upon the plate-glass.

'Mark?' he said.

When First turned, Standing saw his face streaked with tears. The sight terrified him, backed him to the door. He could not speak.

'Come here, Anthony.'

Standing moved slowly towards him and, as he advanced, First too came forward, stepped into the shadow at the centre of the room. He took Standing in his arms, bound him with an embrace that trembled with energy, placed his face against Standing's breast.

Standing, his upper arms pinned to his sides, reached his forearms around his leader's waist, held his head up, tilted it back, not because he wanted to be clear of First, but because he wanted to kiss him, to make love to him, and the impulses that drove these desires horrified him. It would not be an act of degeneracy, he argued, for we would not be stooping to our animal desires, but using our bodies merely to express our energy. It would be a religious act, a ritual to symbolise our unity, our freedom. But for all this rationalisation, the desire rose blunt and physical, and Standing could not understand or control it.

First recognised the symptoms of this desire. It filled him with pride. Had he known how to realise the desire without losing his control of it, he might have submitted to it; but he knew this was a temptation, a weakness. He held the desire and let it lift him. He rose clear of it, and of himself.

'It is beginning, Anthony,' he said. 'The world is bending over, wet-arsed, ready for us. We only have to be true to ourselves and it will all be given to us.'

There had been riots, and Colonel Cheverton had been called in to suppress them. He had done so swiftly and brutally, too brutally for the compromised civil administration who had begun to set him up as a scapegoat for the riots themselves. He had learned that the administration was rotten with corruption, was hated by the mass of the townsfolk, that the riots had been provoked by the duplicity of the administration and that his suppression of them had been greeted with general relief. What he had done was brutal, yes, but necessary to bring some order back into the town.

In the wake of his success he had toured the town as a hero, had been surrounded in the streets, cheered in restaurants. It was only a matter of time before the administration turned actively against him. He had dared them to do it, set himself up alone in his headquarters where they came in a bunch, the mayor, the police commissioner, the political officers. He had outstared them, laughed at them, rejoiced in their fury and their impotence. He had given orders, watched them dragged out squealing to be pistolled in the barracks yard. In the concrete silence, as the cordite drifted off into the afternoon, as the blood trickled out like water on to a drought plain, he had realised what he was about and his heart grew within him like a ripening fruit. He had moved fast, occupied all the vital points, arrested all those who had been connected with the old administration, all those sympathetic to or compromised by it. He imposed curfew, rationing, had secured the approach roads, waited now for something to happen. He hoped it would be battle. He understood battle. He imagined a rabble of mayors and police commissioners and political officers coming down in a squall of fury for him to slaughter massively.

Twenty miles south at Darrington Hall, a hundred young officers were at a charity ball. Lord Darrington held his ancestral estates in these latter days with a mixture of bluff, compromise and simple deceit. There was hardly any charity left, but he sustained the tradition of the ball as a means of keeping in touch. He asked the army because the officers were the only young men of any standing left in the country, and because he was also astute enough to suspect that the army had the next political move. It was far more difficult to find suitable girls, and most of those he had secured were not at all suitable. But they were pretty and sociable, and if they did shout and giggle and get unpleasantly drunk very rapidly, and if they were far too ready to let the army into their underwear, Darrington himself was able, by keeping to the well-lit reception rooms of his house, to sustain a fiction of respectability, to believe that it was, somehow, all going on as it had always gone on, and that the shrieking and squealing that ran down from the upper bedrooms and in from the dusky gardens was just youthful high spirits.

Darrington sat with Commander Fox and a young staff major, talked politics and drank whiskey. The young major watched his commander parrying the pertinent questions which their host threw out as if he were drunk, but which the major, whose name was Catton, knew were based upon some very shrewd gossip.

'You must have contingency plans, Fox, surely.'

'Contingent upon what, Lord Ronald?'

'Contingent upon the whole thing going to buggery'.

'We'd all be in it then, I think.'

And you haven't made sure of your boltholes? I know you buggers far too well for that.'

'We're soldiers, Lord Ronald. We only do what we're told.'

Darrington snorted.

Catton became suddenly bored by this. He excused himself and rose on the pretext of making sure his men were behaving themselves.

'Of course they're not bloody behaving themselves, Major.'

'There are limits, Lord Ronald,' Catton said.

'Go and find yourself a woman, Major.'

Catton bowed facetiously and moved away smartly, drifting as soon as he was out of sight of the others, leaving the house and wandering out on to the terrace, down the stone steps and deep into the garden.

Beyond the glare of the Hall, the night was black and

warm, the air tactile and static. The scents of heavy flowers cloyed him. He passed close to shrubberies whence the progress of ungainly copulations could be marked. By a tree a young lieutenant lay with his sleeping head in the lap of a girl whose face in the shadow seemed bleached and exhausted. A pair of girls approached, leaning against each other and stumbling, giving off as they passed a sour, animal reek. Catton ignored these distractions, steered himself away from them. They too were boring; they irritated him. He felt that he ought to do something about them, engage himself with them in one way or another, but he felt an enormous disinclination to pursue any of these obligations. There was an anger building in him, and any such engagement would focus and release that anger.

He walked out into the centre of one of the large lawns, turned to face the Hall, which glared out like some cruise ship becalmed oblivious in the oppressive night. He longed for something to happen, something that could not happen here, not within the constraints of anything that was happening here now; some cataclysm that would shake all this down, bring some direction to it if only in fending off its destruction. He was a soldier, and he was blunt for lack of action. He had felt this before, never perhaps as acutely as he felt it now, and it frightened him to feel it. He wanted something to leap into, to engage himself. The world seemed stale, living day to day, making do; and whilst it did so, great fissures were opening just under the surface.

He had had a lover once, a girl he had lived with and with whom, at times, it had seemed as if he had found a direction, a whole world of possibilities to be opened. They had made love exhaustively, and he remembered that now with a hot longing. But something had gone wrong. When he had made love to her, he had begun to grow angry, cruel; he had frightened her and she had drawn back. And when he had not been with her, he had felt wearied by thoughts of her. He had outgrown her, perhaps, or perhaps the world in which they had lived had no longer been a place in which such a relationship might function. He had left her, and had been glad to do so. He longed for her sentimentally now, something that was possible no longer but that he wished somehow might be possible again, knowing that it would never be possible, never again this side of a great abyss.

There was a rumble of thunder deep in the night, and Catton lifted when he heard it, roused as if called by it. He turned about and scanned the darkness looking for the lightning, looking for the storm that would come and crash down about him. He wanted it to come.

When it did not come and he turned at last back towards the house, he saw someone running down, one of Fox's orderlies. Catton saw him stop and look about him, urgent. Catton stepped forward and as he approached the orderly, the man recognised him and ran towards him.

On the second floor of the Hall, locked in a lavatory, Rachel Darrington was sitting out the Charity Ball. She was fifteen, and her father had given his permission this year for her to have the freedom of the ball, told her she was old enough now to know what was what. She did not feel old enough, and if she was old enough, her knowledge of what was what gave her no freedom.

She attended a strict church school where she was very happy. Miss Tarrant who took them for Personal Education had told them clearly that to drink alcohol was to put a blindfold over your common sense, that to have sexual intercourse with a man to whom you were not married was to degrade yourself and him. Rachel had seen in the first hour of the party enough evidence to support both these dogmas. She had come up here afraid, and, as the fear had settled behind the security of the lavatory bolt, she had become disgusted. Someone had been sick in her bathroom, and in her bedroom she had surprised one of her schoolfriends licking the penis of a fat subaltern.

She was a prude, they had told her often enough. She only wanted half a chance to do it herself, but lacked the courage. She wondered whether any of this was true. Perhaps it was. She had been to a dance last month and had spent an hour, more, kissing a boy, had liked it, had liked him, had liked his touching of her breasts, had been alarmed but not appalled to realise that he had had an erection and that he was rubbing it against her leg. Certainly, she had been sexually aroused, had drifted in a warm wash of sensation, her body alert and receptive; but, equally certainly, she had had not the remotest desire to go beyond that. Perhaps it was lack of courage, but she knew in herself that to submit to sexual intercourse would be to abandon herself to the crude brutality that she had seen exercised tonight on girls she knew well, had shared secrets and fantasies with, had thought she had recognised as girls essentially like her. Under the casual and efficient embraces of the soldiers, she had watched her friends drowned, annexed, neutralised. Somewhere, one day, she would give herself freely to someone whose touch would make her mean more, not less, than she was now.

Although the lavatory was hardly the ideal place, Rachel was used to solitude and a few hours locked up alone held no frustrations for her. She was a Christian, and in her solitudes addressed herself to God. She did not pray formally. She simply settled herself into an awareness of the presence of God, into the contentment and certainty of herself with which her belief provided her. At such times, the world became very real for her. Time seemed to slow, and her apprehension of reality focused. She could look minutely at doors, at walls, yes, even at a lavatory cistern, and see in them an incredible world of detail. She lost her sense of herself in such times, became her awareness. When she roused from these meditations, she felt calm and refreshed.

Coming out of such a state after she knew not how long, she felt a silence coming from the house beyond her. The party seemed over. Perhaps it was nearly dawn, although it did not feel like it. It was surely too early to venture out. She waited and listened and slowly gathered the resolve to go and see what was happening, planning other boltholes should she need them.

The landing outside was deserted. Her bed showed signs of unpleasant usage, but was empty. She came down the main stairway and saw in the hall a few girls sitting about as if waiting for something that wasn't going to happen.

'Hello, Rache,' one of them said as she descended.

'Where is everybody?' she asked, deciding to yawn and stretch as if she had been asleep somewhere.

'All the soldiers have gone. There's a crisis or something.'

She went and found her father, who was in his study trying to contact someone on the telephone. He saw her and smiled at her distantly. She sat on the floor and waited. Eventually he put the receiver down.

'No-one's answering the bloody telephone.'

'What's wrong, Daddy?'

'God knows. Someone's farted somewhere, and they've all rushed off to have a sniff.'

'Is there going to be a war?'

'I bloody well hope not,' he said, but by the way he said it, Rachel could tell that it was on his mind.

He stood and tapped on his desk, looking into the darkness through the big windows, lost in a rush of speculation. And Rachel, sitting two yards away from him, suddenly began to feel cold and alone. She recalled all the things that had been going through her mind that evening, and suddenly they all seemed completely trivial. Even if I had lost my virginity this evening, she thought, even if it had been as nasty as it could have been, I don't think it would have mattered any more, not now. And this made her very, very frightened.

A week later, Colonel Cheverton realised that he had failed. Militarily he was unassailed. He had the town in a stranglehold, but the days slipped by and he really had no idea what to do next. He had expected the next move to be obvious, had expected that his action would precipitate other actions in which he would be able to identify his objectives and move against them. This had not happened. Nothing had happened. He had the power, but was learning that it had limits.

The townsfolk were not soldiers, and they had gone surly on him. Some had come wanting him to settle old scores, and felt betrayed by his unwillingness to do this. The rationing and commandeering were causing further resentments. Cheverton was learning that any rule, however scrupulously objective, could not fit every case, would breed injustice somewhere.

The days had passed, and the townsfolk grew openly hostile to his men, jeered and threw stones, behaved more and more like a people under occupation. Several of his officers began to call for examples to be made. Cheverton hesitated, felt his great excitement now edged with a panic, a rage, which he held, so far, close within him, but which he was going to have to confront sooner or later. He was going to have to set his heart and follow the logic of his situation. He longed for battle.

Then there came news. An officer from Cheverton's home barracks reached his perimeter. After half an hour with this officer, Cheverton knew what was happening across the country and also why they had not yet been confronted here. His rising had triggered a whole sequence of other risings in army bases throughout the country. There had apparently been a concerted plan in development; Cheverton's action had pre-empted that and the various commanders had moved independently to prevent their being outplayed by their colleagues in the wrangle for power.

At the sports centre, which held three hundred stinking men and women, half-mad with fear and hunger, the soldiers were growing unruly. Their officers had realised what was developing and had sent urgently for new orders, but none had come. Then the soldiers acted. Two women, political officers, who had kept up a barrage of complaints and insults against their detention, were singled out by a pair of bull-sergeants, were dragged out for interrogation, beaten systematically into silence, defiled and humiliated. It took the soldiers nearly an hour to kill the women, whose bodies were then dumped back amongst their friends. The officers had now no effective control over their men, who were busy forming a noisy committee, making plans of their own in the absence of direction from above.

Their wrangling left the sports centre relatively

unguarded. An hour after the bodies of their comrades had been returned to them, the prisoners made a break. It was not a concerted plan. They herded together, muttered, then rushed suddenly at the soldiers, overwhelming half a dozen before the others found their weapons and opened fire. In the confusion, fifteen of the prisoners made their way out into the town; the rest were gunned down as they ran, as they fought, as they stood and surrendered, nailed to the ground with bullets as they moaned and twitched. A young lieutenant who had tried to bring the men back to discipline had also been shot down, and his brother officers had all retreated to the town hall, apart from one who had joined gladly in the slaughter. With the killing done, a sense of anticlimax came over the men, and they wandered away from the scene of their orgy, looking firstly for food, and then for drink. They were even, at first, prepared to pay for it.

But the news of the massacre was out, and the civilians, assuming, not unreasonably, that the soldiers had only begun their killing, began to fight back. Within an hour there was general fighting, and by nightfall the town was awash in an orgy of killing. Most of the population barred themselves as deeply into their houses as they could, but there were fires started, houses smashed open and ransacked, the cowering families butchered screaming in their corners. Out on the streets, there was anarchy. It began with the soldiers fighting the populace, but then looting began, and rape; old grudges were brought into the mêlée; racial, religious and social tensions that had been long suppressed were sprung open in the licence of violence. Soldiers shed their uniforms to blend in with the populace. Every stranger was an enemy and, as the violence grew and grew, all men, all women, became strangers. The desires of humanity, to dominate, to possess materially, sexually, became, as the carapace of social order was ripped off, released, essential: either you became a possessor or you were possessed. In the ache of the long summer's night, fires roared, walls fell, showers of glass burst from plate glass windows; vehicles caught fire or were driven crazily down wrecked streets to bunch against walls, to slam into other vehicles, to career over piles of rubble and turn spinning and impotent like overturned insects. And as the violence gathered its momentum, it seemed no longer instigated but a perpetual motion into which the human beings were sucked as they fought to survive the horror, and in being sucked in fed it further. There was no possible neutrality: the energy of the violence had become the energy of life, and to resist that energy was to succumb to it. Class, sex, race, rank or position, individuality of all shade and degree became dissolved in the struggle.

At dawn the town was devastated. The survivors, those few who had buried themselves deeply and successfully enough, emerged to a world that they did not recognise, and where they did not belong. Mostly thay sat about, waiting for someone or something to come and tell them what to do, or perhaps only to put an end to their wretchedness. The soldiers, or anyone who admitted to being a soldier, had vanished.

But the violence was not over. It had consumed all that it could productively consume within the town and was now spreading out into the countryside. In the neighbouring villages the madness found new sustenance: gangs and bands, mobs hungry and heedless, brought the madness like a plague wind. Anyone who took a stand against it, tried to establish any authority against it, was rounded upon and consumed. Within a week the whole county was in chaos, within a fortnight the cities of the north were afire, the crops were ablaze in the fields and all industry had ceased. Some army contingents moved out to try and establish some sort of order, but they no longer knew to whom they should be loyal, and became, those that held together, loyal to themselves, part of the madness.

As autumn drew on, wet and sour, the violence of man against man was succeeded by the violence of nature in the form of disease and starvation. The populace fell under a great silence – the silence of fear and the silence of oppression. No-one was writing any history of this time, no-one was clear enough to have any perspective upon it. In one real sense, civilisation had come to an end.

In the capital where the army were trying to take control of the streets, Jacob Catton lived in an intensity of rage, driving into the boiling centres of crowds, raking the turbulent bodies with gunfire, setting his heart against the screaming. He did not know whether they screamed their defiance or their terror at him; it made no difference. He only wanted it to stop; but it would not stop, and the more he fought it the louder it became, a molten inhumanity of noise, his rage blistering and bursting against it. He wanted only peace, at any price; only silence, only the end of this if it meant the end of everything.

Rachel, I was frightened by the anarchy in the north, more frightened than I had been of anything; more frightened than I ever was to be again. And behind that fear, although they will never believe or understand this, was a profound sadness for the suffering that the anarchy engendered. I felt responsible for all men. I wanted to rule and guide and protect them. Even the

100

weak and deformed in body and soul were becoming my responsibility. I was disgusted by the personal satisfactions of those who killed for their pleasure or their gain. They had no right to take life, because they did not understand life, and because they were not prepared, as we always were, to give their lives as easily as they squandered the lives of others.

Those whom we killed, and those who died for us, finally deserve the same respect, the same honour. Life is a bright bolt of flame within each of us. We hold it for such a little time. We must respect it and use it, and if needs be spend it freely; and if its use, if its surrender, can advantage the cause of life in others, then its expense has meaning. We sought to concentrate the individual flames into one great body of fire; in this concentration we were necessarily ruthless towards the individuals who either would not be incorporated into our whole, or who were needed to make their sacrifice on the outer edges of our central dominion, to protect and sustain the centre. But we had, always, always, a respect for life; it was our creed. Even in our taking of life we valued it. Death is the consummation of life. Those who deny this, do not understand life fully.

I honour those who died for us and at our hands; and I have the right to lament those who died pointlessly. I grieve for their lack of purpose, the loss of their potential, the squandering of the possibilities that are inherent in every human life. When I remember what was let loose in the north in those months, I am appalled at the horror of it, dream of it at my lowest times, the wound that will not be healed, that soaks the earth and rots it, that staunches the flame. Allow me at least the integrity of these emotions.

THE ARMY

The day the army arrived on the campus, sheets of winter rain swirled about the concrete chasms. There were shots, but an abiding silence settled soon under the weight of the weather and the waiting to see how the world had changed.

Standing and First waited in silence in their room. Standing wanted to talk, to air his apprehensions, but his leader was completely involved in the waiting, listening as if he could hear through the walls, across the concourses, attuned to what was happening. It was this total intensity that, Standing considered, led outsiders to believe that First was stupid. He felt weak in comparison.

At last the boots came into their corridor, and they heard the rooms being opened, heard arguments, blows, huddled footsteps moving away. First did not move, stood with his back to the window, leaning against it casually.

Their turn came, the door flung open and a couple of machine-guns with men in fatigues attached to them entered. Standing, who was sitting on his bunk was told to fucking move. He stood beside First as the lockers were gutted, the beds stripped and prodded.

An officer with a clipboard appeared and they gave their names and positions. Their names were checked against a list and, as they were not apparently on the list, the soldiers left them to tidy up their mess.

'Now what?' Standing asked.

'We wait, and watch, and do as we're told. This place is important to them, but it's useless until they can find someone who knows how it works. They'll come to us in time.'

They were set to work to construct barbed-wire fences about the campus, to dig tank traps and gun pits. It was tiring, mindless work in a world of bitter grey mud, but they didn't complain. Standing kept as close to First as he could, ready to receive the word, should it come; and also because he felt safe beside his leader. One of two of the others made complaints, personal or general, and were treated with immediate violence, knocked down and beaten. The soldiers seemed indistinguishably brutal. There was nothing to be bargained with them.

'They're afraid,' First said to Standing in their room. 'They don't know what they're up against here, and their only response is brutality.'

'I saw Garman today. He tells me they're beating up the blacks for the hell of it, and they've started on the women, although that is officially prohibited.'

'Lucky then, that we have no blacks or women amongst us.'

First liked to watch Anthony's fear, knew that it was going to be tested very soon, for it could not take them much longer to arrive at the Brotherhood. He knew though that his fear was of the unknown, and that

103

when at last they came for him specifically, he would be sufficient.

'Here, Anthony,' he said.

'What's this?'

'A capsule.'

He watched Standing finger the pill, saw him puzzled for a moment, then smile; and he knew he had been right.

When they came for Standing in the work line, First did not even lift his head. Standing would have come readily, but it was part of the ritual to drag him and hit him. They threw him into an interview room and left him there for an hour to examine his bruised kidneys.

A major arrived eventually, a tall, sour-faced man who smelt of semen, with the two morons who had collected him to do the physical necessaries.

'Anthony Macdowell Standing?'

'Yes.'

'You ran an organisation called the Brotherhood.'

'Hardly an organisation, Major.'

'What then?'

'An . . . affectation, I suppose. A group of friends who did things together, discussed things. It all seems quite trivial now.'

'Give me the names.'

'Oh . . . there was Jack Robinson . . . Bill Wright . . . Tom Deverill. Most of them left before you arrived.'

'Why did they leave?'

'I expect they were afraid of you, Major.'

'And why didn't you leave?'

'Because I don't think that I have anything to be afraid of. I'm really quite glad you've come. There was the most piss-awful mess here, you know.'

'Don't patronise me, you little cunt.'

'I'm sorry, Major. I really didn't mean to patronise you.'

'Who was the leader of this organisation?'

'Well, I suppose I must admit to being that.'

'I have here a transcript of one of your speeches, Standing. You talk about the leader: I quote, "The man of ultimate integrity, the man whose silent strength is within us all." That isn't you, is it? Is it?'

'No. I probably didn't have myself completely in mind at that point. I tended to make up those speeches as I went along, inspired by the rhetoric of the occasion. I don't think any of it meant very much, I'm afraid.'

'So you're denying that there ever was a leader, someone behind the scenes, someone to whom you were answerable.'

'Who on earth can you have in mind?'

'Answer the fucking question, Standing.'

'What fucking question, Major?'

The morons moved forward, but the Major held them back.

'Is there or is there not a leader of this Brotherhood, apart from yourself, over and above yourself, to whom you were, and presumably still are, answerable?'

'Oh. That fucking question.'

'Well?'

'No.'

'There is no leader?'

'No.'

'No, there is no leader?'

Standing felt himself lift out of this mess, set himself straight at last.

'No, Major. No, there is no answer.'

'Very well. You have twenty-four hours in which to find an answer. If there is still no answer, I will have it extracted from you. This will be very painful. You will beg me to put you out of your misery and, when I have the information I need, I *will* put you out of your misery. Am I clear?'

'Quite clear, Major.'

'Take him down, Sergeant; and Sergeant?'

'Sir?'

'Don't hit him any more. Not until I say so. Understand? Do you understand me, Sergeant?'

'Sir.'

'Bad luck, Sergeant,' Standing said as they dragged him down into a cellar.

In the rank darkness within which he was confined, he felt that he had acquitted himself with honour. He hoped distantly that one day they would know and would be proud of what he had done. They had searched him, but had allowed him to keep his watch. It had a little light which illuminated the digits, and this became a point of stability in the darkness that swirled about him. He believed that the Major was a man of his word. He counted off the hours. He had the capsule still tight in his anus. Thirty minutes before they came for him, he would recover it and crack it open between his teeth. He sat on the stone floor and determined not to go to sleep. He could not waste these last hours in sleep.

It amazed him that he was without fear. He faced his extinction without the slightest tremor. The life in him was strong and clear, rushing through him even in this silent darkness, concentrated and pure: the knowledge that it would soon be snapped off intensified it. He felt limitlessly strong and certain. Three years ago he would have submitted to the merest threat. Cowardice, he reasoned, is only for those who do not understand life, who think always that with a little more time they can find out the secrets, whose hearts are still clotted with the indulgences of self. He played out in his mind the moments of his triumph, the rallies when he had been possessed with the inspiration of speech, the battles along the walkways when he had ridden the adrenalin of violence, the secret meetings when the nakedness of the truth had been caressed like a willing woman. He thought too of real women, was distracted briefly by this and masturbated quickly and efficiently to clear himself of the distraction. He could think then clearly of the great love affair of his life, of Mark First, for whom he was glad now to be able to die, by whom he would be remembered, in whom he would live forever. He felt the emotions galloping through him, the great dragon of energy that devoured him and freed him. He passionately wanted the moment to be upon him, and in this anticipation he was greater than he had ever been.

First gambled on the fact that they would allow Standing some time to sweat before they went to work on him properly. It was a gamble of some uncertainty: Standing might already be dead. If it was necessary for Standing to die, then First trusted that he would have done so cleanly. He would mourn his friend, feel the personal loss deeply, would be made harder and tighter by it. But they were playing with their lives as stakes, and Standing knew this. So First waited calmly and in the evening made his way to the military command centre.

The military command centre was a detached house within the campus that had originally been the medical centre. It was well guarded, and First was stopped a hundred yards from the entrance by men who materialised out of the darkness. They forced him on to the ground, put a boot on his neck as he was searched, but they did not hit him, and this told First that here were professionals. They pulled him back up onto his feet.

'Out for an evening stroll then, Mr First?' a suave officer asked him, examining his identity card minutely.

'I would like to see the Commander.'

'I don't think the Commander would like to see you, however.'

'I have information that will be of interest to him.'

'What information?'

'Information that I would not be prepared to discuss in the open here.'

'Then we will go somewhere where you will be prepared to discuss it.'

'I am familiar with Major Radcliff's methods, Lieutenant; and I promise you they will not work on me. If you go on treating everyone here as your enemy, then you will lose the advantage you gained by securing this establishment. There are some of us who are glad of your arrival, and who are willing to work with you. You have done a great deal of stupid damage already. Please. Tell the Commander that I want to offer him my services. He can, of course, have me shot at any time.'

The lieutenant considered this, took out a packet of cigarettes, offered them to First who declined, lit one himself and then, casually, went back into the house.

First did not look at the men who guarded him, stood straight and still and watched the door at which, eventually, the lieutenant appeared.

'Bring him in.'

He entered then, for the first time, the office of Commander Gorham. Gorham was small and fat, quite predictable. First was reassured. He sat at his desk in a pool of light. His face was bloodshot, and First smelt the brandy, the sweat, the claustrophobia of a command exerted only with the bluntness of violence. He smiled.

'Well? Who are you?' Gorham said.

'My name is Mark First. I was a senior information officer.'

He could see that Gorham, in the light, could not see him clearly, and that this was an advantage to him that Gorham did not immediately know how to redress.

'You have five minutes, First, to convince me you are not wasting my time.'

'Very well, sir.' He was prepared. 'You have a good friend of mine under interrogation. Anthony Standing. I assume that the reason he has not been released from interrogation is that he has refused to tell you something you wish to know. I assume that what you wish to know, sir, has to do with what has come to be called the Brotherhood. Anthony Standing will, I'm afraid, not give you any information. He has a binding loyalty to the leader of that movement, and he will die rather than betray that loyalty. So. I am the leader of that movement, although you will not find my name on any records the previous administration have compiled about us. I have been very careful. The Brotherhood is a political movement which has been working actively for the past three years against the government. We have been open in some of our activities, but concealed in all our important operations. To put it briefly, sir, we have been waiting for three years for you to arrive here; and now that you are here, we welcome you and believe that we can be of great assistance to you. I apologise for not coming forward before this, but I hope you will appreciate our caution in times such as these.'

'And how do you imagine you can possibly help me?'

'We are disciplined and independent of anything that

has been going on here officially. We know the workers here very well. We know who to trust and who to avoid. If you were to make use of us, we could impose order on the mess here from within. You can only impose it from without, and, with respect, this limits what you can do. But, more importantly, we can work the information system. We can give you absolute access to the heart of the system, to all its information and to all the power that is locked in it. We know what information is false and what is accurate. We have developed a very considerable command of the system, far beyond what we ought to have done, I'm afraid. We knew, for example, what Colonel Cheverton had done in the north before the authorities here knew of it. Our organisation went underground, therefore, some months before you arrived; which is why you have taken so long to connect with us.'

He had made Gorham angry, he could see that. He had expected it: Gorham could not trust him and, not trusting him, but needing exactly what he offered, he had no other resource but anger.

'Lester?'

'Yes, sir.'

'Get Radcliff over here. I don't care what he's doing. Now.'

Lieutenant Lester smiled slightly, and turned to go.

'And take this little shit out of here until you return.'

This time he was allowed to wait in the outer office. He surveyed it strategically. It would not, he concluded, be difficult to get to Gorham.

Radcliff arrived half an hour later, obviously from some indulgence the interruption of which made him very angry. He looked at First.

'Who the fuck are you?' he said.

110

'I am the leader of the Brotherhood, Major Radcliff.'

Radcliff paused, open-mouthed.

'In that case,' he said, 'you're going to be shot.'

First bowed his head submissively, and Lester took Radcliff through to see Gorham. He could hear voices raised in there. He knew enough about the power games at the centre of the military command to guess what was going on. Radcliff was becoming powerful, and Gorham resented this. Radcliff wanted to shoot First, as perhaps he had already shot Anthony Standing, as he shot anyone who identified themselves in any way. Gorham would be using First as a shield against Radcliff's power. Gorham was stupid, the typical dull officer who, now that he had no-one to give him orders, had no idea what he was doing, knew nothing but power. First did not think that Radcliff was yet strong enough to defy Gorham. Lieutenant Lester was new to First and was interesting; an intelligent young man who might be of use.

Ten minutes they took, before Lester came to fetch First.

Gorham seemed more sober than before, and Radcliff was at the edge of the room like a chastened schoolboy.

'You are to report to Lieutenant Lester at 0900 hours tomorrow,' Gorham said. 'He will take you to the information rooms and will require that you give him access to certain information. He only has to suspect that you are playing any sort of game with us, First, and I will have you shot out of hand.'

'Thank you, sir,' First said.

'And,' Radcliff said emphatically, 'you will provide Lieutenant Lester with a complete list, a complete list, First, of all those who were members of your organisation and who are still here.'

'Lieutenant Lester already has that list, sir,' First said.

111

'It was with my identity card. I thought you would ask for it.'

Lester stepped forward, a little embarrassed, and picked the list up off Gorham's desk where he had deposited the contents of First's pockets. Radcliff snatched at it and went down the list rapidly.

'I've never heard of any of these,' he said.

'We . . . we were careful to cover our tracks, sir. You will appreciate our caution. You have had to scour out certain undesirable elements here, and have necessarily been inclusive in your actions. We did not want to be caught up in that.'

The three officers seemed embarrassed by this. There was a pause. Gorham cleared his throat.

'Right,' Gorham said. 'Very interesting, First. Off you go now.'

First did not move at once, looked thoughtfully at Gorham.

'What're you waiting for?'

'Anthony Standing, sir.'

'Oh yes. Do we have this man under interrogation, Radcliff?'

'Yes, sir.'

'Well, First, we'll look into it. Off you go now.'

'I would be very unhappy if anything were to have happened to Anthony Standing, sir,' he said quietly.

The atmosphere changed steeply.

'Are you dictating conditions to me?'

'No, sir. I am merely stating a fact. I would be very unhappy if anything were to have happened to him. He is a man of immense integrity and a close personal friend. He is not, nor has he ever been, any threat to your command. Goodnight, sir. Major Radcliff. Lieutenant Lester.'

★   ★   ★

Standing stood in the centre of their room and shook with an uprush of emotion that he could no more control than he could understand. First held him in a rigid embrace, clasped him as if to hold him together. The pain of the beating Radcliff's men had given him in lieu of the bullet, made him wince, and he used the pain to mask the emotions.

'I nearly took my pill, Mark. When they opened the door, I thought they had come for me. I . . .'

'Quiet now, Anthony,' First said. 'We have come through that.'

Standing was released from First's physical embrace, allowed to sit on the edge of his bed. First drew up a chair and sat before him, leaning forward and speaking closely to him.

'Listen to me. We are going to come out into the light at last. We must move secretly amongst our brothers and tell them. We must have a meeting, but carefully because they will be watching us. They do not trust us, and so we must be perfect in every detail. We must live for a while in the open with clear space all around us. It will be a time of trial for us, Anthony. It is easier to be unified when we are secret, when we can have the intimacy of midnight together: it is hard to stay united when we move clearly in the sight of the others who dislike and distrust us. We must submit ourselves entirely to this new power.'

'Why?'

'Because they are strong. They have no ideals. They will do anything to anyone so long as it works. They are absolute in their intention; and their intention is power. This is good. But they have no ideals, power is a means to an end that they do not think about; there is an empty space below them that, in the necessity of their grabbing and holding control, they are not aware of. They will be forced to think in time, and then many of them will become aware of the empty space. Then some will fall into doubt, will feel compromised by what they have done, will go against what they have become: others will grow greedy, indulgent, trying to cash in their power for money, or live on the simple intoxication of it; some will, perhaps, come towards us. Then we will be ready. But until we are ready, we must creep about in their shadows. We shall take any power they offer us, but we must use it softly, unwillingly. We must work hard, Anthony. We must become the machinery of their power.'

'And then?'

'Then . . .' and he put his hands out and gripped Standing's wrists. 'Then we will come into our birthright.'

The winter came and went. An uneasy peace settled over the country. The north was a desolate anarchy; ragged trails of refugees made their way south where were now small military areas, none of which welcomed the influx of stragglers. The refugees were often moved on, sometimes herded into detention camps, sometimes, where the central command was weaker, they found places to settle and be absorbed into the local towns. There were bands of them, though, who were always on the move, prone to violence both from and upon the settled and nervous communities through which they passed.

A man called Ben Wallis travelled in one such band when they broke into and looted a large estate. The owners had fled, and they spent three days gorging themselves on hoarded food and wine before a company of militia arrived to dislodge them. Wallis had stayed sober, and when the militia arrived, he was one of the few of the band who realised that they were not merely going to be turfed out and sent on their way. He slipped away and hid in the cellar of a dilapidated outhouse, from where he could hear the shooting and the screaming, smell the smoke and the cordite.

It went on for hours, and the longer it went on, the worse it was. The terror came to the very door of his cellar, the boots kicking and the voices thick with the intoxication of their butchery; but they passed over him. He waited two days, his terror defrosting slowly. At times he regretted hiding, wanted to be quickly dead, afraid of what was still to come, knowing that in submitting to his instinct for self-preservation, he would make it worse for himself in the end. Hopelessness was the condition of the time: those who hoped for anything were the ones who suffered.

At midnight, at last, he surfaced. The moon shone and there was a sharp ground frost. He kept to the shadows. Bodies lay glittering in the moonlight. He dreaded identifying them. He felt as if he had survived the end of the world. He went up to one of the upper bedrooms which was wrecked but, thankfully, had not been used as a killing ground. He bundled up in anything he could find and slept curled up on the floor, shaken by a fever of tears that he could not understand.

In the morning, he woke to find himself watched by a girl. She was slim, clean, well-dressed and beautiful. He did not believe she was real; and if she was real, she would destroy him unless he destroyed her first. The instinct for that rose in him, but he was too weak, physically and emotionally, to direct it. He found himself crying again.

'I thought you were all dead,' she said.

'I . . . I hid,' he said.

'This used to be my home. My father was Lord

115

Darrington. He's gone abroad.' She spoke softly, distantly; perhaps she was mad.

'Are you alone?'

'Yes . . .' Then she became afraid, began to move away. 'No. I'm not alone. There are soldiers in the courtyard. If I cry out, they'll come and kill you.'

He rose to his feet, unsteady, giddy, hungry and wasted.

She watched him, caught between her fear and her curiosity, and perhaps, Wallis thought, responding to a simple humanity that was the gift of her privilege. He wondered how such things had survived so much.

'What's your name?' he asked her.

'Rachel,' she said, then looked at once as if she had given something away, then looked defiant. 'Lady Rachel Augusta Darrington,' she said, 'and who might you be?'

'I . . . I think I lost my name . . .'

'That's stupid. You must have a name.'

'Ben,' he said.

They looked at each other for a while. The possibilities of what might happen between them crowded at the edge of their stillness, but did not break in just yet.

'Will you help me, Rachel?' he asked at last.

'All right,' she said.

I never had anything but contempt for the army, for all armies. No state that has any real integrity has a professional army. All armies are implicitly or explicitly instruments of the dominance of a vulnerable and cowardly elite over the hearts of the people. In our state, all men were soldiers, trained and prepared to do battle at any moment; it was a right and duty of their

116

belonging. We fought because it was our nature to fight, and never for any other reason. That is why we were so strong and also why, at the last, we were so open.

Professional soldiers are dogs in human costume. They stand, thick in braid and clanking with insignia and with all the honours they give each other, with so much to prove and all of it on show like some charlatan's shop window. And when they are not dressed up in their medals, here they come with all their weapons, all their fine technology, their machinery which is so complex to operate it stops them having to think of its purpose. They hide behind everything they have to try and avoid revealing the emptiness, the nastiness, the pettiness of their nature. At best they are no more than dumb operators of their machinery, dumb mechanics of blind brutality.

They are, and always have been, the proof of my assertion that power without idealism is futile and destructive. What else can they do but kill? What else is their function? And when they are not actually killing, what else is their purpose but to threaten to kill? And what is the purpose of their killing? Without killing they have no motivation, no reason to exist, so they have to keep killing, to keep threatening to kill, or they will have to face the reality of what they are; and then they will disappear.

They take the basest instincts of man and dress them up with ceremony and tradition, with the stupidity of nationalism. If they are heroic, it is the heroism of the stupid. It is not difficult to throw yourself into destruction if a million others are throwing themselves at the same time, if you have been drilled out of thought, conditioned to respond to a shout, a slogan, a symbol or two. Heroism, real heroism, is an act of personal will, a conscious, deliberate offering of yourself to

117

something higher. The depth of the heroism does not depend on the action, but on the strength and clarity of the will that motivates that action. We lived and fed on a current of pure heroism, from the beginning to the end, and on and on into the future.

Never trust any professional soldier, Rachel. They are loyal only to the man above them, and only then out of fear and conditioning which deprives them of the courage to think for themselves. I am sure they are now trying to make you into some symbolic victim of our beastliness. Do not allow yourself to be so used. They will make you comfortable; they will regale you with lies about us. Keep yourself free of them. They are incapable, morally and physically incapable of any truth that does not come out of a gun; that is their nature.

Remember us as we were, as we are, as we always will be – true to the fierce angry spirit of life, to its ecstasies as well as to its horrors. We were never an army.

REALISATION

STRONGHOLDS

The Brotherhood emerged quietly. They took to wearing white scarves over their fatigues and moved amongst the others with an air of quiet authority, although they were scrupulous in avoiding any open assertion of themselves.

The power of the military was never challenged, but First carefully and gradually began, whilst opening up the information system, to suggest to the reasonable mind of Lieutenant Lester that there were better ways of doing things. The information system revealed the identities of all who might cause trouble and who had submerged successfully amongst the mass of the workers. First suggested that, rather than have them shot, they might be dispatched to work camps to do menial, physical jobs. The camps should be small and widely separated; those who were sent there could be deprived of any social or intellectual privileges. Those who could not be relied upon to support the new order could expect a life of digging gravel, picking vegetables, sawing lumber, mending drains and fences, living in bunkhouses that were searched regularly, changed

121

regularly, and stripped of anything personal that they might seek to establish there. They had to be grateful for being alive if they wanted to go on being alive. The hidden advantage of this system to Lester and Gorham, which First foresaw but which he did not specify, was that it would divert Radcliff's security thugs off the campus where, in truth, they were finding objects for their brutality where none really existed, and under which nothing productive could be effectively achieved. First drew up a detailed scheme for the camps, which Lester passed on to Gorham, and which Gorham dictated to Radcliff.

With the pressure of Radcliff ameliorated, the Brotherhood, models of industry and rectitude, began to make the campus work again as it had worked before. They became the channel of communication between the military and workers. Radcliff periodically blundered about with paranoias of a great plot to take over and shoot everyone, but Gorham knew that this was his frustration. The soldiers came to like the Brothers, Anthony Standing particularly; and First, if he was the leader as he claimed to be, seemed to be content to be Gorham's office boy, limitlessly deferential and efficient.

Quietly but not secretly, they began to recruit more members. You did not, of course, offer yourself: they approached you if they felt you might be suitable. The basic qualifications of race and sex were required, of course. The number of the Brothers grew steadily, from about two hundred originals to over five hundred. Those who did not wear the white scarf began to murmur against it; some even went to the military to complain about some injustice they felt the Brothers had committed. Such complaints were always passed directly on to them, and their authors were confronted, singly, told to behave themselves, told that their liberty here was provisional, that there were camps for people who did not want to belong to the new order of things.

There was a terrace of small, single bedroomed houses on the old campus, and Gorham had agreed to First's commandeering them for his headquarters. One night, Anthony Standing was on the way to bed when he found First sitting in the small living room that each of the houses possessed. Such a visitation was not unique. Standing went to his kitchen and brought a glass of mineral water for his guest, pouring whiskey for himself. They sat slowly drinking for some minutes. Perhaps First would finish his drink and then go home to bed, without saying anything. Perhaps there was something new tonight.

'We have not got the question of women right, Anthony.'

'Your principal is absolutely sound, Mark.'

'No. If it was sound, we would not have alienated the best of them. They would submit and come to us gladly, accept their status and be part of us. If a principal is sound, Anthony, it works.'

'Human frailty, my dear Mark, human frailty.'

'We have outmanoeuvred human frailty. We are not imposing our power: we are releasing the power that is in all men. But we have not worked out the women yet.'

'Are we . . . to admit them?'

'No. Anthony, the answer is much simpler than that.'

Standing waited for the answer, smiled in anticipation.

'Anthony?'

'Yes, Mark?'

'I want you to get married.'

'Good God. Who to?'

'To Muriel Jarrow.'

Standing was speechless. He did not think of how it might be done, for he assumed, as with everything First said, that it would be done; his thoughts therefore tumbled in a confused imagining of life as the husband of Muriel Jarrow. The idea was enormous, complex and bewildering and, to begin with, his heart sank; but then he looked up at First, who was smiling at him, and he surfaced bright and laughing.

'It is not . . . not a physically difficult proposition for you, Anthony, I hope.'

'We have gone beyond that, Mark. And anyway, Muriel Jarrow is . . . is by no means a difficult physical proposition. As an intellectual proposition, however, she might be very difficult.'

'Ah well, I thought you'd appreciate the challenge. And, Anthony, you must succeed. After you, there will be many marriages. We must give our brothers a domesticity rather than all this random fornication. They must all be married, all of them.'

'But not you, Mark.'

'Oh no. I am outside all that. Goodnight, Anthony.'

When, next evening, at about nine, which was late for visitors, Muriel Jarrow heard a small knock at her door, she assumed it was at last the inevitable knot of soldiers with the order for her removal. She did not understand how she had been spared for so long; so many of her close friends had been taken months ago. She knew the scenario: they would march her out to a van with its engine running and they would drive her into the night; they would stop somewhere and rape her, telling her it was the last fuck she would ever get so she might as well make the most of it; then, if she survived that in any state of awareness, she would find herself dumped into a barn with a hundred other women, some of whom she would know, none of whom would have the spirit to recognise her; she would then have to hoe fields from dawn to dusk; in a year she would age a decade; in two years she would be dead. The processes of the camps were officially secret, but when pushed for information they were quite frank about them; there was a deterrence to be generated from them, after all.

She did not answer the door. She lay on her bed and endeavoured to compose herself for the inevitable, but the fear possessed her like a fever. I do not oppose them, she pleaded to an imaginary inquisitor, I simply cannot give in to them. I understand what they are doing, and I admire them in a way, but I cannot surrender what I am to be a drudge or a whore for them. If I have opposed them, it has only been in defence of my own integrity. I am no threat to them. Please leave me in peace. Please.

When the knocking came again, insistent but not forceful, she began to hope.

The soldiers would not have taken her refusal to answer their knock as a barrier to their progress. The knocking was repeated. In a sudden reckless rush she rose from her bed and unlocked the door.

'Forgive me for disturbing you so late,' said Anthony Standing. 'I wanted to talk to you alone, on a matter of some importance.'

She went back into the room, sat heavily on its only chair and left the door open for Standing to come in or go as he chose. I'm going to get a warning, she said to herself. All right, I'll take their warning. Keep your mouth shut. Bastards.

Standing came in circumspectly, closing the door behind him, looking round and sitting himself on the

125

edge of her bed. He took the scarf from around his neck and laid it down neatly on the bed beside him.

'Muriel, I would hate to see you taken away from here.'

'Is this an official call, Brother Standing?' she said, biting deep into her lip as soon as she had said it.

'No. It's a personal call, although I don't expect you believe that.'

'I fulfil your expectations there, Brother Standing.'

'Please don't call me that, Muriel.'

'Is it forbidden?'

'No. You can call me what you want to call me. It's just that the way you say that is . . . hurtful.'

'Is what?'

'Hurtful. The sarcasm. The contempt.'

'Standing, you come up here to threaten to have me sent to a work camp . . .'

'I'm not threatening you, Muriel. I have no official purpose here. If you tell me to go, I will go. I have a respect for you that I would give anything to make you appreciate.'

'Then give me back Jenny Wilkins. Give me back Annie Lowther. And Mary Berryson.'

'Muriel, they've gone. You know that. They can't come back. I can't make them come back. You know that too. We are not in charge here, and even if I had the power to bring them back to you, I couldn't do it. They were corrupt, they were dangerous . . .'

'Mary Berryson? Dangerous?'

'What can I tell you about her that you would believe? True, she was not political, but she was corrupt, very corrupt.'

'She was . . . she was . . . only a child . . .'

'Far from a child, I'm afraid. Your tears for her do you

126

honour, but you must not squander your tears on things that are passed and cannot be recovered. You are not like her. That is what I have come to say to you. I would be hurt more than I can say if you were to throw yourself stupidly after your friends. Listen to me, Muriel. When the army came here, a whole world ended; and where a world ended, another is beginning. It is frightening to think of these things, but it is the only truth now. It requires immense courage to face that truth. It is easy to give in to desperation. It might feel like a brave thing to do, to throw yourself against the new power; but it would be, for someone as intelligent and strong as you are, not courage but cowardice, to surrender to your own weakness and desperation. Please, Muriel, please don't do it. I must go now. We must talk again. There is a lot to be done, and you could have a part to play in it, if you have the strength for it. Think on what I have said to you. Goodnight, Muriel.'

He left her then to her misery, which was acute, which twisted inside her like something trying to get out of her. When she woke in the morning, she felt unclean. She went over and over what Standing had said to her, and could not rid herself of the notion that he had come to seduce her. At thirty-five, having remained defiantly a virgin throughout all the sexual squalor of the campus, the image of Standing as a lover disgusted her. They all disgusted her, all the Brothers. Her image of manliness was young and reserved, sensitive, and there weren't any of those left now. She remembered once finding Mark First attractive when they had worked in the same data pool some years ago, but the scarf had appeared around his neck like a poisonous snake and, she told herself, she had always known there was something wrong with him.

Later she calmed, told herself she was being silly about this, frumpish. She came to consider what it was really that Standing had been doing in her room last night. She recalled his offer, veiled though it had been, and began to grow distantly curious, at least about its motives, which were surely not simple. Were they going, at last, to offer their bloody scarf to women? She couldn't believe that, and even if it were to be true, she wouldn't wear one, no, not to save herself from the camps.

She kept meeting Standing over the days that followed. Perhaps he was looking out for her, perhaps she was just sensitive about him, for every appearance made something jump inside her. Whether consciously or not, she took very great care with everything she said and did, aware of being watched. Her friends noticed and asked her what was wrong, at which she grew irritable.

She would sit with her friends in the bar most evenings, unwinding, talking, airing grievances. One evening, about a month after Standing's visit, there was a larger than usual group of Brothers there. They were having some sort of celebration: they were not noisy, but they were exclusive. Watching them, she could see some sort of ritual of drinking and making pledges in progress. They were never more ominous than at times like this. At last one of her friends, Paula Wright, a woman prone to aggressive melancholies, especially when she had been drinking, rose from her seat and lurched over to them. Muriel rose too, wanting to hold her back, to protect her; but Paula had gone too far, had barged in amongst them and had begun shouting.

'Perverts!' she yelled. 'You'll have to get rid of us all, you know, every decent woman will have to be got rid of. And then you'll have to fuck each other. And then you'll have to get rid of yourselves too. You're like a disease. You're like cancer.'

Muriel reached and drew her back, took her out into the air where she collapsed in a sobbing terror.

'Help me, Mu, help me. I don't want them to take me away. I don't want anything. I only want to live a normal life again. Why is that so dangerous to them? Why? Why?'

Muriel took her back to her own room and let her sleep in her bed, curling up on the floor with a blanket. Paula slept, but Muriel lay awake. She had to go and see Standing. She tried to argue herself out of this conclusion, but she could not with any honesty. It was late, half an hour before curfew. She did not like to leave Paula, but she knew they would have to clear her removal with the military, and they wouldn't be able to do that tonight. She woke Paula and told her that she was going to try and get some help. Paula begged her not to leave her alone, but she told her to trust her, not to open the door to anyone. Then she went.

Standing was pleased to see her, asked her in at once. He had a group of young men with him, some of whom she was sure had been in the bar. She stood back, wretched in their scrutiny of her.

'Forgive me, Brothers,' Standing said to them. 'We'll meet tomorrow. Goodnight.' They parted, each with a small embrace that made her cringe to watch.

When they were gone, he offered her a seat, which she accepted, and a drink, which she refused. He poured himself a glass of whiskey, which looked to her very good.

'I assume I would be deluding myself,' he began, 'if I thought you had come to see me for a purely social purpose, Muriel.'

'I've come to see you about Paula Wright.'

'Ah. I thought that's what it would be about.'

'Please don't have her sent away.'

He paused, sipped his drink, considered seriously.

'Can you vouch for her, Muriel?'

'What do you mean, can I vouch for her?'

'What we are trying to achieve here is infinitely complicated, far more than you can begin to realise. We cannot allow subversives to endanger that.'

'Paula was drunk and unhappy, and she shot her mouth off. And now she is terrified. She is not a subversive.'

'In that case, she has nothing to be afraid of.'

'You won't have her sent away?'

'You have told me she is not a subversive. I have told you she has nothing to be afraid of. I accept your word. Please accept mine.'

'Thank you.' She grew weak at the relief of this, had come down here on a surge of adrenalin that now leaked out of her system leaving her limp and tearful. She struggled to master herself.

'Now. Will you accept a drink?'

She did so without making any real decision to. The whiskey was as good as it had looked. It was ten years since she had drunk anything as good or as strong as this.

'I am grateful that you came to see me about this, Muriel. Please. If there are any other difficulties, come again. There is so much misunderstanding about our organisation, and it leads to confrontations, and perhaps even to injustices, that could and should be avoided. Come and see me, Muriel. And if I have any difficulties, may I come and see you?'

Thus Muriel Jarrow became the women's voice amongst them. Standing was true to his word. Any woman whose behaviour became suspect he referred to her. Muriel defended the women strenuously, and Standing always agreed to accept her word on their behaviour. This led to Muriel having to take the errant women to task.

'Whose side are you on now, Muriel?' they would ask her.

'It's not a question of sides. It's a question of survival.'

'Are you sleeping with him?' she was asked.

'No. I only drink his whiskey.'

They didn't believe her, of course, and it made her angry, filled her full of resolves to keep their meetings functional and open as far as possible. After a while she ceased to be angry, became contemptuous of those who couldn't see beyond sex.

In spite of herself, she was beginning to like Anthony Standing, to be aware of the man below the organisation. She found that she could relax in his company, and she began to enjoy doing so. They met often, and not always on matters of business. He was educated and well-mannered, leant her books, was prepared to discuss anything with her in an atmosphere of intellectual freedom that she had thought had gone forever.

'Why don't you admit women into your organisation, Anthony?' she asked.

'It's essentially a brotherhood. What binds us together must be beyond the complications of sex. We do not believe that women are intrinsically any less intelligent or strong, or any more unstable than men. Perhaps there ought to be a reciprocal sisterhood, exclusively female. You should think about that, Muriel.'

'I don't think I'm a joiner of movements, Anthony.'

'That's foolish. Individualism is a dead end.'

'Tell me,' she said, as casually as she could manage it.

'Do you see yourselves taking over from the military one day?'

'Oh yes. One day. Not too long to wait now. We will step up to the top of the mountain. There is, after all, only an empty space there at the moment.' He reached over and filled up her glass. 'There now, Muriel. You have an admission from me that the army would be most alarmed by and interested in. You could denounce us. Gorham would not be unhappy to suppress us.'

'Perhaps a spell in the camps would do some of you good,' she said sourly, instinctively unwilling to have this sort of confidence.

The deportations to the camps had virtually ceased for men as well as for women, but Muriel knew that the time would come when there would be a woman whom she could not defend on any other grounds than simple humanity and, knowing Standing now very well, she knew that that would not be enough. It would be the time of testing, of him and of her.

Sue-Ann Jones was the deciding case. She was a large girl, unintelligent and promiscuous. She worked in the kitchens where she pilfered food and overate, was probably the only person on the campus who was actually growing fat. She, it was discovered, was suffering from a venereal disease; she was also accepting small sums of money to make her genitals available to anyone who wanted them.

Standing came to Muriel with this information, offering it flatly, careful at this stage to make no case. Muriel went at once to the sanatorium to try to find something in this girl with which she could defend her against what seemed to be the inevitable. Muriel tried to convince her of the immorality of her actions, but was

132

countered with, 'Well. I bet you're doing it too. Or perhaps you haven't got the guts. Perhaps you're a lesbian. Eh, Miss Jarrow?' Muriel then mentioned the very likely possibility of her removal to the camps, and Sue-Ann dissolved into disgusting tears, not of contrition, but of simple fear. However hard she tried, Muriel could find nothing to fight for in this girl. She returned to Standing.

'Anthony, I can't see the harm she's done, not the real harm. There's not enough intelligence for her to be subversive. Have you met her?'

'She has done harm, tangible, physical harm.'

'To men who have used her as some sort of sexual receptacle. They are as culpable as she is.'

'They are certainly culpable. Perhaps they should all go to the camps, apart from the fact that most of them are soldiers and Gorham won't send his own boys off. Come now, Muriel, you cannot really have any respect for that woman. She is a source of moral as well as physical infection. You have done miraculous things in the past months. You have taken the anger out of our relationships with women. How many do you reckon you've saved from the camps? Thirty? At least thirty. Probably more who have come under your influence. But if I were to give you this woman, this obscene and useless woman, our relationship would seem, to put it bluntly, corrupt. Your influence would be diminished.'

Muriel wept at her defeat; not merely at her defeat on behalf of Sue-Ann Jones, but at her own defeat, her digestion within the system, her betrayal of herself. She wept and Anthony Standing brought her whiskey, sat beside her and placed a protective arm around her shoulders. If he asks me to share his bed with him now, she thought, I will do it. She saw herself leaning up

133

against a wall like poor Sue-Ann, the receptacle of the Brotherhood's masculinity. In a twist of self-disgust she wanted this.

Then Standing released her and she looked up to find someone else in the room. He could not have been there when she arrived, and he had entered without knocking or announcing himself. She grew angry at having her private hurt thus observed. The observer was Mark First.

'Good evening, Mark,' Standing said, as if he had been expecting him.

'Anthony. And Muriel. How are you, Muriel? It's been a while since the Third Section Data Processing Unit.'

He sat down before her. Standing had left the room. First did not seem to notice her obvious emotional state, or else he ignored it; at any rate it did not embarrass him as it did her, considerably. She dried her nose and eyes on a handkerchief and set her mouth hard. She looked at First who was leaning back in his chair regarding her. He was small and stocky, as she remembered him. His hair was black, cropped back from his receding forehead. She remembered his features as softer than this. She remembered being attracted by him, but there was none of that left now.

'What are you doing now, Mark?' she managed to ask him eventually.

'Oh . . . looking after things. I help Commander Gorham, mostly.'

Standing returned with a glass of mineral water, which First took without acknowledging. There was a silence then, but not an awkward silence; it was as if the situation in the room had suddenly become important. Muriel looked to Standing, but his eyes were down. Eventually, First began to speak, clearly and directly.

134

'You're a remarkable woman, Muriel. Don't be afraid of being identified with us. We are proud of what you have done, proud to have your advice and your humanity, proud even to receive your criticisms because they come from your inner strength and beauty. Try to be proud of yourself. Try to be proud of us. I envy Anthony your friendship. You have made him a stronger and deeper man. Thank you, Muriel. Thank you.' He drank from his glass, placed it down on the table before him, rose and left.

Muriel found herself trembling under this acclamation. It seemed suddenly to have placed her out in an open space, exposed, with everything she did of significance. She looked at Standing who was now considering her closely, watching her from a cautious distance. She found herself wanting his physical reassurance at this moment.

'Mark is our leader, our inspiration,' he said slowly.

'I . . . I didn't know that.'

'He sent me to you that first time. He understands everything.'

'He frightened me.'

'Oh yes.'

'May I have some more whiskey?'

He brought the bottle over, filled her glass, stood above her as she drank. She looked up at him, then rose to face him. He put his hands gently on her shoulders and she leant against him.

'May I stay the night?' she said.

There was no response to this. She felt that she had said something appalling. She felt herself blushing deeply, felt the tears rising into her eyes.

'I'm sorry, Anthony,' she said.

'No. No. Dear Muriel. There would be no greater joy for me than to . . . to make love to you.'

'That's what you think. I'm thirty-five and a virgin.'

'Hush. That's stupid talk. Now listen to me. I will walk you back to your room. You're reacting emotionally now, and though your emotions may be true, they may not be. I would not want to degrade you by taking advantage of you tonight. Come and see me tomorrow evening and, if you still feel as you do now, on reflection, calmly and clearly, then we will be married. You will come and live here and share my life, be a part of the future. Those are the only terms on which you ought to give yourself to me, and the only terms on which I should take you. You know that this is true. Finish your drink now, and I will take you back to your room.'

'Yes. Thank you, Anthony, thank you.'

Rachel Darrington took Ben Wallis out of the big house where she had found him, and led him over what seemed like miles of park and farmland. The day was misty, and she drifted along beside and before him like a wraith whilst he stumbled and struggled and identified shapes in the mist as his waiting destroyers. She brought him at last to a small cottage hidden in the woods. She fed him bread and cheese and milk which he could hardly swallow, then she took him up to a bare room where he slept on an old mattress.

How long he slept he did not know, days certainly. He was not physically ill, but he was emotionally exhausted to the point of disintegration. He swam in a flood of nightmare and memory, writhing through stifling heat and bitter cold, longing through empty hours for death to come and liberate him, wrestling with monsters who leapt from his mind to choke and stab and crush him. He was aware at times of Rachel who came to sit with him, to bathe his forehead, to change his blankets. At times he was terrified of her, at times he knew she was an angel of whom he was pathetically unworthy; at times he wanted to leave, to rid her of his corrupting presence; at times he wanted to drag her down and fuck her.

He woke one morning clear of all this, drained and weak, his limbs and head throbbing, but free of his terrors. He went down to find her in the room that occupied the whole ground floor of the cottage. She was darning clothes before an old cast-iron range. She smiled at him and he sat across the table from her. Her hair was swept off her forehead and tied in a neat bunch that hung down her back. She was beautiful – young, neat, precise in her movements. She belonged to another world.

For Rachel, Ben was a gift from God. It was her faith that had saved her, and now her faith was rewarded.

In the panic of her father's preparations for flight from the Hall, she had been wretched. She felt that to leave was cowardice, that her father was a coward, an opportunist, that he owed it to the estate, to the house, to her, to stay and outface whatever happened. She loved her father, but in those days she had realised that she did not really know him, that her love was for a distant image of him that did not correspond with the reality. In his plans for flight he had seemed to consider her as little more than a part of the essential baggage. She had thought and prayed and she had determined to stay; and having taken the decision she had become at once lighthearted, happy, excited.

It had been easy to slip away, to be forgotten in the confusion of the departure. When she had surfaced again, her world had been empty. The great house was full of new echoes, its pregnant familiarities growing day by day stranger in the emptiness. She had wandered through the rooms for hours, for days, coming inevitably to realise that in its escalating, dusty silence it was no longer her home, and that her childhood was over.

She had gone to live in the old cottage at first, to avoid the search that she assumed would shortly be sent after her. It either had not come or she had managed to avoid it completely. She kept contact with a group of local Christians who met quietly, and through them she learned of the terrible things that were happening in the north, that were sweeping south, that would soon overtake them all. She had no defence but prayer, and she fell back amongst its quietness, feeling strong within it. At times she was mortally afraid, but a few moments settling into the stillness of her devotion restored her quietude.

She was strong-willed and resourceful, and the Hall was well-stocked. The seasons changed and whatever raged beyond the circle of her territory, miraculously it never came near her. A year passed, then another. She was lean and healthy, living on vegetables which she grew, on eggs and milk from which she traded with local farmers. She grew to love her solitude, the strong simplicity of her life.

She would hold long, intimate conversations in her head with an imaginary figure, discuss the problems of her life, the decisions she took, share the moments of her joy and bring to light the shadows of fear and complexity that came to her. At first this figure was her father, but her sense of him slipped as the months passed, and then, perhaps, it was God to whom she opened herself; and then, imperceptibly, she realised that her companion was a lover, a man. She was no anchoress. She yearned for and believed in a time when all her growing would be shared. She dreamed vividly of the weight of a man upon her, her pleasure rising like a sea to swallow him. She woke blushing, admonishing herself, disciplining herself with lots of hard work, but laughing at herself as she did so. The locals who wandered past her cottage sometimes, who liked to keep an eye on her, this strange, beautiful, generous girl, would sometimes hear from the cottage or from the garden her quiet, private laughter.

The night the renegades arrived to sack the Hall was a night of dense terror. She hid in the woods and saw the lights from the fires they lit, glaring like devil's eyes from the windows. She heard the noise of breakage, the shrieks, each sound coming like a blow, bruising her. She went back to her cottage, barred herself deeply within it in silence and darkness and prayed; but her prayers were not now strong enough to still the terror, to hold the imagination of what was happening, what was coming. She felt abandoned, betrayed, desperate.

Then she heard the guns. She did not know what they meant, only that there was fighting, that someone was opposing them. She did not know what to feel. She wanted them driven out and perhaps that was happening, but the thought that people were dying up there appalled her. She wanted to be able to go and say, 'This all belongs to me. You are welcome to it if you will leave everything else in peace.' The weakness, the impossibility of this shrivelled her.

When the guns ceased, she waited and then crept out. From a distance she could see the stains of the damage on the face of the building. There was a great silence there now, a new, ominous silence. The mist lay across the lawns like poison. She went back to the cottage and waited, although she did not know what she was waiting for, knew finally that she was waiting only for the courage to go and face whatever had been done there.

The dead lay in the yards and shrubberies, caught where they had fled or in huddles where they had been grouped and butchered. They lay with the brute terror sinking in their blank faces, a sickly rime of frost covering them. Rachel had never seen the dead before, and their hideous inhumanity tore her open. She knelt on the ground on the instinct of prayer, but it was beyond the reach of her prayers. She was stamped simply with the wretchedness of it, with the sense that her own life was trivial and selfish in the face of all this blind butchery. She felt as if she had no meaning any more.

Thus, when she came upon Ben, huddled and trembling in her own long-abandoned bed, her course was obvious. She tended him through his fevers with a solicitude that at first was merely repaying some of the debt she felt she owed the dead. As the days passed, however, as he became strong enough to talk and to be with her, his masculinity began to become an issue. It seemed as if the terrors of that night had been designed to bring him to her; this conclusion was facile, and she did not trust it consciously for a moment. She found him beautiful, but that too was facile, for she was without any serious experience of men. She could see how he watched her, knew that he wanted her, expected, day by day, for him to reach for her. That she wanted this to happen frightened her. She was terrified that she would allow the emotions that lifted within her to surface, would give herself to him in a sudden abandon that would lose her everything she had.

Meanwhile, they slept in separate rooms across three feet of stairhead and kept a functional and absolute modesty in their living. He was practical and useful, and her little life expanded substantially with his help. She began cautiously but with what, just below the skin of their life together, was a desperate urgency, to try to know him.

He would not, for a long while, talk about himself. She learnt the facts of his childhood, knew that he had been in the army, knew that for the last two years he had been living wild with the renegade gangs; but he would not go into any of that, and the more he resisted her questions, the more she felt that she had to know.

'They were like night,' he would say, 'a night that lasted two years, full of nightmares, fevers. What happened then is over now, for me at least. I can't go back there.'

'Ben,' she pleaded, 'you won't be able to rest until you've brought it out.'

'I rest better than I have ever rested.'

'Well,' she said, looking down. 'I won't be able to rest then, not until I know what I'm sheltering under my roof, all of what I'm sheltering, not just the easy bits.'

So, gradually, he began to tell her. At first he was brutal, as if to shock her into closing her mind against what he had seen and done; but, although he could make her cry, make her wince with the horror and filth of it all, he could not shake her off. She came back with questions and, if ever he had assumed a bravado about his fighting and fornicating, she outfaced that and watched the shame catch him.

'Why did you do that, Ben? Why?' she said. 'You are not like that.'

'I became like that. I had to survive, not only physically, but emotionally. When brutality is the currency of the times, you have to trade in brutality or you have nothing, you are nothing, you become useless and you die.'

'Could you become like that again?'

141

'I don't know. I . . . probably . . . I don't suppose there's much I have had in my life that means more than surviving. Maybe one day there will be. I hope so.'

At moments like this they became still, apprehensive of each other. At night she could hear his restlessness. It's going to happen soon, she said to herself, filling with delight as the possibilities of it flooded through her imagination, bursting with a gratitude that filled her prayers.

Coincidentally, two hundred and fifty miles apart, the two marriages were celebrated on the same day. The sun shone across the whole country, the sky was cloudless and open, everywhere was quiet.

Anthony Standing and Muriel Jarrow had a ceremony in an old lecture hall. The senior Brothers were all there, over two hundred of them. There were women there too, fewer, but a significant number nevertheless of the more responsible women, the ones Muriel had worked for, the ones who had laughed at first when she had told them of her engagement, but who later had come to admire and even, she felt, to envy her; she was happy to see them. She was surprised, however, to see amongst the Brothers a number of the younger army officers. Gorham and his senior staff were not present.

The civil servant who officiated had been selected for his dignity and for the sonority of his voice. The audience, on the cue of the Brothers, rose to stand silent as the vows were exchanged, then broke into dignified but prolonged applause. Muriel, who had refused to wear white, found the whole thing absurd and looked to Anthony for some echo of her feeling, but found him monumental in his dark suit, draped with the gleaming

142

scarf like the token of some ancient cult. At this point she began to be nervous.

At the reception afterwards, when she had drunk several glasses of wine, when she surveyed the way her friends and the Brothers were talking and laughing together, she felt a little better. Anthony was there with reassuring touches, of her hand, her shoulder and once, when no-one was looking, he ran his hand over her backside which made her giggle. Then Mark First came up to her and Anthony as if it had been arranged, drifted off for a moment.

'Don't be afraid, Muriel,' he said. 'We have a lot to learn about functions such as this. We are not used yet to celebration. Nevertheless, we honour you here and welcome you.' He embraced her and she burst into tears, and Anthony came to take her and protect her, and she clung on to him to a small ripple of local applause.

Rachel took Ben that sunny morning to the Christians, who read the old marriage service over them, who kissed them and gave them gifts of old household things burnished up for the occasion. They drank cider and laughed and wandered back to the cottage, some of the congregation walking a little of the way with them, but leaving when they came within sight of their home.

When they entered the cottage, coming into the cool shadow, Rachel began to lay out the meal they were to share, things saved up specially. Ben came and halted her with an embrace, lifted her off the ground and turned her round. They covered each others' faces with kisses.

'If you want to go upstairs first . . .' she said.

'Yes.'

'Tell me what to do.'

She lay still and straight under his touching. Her nakedness seemed so fragile and delicate that he was

143

afraid of his desire, which seemed, as he had always known it would, gross and brutal. He held her face to his and they kissed amidst the close tension of their breathing; and as they kissed he slid over her and she gasped at his weight, and gasped again as he entered her, gripping on to him, biting her lip and letting tears spill down her face; but he felt, as he moved slowly and carefully within her, how the tension of her fear became resolved into the tension of her pleasure, how her restlessness under the burden of his body became coordinated about the soft surges he imposed upon her, how her breathing responded to the movement and seemed to come from deeper and deeper within her.

Afterwards they lay naked until late in the afternoon, touching and looking and talking, before going down to eat and to begin the domesticity of their life together.

Muriel writhed and cried out and struggled about Anthony's deft and experienced penetration of her. If it was pleasurable, and she certainly felt later that it had been, then it was pleasure achieved out of effort, out of an active, losing fight against him. She seemed to struggle against the pleasure, intensifying it, accepting the climax into which he drove her as a physical defeat.

Afterwards they drank whiskey and laughed like amicable competitors after a hard-fought match. Anthony showed her his back where her nails had drawn blood. She dabbed ointment on to him, and he winced. She rather liked the idea of covering him in the scars of their lovemaking.

In the adjacent house the next morning, First sat in a strange glow of contentment. Through the thinness of the adjoining wall, he had attended the physical celebrations of Anthony and Muriel's union. He had been almost embarrassed by this access to begin with, but embarrassment was not an emotion he could countenance. He had set himself, and had come to feel himself, a silent celebrant of their joys. Thereafter, night after night, he listened closely. He came to hear the sounds of Muriel's pleasure as a sort of song; the song of human rejoicing in the glory of the nature of life. It soothed him, and reminded him that at the heart of everything they undertook there was joy and there was fulfilment.

I had known Muriel many years. She had worked under me, and I had always admired her integrity. She had kept herself aloof from the cross-currents of amorality of those times. She was certainly repressed, but not, I felt, through any neurosis; simply because she would not allow herself to be swept along by anything. I sensed a moral outrage below her reserve, an anger at her inability to bring others into the clarity of her own life.

She was attracted to me in those days. She would linger and talk to me, always about work, but I sensed other emotions behind her lingering. I found her, also, attractive. In another time and place, I might have ventured to explore these attractions. If I had been able, without compromising either myself or her, to have seen her naked, I think it would have given me pleasure. She was one of the possibilities of life that I had to renounce.

I never lost sight of her, however, and when the army came, when we began to move into the open, I watched sadly as she shaped herself into a considerable figure against us. I watched all that repressed rage turning bitter in her. Several times I was on the point of organising her removal, but I could never take that decision. It seemed, for all her awkwardness, all her anger, that there was something she might do for us, some part for her to play. It all fell out as if it had been planned.

When Anthony told me that she was still a virgin, I was happy for her, and happy for us that we had recovered such perfection from the wastage. There were some things of which I was always incapable, and the wooing of Muriel Jarrow was such a thing. Perhaps I never admired Anthony more than in those days. He achieved so many things over many years, but I watched that with a personal eye, grew secretly sentimental for him. I felt in a way that he was wooing her for me; and in a way he was. He was wooing her for the Brotherhood, and I was the Brotherhood. In those first years, I was an intimate part of their marriage, delighted in their delights, accepted their union as an offering made to me.

Although at the end she was to fail us, yet, as she was in those days, Muriel was of course, dear Rachel, your forerunner.

ALPHA

Gorham in time came to hate First with a frustrated intensity that bloated and blocked him. First was a drug to which he was becoming fatally addicted. If only it hadn't meant giving in to Radcliff, he would have destroyed him. He dreaded First's regular visits to the house, to which he found himself now almost confined by his own inertia. A short man himself, Gorham was easy only when confronting tall men whom he had at a psychological disadvantage, always seeming to be able to see below them. With First he was confronted with a man who balanced his stature; but where First was stocky, Gorham was flabby; and First had a way of sitting, a way of moving himself in and out of the room, that always emphasised this distinction. He had a solidity of bearing that made him indigestible in any atmosphere.

Gorham hated his immaculate deference; he knew that it was offered with the most consummate sarcasm, but he could never break the skin of it, grew angry and stupid and futile in his attempts to break it. He hated the way First never suggested anything directly, but always managed to move Gorham exactly where he wanted him. He had tried, even with a tape recorder, to work out how First achieved this manipulation, but the best explanation he could come up with was that First made him so angry that he would do anything to get the little shit out of his office. He came at times, usually when he was very drunk, to the point of giving in to Radcliff, vowed that he would one day, wished he had done it last month, last year, when they had first arrived, knew that he could not do it now. Shooting First would be to put his whole command in jeopardy; at times it seemed almost worth it. At times it felt as if only his lack of courage held him back from it.

As the Brotherhood colonised more and more of the complex, as the army became more and more idle custodians, Gorham began to drink seriously, began to live in the softness and warmth of the brandy, began to despise himself sober, when the world seemed black and sharp and his thirst made him ill and exhausted. If only First would drink, if only once he could see him drunk and stumbling; but he was incapable of that, quite incapable, and that made him seem at times to Gorham inhuman. Perhaps he couldn't be shot, perhaps the bullets would just bounce back off him. At times Gorham was afraid.

He hated Radcliff too, found himself often having to interpose between First's quiet practicality and Radcliff's outbursts of paranoid spleen, having to struggle to assert himself, to prove that he was still the commander here, absolutely, that he could have them both, have anyone, shot on a whim. One day he would do it. One day he would take his pistol from the drawer and blow the head off someone: First, Radcliff, anyone, just so they knew what he was.

'And what's your problem today, Major Radcliff?' he

148

asked from behind the ache that seemed to be pulling his eyes together.

'This is of the utmost importance, sir, I do assure you.'

'You're always assuring me of something or other, Radcliff. You're becoming a depressing little turd. Well?'

'The man First, sir.'

'Bugger First.'

'Are you aware, sir, that over thirty of your officers and over a hundred other ranks are now members of his organisation?'

'What d'you mean, members of his organisation? How can soldiers be members of the civilian administration? What are you talking about?'

'Sir, First has used his positions within the civilian administration to develop serious and advanced ambitions to stage some sort of armed coup.'

'Armed coup? Bollocks, Radcliff, bollocks. Where's that little cunt First? Get him in here. Lester! Lester!'

Lester went as ordered down to the terrace to fetch Mark First to his commanding officer. He found First, as usual, going over a stack of security files and making minute, cryptic pencil notes upon them.

'Good morning, Lester.'

'Gorham wants to see you, First.'

'What's troubling him this morning?'

'I'm afraid . . . Radcliff's making his move.'

First put down his pencil, concentrated briefly.

'Has Radcliff put any units in place yet?'

'I don't think so. I checked briefly as I came down, but if he has, he's been more subtle than usual. I think he's gone to get clearance before he does anything, or at least to give Gorham the chance to respond before he moves.'

'We'd know if he was seriously ready for us, wouldn't we, Lester?'

'Oh yes.'

'Wouldn't we, Lester?'

'Yes, First, we would know.'

'Good. Then get back to Gorham and stall him for half an hour. Tell him I have a serious discipline problem that I cannot leave, but I'll be there the instant I'm free. If Radcliff has wound him up to the point where that won't work, find some way to let me know at once. I don't want a slaughterhouse.'

'Right, First.'

'Radcliff will know, I assume, of your involvement with us.'

'I don't see how he could know.'

'Don't rely on it. He may be a thug, but he can be thorough. Just be certain that whoever I have with me will not be searched before we go in.'

Anthony and Muriel were having a late breakfast, sitting in loose dressing gowns through which substantial expanses of their bodies were on mutual display. When First appeared they blushed, rose and pulled themselves together.

'Go upstairs and get dressed, both of you. Radcliff's moving, and we will have to reclaim the advantage. We may have to make our move. Today. Within the next hour. Hurry now.'

They went upstairs and he followed them, talking as his mind worked. Muriel was appalled at having to dress with him there, appalled at the exposure of her husband's body with all the indentations of her struggles upon it; but their leader was not looking anywhere but into the burning future: they might have been copulating, and it would have made no difference to him. He was lit with

150

danger. She had sometimes wondered whether his power was a delusion, fostered merely by the adulation of his Brothers; at this moment she felt that his power was intrinsic and terrible.

'He's too early for us. He can't be ready yet. He's gone to Gorham on the gamble of panicking him into moving against us. If I go and argue, I could buy us more time, a week, a month, but with Radcliff out in the open on us now, there would be little hope of concealing anything. He will use his search powers, in defiance of Gorham if necessary. We will *have* to move today. There will be more bloodshed than we had hoped, but if we don't move, if we give Radcliff time to put any security in place against us, we will have battle here. Anthony, rouse the Brothers. I want everyone armed. I want no action until I have seen Gorham. Be ready for my word. The word is *Alpha*. At that word, neutralise those on the list and only those, unless there is definite reaction. I don't want carnage, but I don't want any margin for error. Quickly. Isolate your targets and be ready for the word. *Alpha*. I'll take Danmore with me. Give me one hour, and if I've not sent word, then move on your own.' He paused and smiled. 'And if I . . . lose the advantage, Anthony, then it's all yours. I have absolute confidence in you.'

He stepped over then and clasped Standing.

'Well? Are you afraid, Anthony?'

'I've never been more alive, Mark.'

'This is the greatest day of our lives.'

Then he turned to Muriel, who watched and heard aghast. He came to her and put his hands on her shoulders. She shuddered.

'Muriel, you know what this is, don't you? This is the day we come into our birthright. There has to be blood, you know that. They are bloody men and cannot be

151

persuaded with truth. You know their degeneracy, the degeneracy they permit and protect. I know you are afraid. You must be afraid for us. When I have gone, when Anthony has gone, go amongst the women. Be ready, and when it begins keep them calm, keep their fear amongst them, share your fear with them. No woman wil be touched, you have my word. This is the moment, Muriel. Be strong now.'

He turned and went down the stairs. She stood motionless in the space he had left. Her husband came and clasped her. She spun round and clung on to him, gripped hold of him to protect him, to fight him down, to claim her share of him, to master him to her own power against the power which now possessed him. He struggled at first to free himself, laughing at her tanglings of him; then moments later they were tearing each other open, sprawling on the bed, fucking like engines. She felt as if she had fallen off the end of the world.

It was quickly done. He rose from her, changed his smeared trousers. She sat up on the bed with her legs open and her head in her hands, gasping and numb, trying not to scream out, trying to reconcile her loathing for what was happening with her desire that he, her husband, should go out and cover himself in the hot gore of his enemies.

When he was ready, having checked himself in the mirror, brushed his short hair, he turned to her, regarded her.

'Muriel,' he said, 'you are my liberation. Come on. Come down and see me off.'

She pulled herself up and shuffled limply downstairs after him. When she came into the living room, he was kneeling at one of the floorboards.

'Here,' he said, handing her a small automatic pistol.

'Fire it close range and go for the head. There's not much kick, but it makes a lovely big bang, so hold it away from your face. There's the safety . . . you see? It's loaded. Six shots. But only if you have to, my love, only if you have to. Be brave now. Set yourself to it if you have to.'

He stood and watched her handling the weapon, puzzled, flicking off the catch.

'Careful, my love.'

She looked up at him. In a moment of imagination she had raised the gun and shot him dead. She turned away and put the gun on a table, walked to the window. He picked up the gun and made it safe. She took deep breaths and put her hand to her forehead. I nearly killed him, she thought, I nearly stopped him. Why didn't I? But she knew why. She knew that she had not wanted to stop him, merely to kill; she wanted to know what that felt like. The realisation made her feel sick.

He came behind her and slipped the gun into the pocket of her dress. She felt its weight like an erection on her thigh.

'You'll be alright, my love?'

She nodded, her mouth tight to contain the bile.

He put one hand on her breasts, the other between her legs. He breathed a hot kiss on her neck, turned and left quickly.

She stood for a long while in a limbo, without thought or movement. Then suddenly she looked at her watch. It was thirty minutes since First had left them. She had to go. She had to go to her women and prepare them. It might already have begun. She might be too late. She might have missed it.

'Can't this wait until after lunch, Radcliff?' Gorham said. He was bored by the waiting. When he had heard that

First was delayed he had been angry, had relished the idea of tearing into the little shit for his insubordination; but that had cooled now, and his headache was worse. He wanted a brandy, but it wasn't ten yet and, still determined to maintain that he was a social drinker, he was holding off until noon, or half-past eleven at least.

Radcliff did not answer his question, stood uneasily before him, looking more and more of the prat that this whole thing would prove him.

'First will prove what you say totally absurd. You know that, Radcliff.'

'We shall see, sir, we shall see.'

'What would you have me do, Radcliff?'

'Have him shot. And Standing. And Williamson, Garman, Lovell and Peters. For a start.'

'You enjoy having people shot, don't you, Radcliff?'

'At least allow me to detain him whilst I tear his quarters apart, sir.'

There was a brisk rap at the door that was immediately identifiable.

'Come!' Gorham bellowed.

'My apologies, sir, a matter of internal discipline. I have the culprit with me. It is in fact quite serious. I'm glad you're here, Major Radcliff, because I don't think I can deal with it on my level.'

'In a moment, in a moment, First. Major Radcliff has brought me some information that I find rather disturbing.'

First glanced at Radcliff in surprise. Radcliff sneered and looked away.

'He tells me you are recruiting my soldiers into your organisation.'

'Into the civil administration, sir? May I ask Major Radcliff why I should care to do that?'

'I have information, First, that leads me to suspect you of treason. I intend to have you locked up until I have completed my investigation, which will, I promise you, be very thorough.'

'Wait a minute, wait a minute, Major. You have information? May I know what information, please?'

'You have weapons.'

'What weapons?'

'Weapons you have stolen from the military. You know it is a capital offence to possess weapons. It is a capital offence to steal from the military authorities. You're going to be shot, First, you and as many of your fucking Brothers as I can catch hold of.'

'Major Radcliff. I have no idea who has been talking to you, nor what you have been told. I assure you that your informant is under some sort of delusion. I have no doubt of my own disposability, nor of those of my friends, but . . . but we have run this place in peace and security for almost three years. By all means indulge your paranoias, but I do feel a responsibility to those under my authority, even if you don't.'

'You conniving little shit. I've been watching you and your friends from the day we arrived here. I'd've had the lot of you shot then, if I'd had my way. You've run this place as your own little parish, lining your own nest, living like leeches. You despicable little shit, First. I'm going to put the fucking bullet in the back of your fucking neck personally.'

Radcliff, now screaming, had advanced during his tirade to within reach of First, had clenched his fists. First eyed him evenly, put his head on one side.

'May I speak with you alone for a minute, Commander?' he said quietly.

'No, you fucking may not,' Radcliff yelled.

'Please, sir,' First said, moving a little further from Radcliff.

'For God's sake, Radcliff,' Gorham said.

'He's armed!' Radcliff yelled. 'He's got a gun!'

First lifted up his arms and opened his hands. 'Search me, if it will entertain you, Major. Lieutenant Lester did search me before I came in, as he always does, but then perhaps Lieutenant Lester's in my pay now?'

'Of course he is!' Radcliff said. 'Of course. That's how . . .'

'Get out, Radcliff,' Gorham said at last. 'Get out and cool down. This is becoming bloody absurd.'

'I'm warning you, sir. . .' Radcliff spluttered.

'Out! Out before I have you shot,' Gorham said through his teeth.

Radcliff turned on his heel and barged his way out through an imaginary crowd. As he went he unbuckled his holster and drew his pistol. In the outer officer, Lester sat behind his desk. Radcliff went straight to him and shoved the barrel of the pistol under his nose.

'Out of there, you,' he said. 'We're going in to see the Commander.'

Someone stepped out behind Radcliff and shot him in the head. He collapsed in a pile as if he'd been deflated all at once. Lester hissed, reached over, flicked a switch on his desk console and slumped back in his chair. Brother Danmore stepped over and put another bullet into Radcliff's torso, causing the body to writhe under the concussion.

'You got him first time, Brother,' Lester said.

'I just wanted to see what it was like, Brother.'

'Shush now. Go back and watch the front. I want to hear how Gorham dies.' And he reached over and switched on the intercom again.

156

Gorham had poured himself a large brandy. He sat down at his desk and faced First who had not begun his defence yet, which surprised Gorham slightly.

'I must stand by my officers first, First,' he began, twitching at the repetition which made what he said seem silly, which made him cross. 'I won't let him shoot you, of course, but I'll let him hold on to you for a few hours whilst he ferrets about, if that's what he wants. Then I can transfer him and we can be clear of all this nonsense.'

'Major Radcliff's dead,' First said.

'What?' Gorham had heard, but it didn't make any sense.

'I had someone waiting out there for him. If he was still alive, he'd have come back in by now, I think.'

Gorham gaped, then began to choke. The truth seemed to erupt inside him physically. He began to fumble at his desk drawer. First stepped round and neatly, with almost no effort, tipped his chair over and sent him sprawling across the floor. Then he reached inside the drawer and collected the gun, an old-fashioned automatic, heavy, large calibre.

'It's not even loaded,' he said, rectifying this. 'You really have let things slip, haven't you?'

'Get out. Get out of here. What do you want?'

Gorham, who had fallen on his back, began to edge himself backwards along the floor. First stepped across and shot Gorham in the stomach. The noise filled the room, and when the booming had died down, Gorham was groaning and gurgling, clasping his hands to his wound, then bringing them to his face as if he could not believe them. First watched him curiously.

Lester appeared almost at once.

He's not dead, First.'

'He will be soon. Could the noise be a problem?'

'Everyone within earshot is ours.'

'Good, Lester, very good. Send Danmore in here. The word is *Alpha*. Go to Anthony Standing. He's in the committee room. Give him the word. *Alpha*.'

'*Alpha*.'

Lester left, and Danmore came in. First had righted Gorham's chair, and sat in it watching the old man twisting about on the floor about his blown belly, trying to lift himself up, trying to hold his guts in, choking and spluttering, wallowing in his own bloody filth. Danmore came and looked down. First watched him grow pale at the sight.

'D'you want me to finish him off, First?'

'No. You're here to make the tannoy work. I wish to speak to the complex at midday. That gives you an hour and a half. Did you lock the doors?'

'Yes, First,' he said. He looked at Gorham and whistled. 'The tannoy. I wondered why you picked me. I've never even fired one of these before.'

'You had no problem?'

'Oh no, First. It was easy as easy.' He raised his gun and made a popping sound, then laughed.

'Beware of that, Danmore. Fix the tannoy, then we can watch this corrupt old man die here. You will learn something from that. There is a justice in shooting his belly out. It is foul and cruel, but it is just'.

First rose and walked over to Gorham, looked down into the old man's watery eyes as if trying to see behind them; then he knelt and pressed both his hands down into the wound. Gorham screamed, a high-pitched shriek that came from deep inside him, a child's scream, an animal's, as if the pain had driven him back deep into the labyrinth of his evolution. First rose steadily and wiped his hands down the length of his scarf.

158

Danmore, watching this, snatched quickly at Gorham's brandy bottle and emptied a substantial amount of it into his mouth, swallowing it and finding that it had neither taste nor strength as it went down his gullet.

He did not have a pleasant hour, and the brandy had made it worse. He asked to be excused. First would not excuse him, and he vomited in a corner of the office. He was ashamed of himself, afraid that he had failed; but he had not failed. He was very young, and his disgust did him credit. First wanted him to go through that, did not want any of them to become used to brutality, to avoid its consequences, for it ever to become blunted within them. This is what it is to kill a man, First told him. This is what we are about today. Watch him, and be constantly prepared to suffer as we have made him suffer. In the end, all you will be is a quivering bag of bloody filth, there, like that. Look at that and ask yourself what more you have, now, at this moment; your life. And what is your life worth? What is it that makes you better than him? No, it is not that you have won and he has lost, not that you will go on living and he shortly will cease to go on living. Your life, for as long as you have it, is a power, a privilege, a truth which you must always honour.

Alpha

They move quietly into place, waiting, watching. Above the complex the sky is grey, the concrete is darkened by the damp of a settled mist. The day proceeds through its customary routines, dull and unremarkable. Small hopes and small frustrations rise and turn in offices and workrooms, out in the guard houses and down in the stores; but below the surface, the chosen hearts are driving, generating a stored power that is about to be monumentally discharged. They know that the great

159

moment has already happened. It happened with the word – *Alpha*; they know that what they are to do will merely be to respond to the moment. Their loyalty and obedience absolves them, liberates them, gives them the power beyond themselves. They know that the emotions which strive in them for release are not their emotions, but the emotions of the movement, the brotherhood. They do not look at one another; they have no need to: a telepathic imperative unites them. They are faceless and invisible, incapable now of individual response, and this is the greatest feeling in the world, beyond material possession, beyond the most profound physical pleasure. What was promised them is, this day, delivered to them. They are to be gods.

Eleven o'clock. Eleven hundred hours. The eleventh hour.

An office door opens. The colonel looks up, surprised at the unannounced arrival. He sees a young man whom he vaguely recognises. He is about to assert his authority when the young man swings up a pistol between straight arms and fires into his head which is thrown back, the chair on which he sits rolling back on its casters to meet the filing cabinet behind. The colonel sits on the chair as if he has been dropped down into it from above. The young man keeps the gun raised, notes where the bullet has struck, just to the right of the mid-line of the forehead. It is enough. He turns to go, joining another young man who has held a pistol to the head of a secretary-clerk who sits open-mouthed. The only sounds are of the ticking buzz of the information console and the trickle of urine onto the floor under the clerk's chair. As the men leave the telephone rings, but the clerk is incapable of answering it.

The captain is late on his rounds, harbouring a petty

irritation that he wants to exorcise on someone. When he reaches the gatehouse, no-one is in sight. 'This place is open like a convent virgin,' he yells, stopping with his hands on his hips, waiting for them to come creeping out from whatever they have been indulging themselves upon. Two young civilians appear from the door, stepping out decisively. A survival instinct turns him and darts him for the cover of a wall. He trips, however, and when he looks up he sees one of the young men moving round in front of him, lifting the pistol.

Two young lieutenants sit with their fiancées in a secluded part of a coffee house reserved for officers. They are intelligence officers, and are telling the girls little secrets that titillate them and make them giggle. One of them has his hand under the skirt of his fiancée, and is pressing his fingers into the taut cotton before her vagina. His comrade suddenly shakes his shoulder. He looks aside, irritated, to see his comrade's face fall comically into a plate of cake. His girl shrieks and pushes him away. A bullet slashes through his cheeks. He doesn't feel it, suddenly finds blood gushing from his useless mouth. He looks up at the girl, uncomprehending, then a second shot drops his head down into the lap of her white dress, and the blood spreads by a rapid capillary action up across her belly and down her thighs. She shrieks and shrieks and shrieks.

In the security command office, four interrogation officers are waiting for Radcliff, who ought to have been here an hour ago. They have things to do, and argue whether they should wait for Radcliff or get on with it; either way, they know they will incur his wrath. There is a small knock on the door. They exchange glances, and one of them heaves himself up and goes to answer the knock. He opens the door slightly, talks to someone and then is flung back as if punched. The others dive at once for cover and for their pistols. The room is suddenly full of silent, purposeful figures. One is fumbling with his holster when he is dropped, face down. Another manages to draw his weapon, turn and fire into an empty space where, a second before, a dark figure was standing. He doesn't have time for a second shot. The last one has crashed straight through the door into Radcliff's office, manages to turn and train his gun on the door frame. He waits, ready. Nothing happens. The lights go out in the outer office, which, unlike Radcliff's office, has no exterior windows. The door frame is a black space into which he fires, once, twice, three times. He begins to edge away from the door. He doesn't hear the shot, but he feels it enter his groin. He fires again, once, twice, but knows his shots are going into the floor, into the wall. The pain in his groin is massive and it buckles him down, presenting the back of his neck for the figure who steps now quickly in over him.

The adjutant is crossing the concourse with a stack of papers under his arm, requisition orders which he must have signed this morning. Someone calls his name. He doesn't stop, turns on the move, collides with someone. His stack of papers slips from his hands and fans out on the wet pavingstones. He swears and kneels at once to gather them back together. Someone steps over him, he assumes, to help him.

The two military policemen notice a cluster of young men by the ornamental steps down by the refectory. They exchange glances and, tapping their riot-sticks in their leather palms, they go down towards the cluster. Some feet away, they stop. 'Shouldn't you fuckers be at work, then?' The cluster breaks open at once and forms a line in movement that might have come out of a musical.

The drill sergeant goes down for his mid-morning bowel movement. There are a couple of young men in the latrine, one of whom he recognises and greets. He peers into various cubicles to select one that is not too sordid and, having selected, is just turning to shut the door when it is pushed open against him.

The deputy-quartermaster is lying in. He is half-asleep, lying on his side, trying to muster the resolve to get up and empty his bladder, slipping in and out of awkward dreams in which someone comes into his room, places a cold, steel finger at his temple.

A big corporal breaks out of the resource building and runs across the concourse, yelling. 'They're murdering us! They're murdering us!' He stumbles, falls, covers his head. He does not attempt to get up, lies there writhing about, sheltering from some invisible terror. A crowd begins to gather around him, keeping their distance as he twists and pleads with them. 'Stop them! Stop them!' A young woman, a nurse, comes forward and kneels before him, reaches out her hand. He looks up at her. 'It's all right,' she says. She feels hands under her shoulders, lifting her. She looks to see two young men regarding her with ironic smiles. The corporal, sitting askew on the pavingstones, sees the young men and whimpers. 'You're not going to kill me, are you?' They drag the nurse out of the way, deposit her, but she rushes forward and grabs at their jackets. One of them turns and stabs a fist into her stomach. She goes down with a moan. 'Sorry, love,' one of them says to her. She watches them step towards the corporal. 'Don't kill me,' he says. One of the young men shoots him in the foot. He screams. 'Don't piss about,' the other says. His companion rams the pistol into the corporal's mouth. 'One, two, three,' he says slowly and then blows out the back of the corporal's head. 'He might

163

have been armed,' the other one says as they move back through the stunned onlookers. 'Bastards!' the nurse screams. The killer turns back, but his companion drags him away.

Alpha. It is eleven-fifteen.

The resonance of the killings spreads rapidly. Few of them have actually been witnessed, but the knowledge of them blows through the complex like a cloud of gas. Everything begins to stop, like a terminal heartbeat. Everyone looks at their neighbour. Something has happened. Are they part of it? Are you? Am I? A cold quiet comes amongst them, a taint. Perhaps that was a shot. Someone is screaming somewhere. Someone is moving fast down the corridors, across the terraces, up and down staircases; one pair of feet, two pairs of feet in step; not running, but moving with purpose, moved by it, driving it, driven by it. They come closer; they move away. A door opens, everyone turns, everyone turns away. Someone is looking, searching for someone. It is me? Is it her?

That it is enormous, that it is beyond reaction, seems self-evident. No-one wants to know anything about it. A slow stun grips them, each one, separating them from each other, from everything that an hour ago they were a part of. They wait for someone to tell them what to do, to tell them who they are now, to tell them that they have survived it, if they have survived it, if it will be possible to have survived it.

At last the loudspeakers crackle and a voice comes amongst them; and as it comes, everyone knows that this is what they have been waiting for. They look up at their loudspeaker and as the voice delivers its slow, clear rhetoric, they can visualise the face behind the voice, feel it talking to them personally, feel it claiming and defining them.

'*Alpha, Alpha.* It is a beginning. You are now free. Everything that held you back, that repressed your strength and truth has been destroyed. I welcome you to a new world. You are reborn today, members of a new unity of ideals and power. The birth pangs of your new unity have not been without pain, not without cruelty. How could they have been? To that which is weak and corrupt within us we must be cruel. How else are we to be free of those parts of us that do not live up to our highest realisations of ourselves? In your name we have killed today thirty-seven men. We have broken the links of the chain that bound you. Some of you must mourn those who have died. Do not be afraid to mourn. Do not be ashamed to mourn. Accept your pain, accept it proudly and freely. Clean yourself with suffering so that you are fit for the trials that lie ahead of you. They will be many. What we have begun here will arouse fear in the hearts of the corrupt and the degenerate. They will bring all their powers against us. But they will not overcome us. We are the inexorable. You are the inexorable. Those who wear the white scarf are your guides now. Greet them as brothers. Be strong to give them strength, and be strong to receive the strength they have to give. Exonerate them in your hearts for the pain they have caused you. Honour them for their courage. Unmask your own courage to be able to walk with them. Go about your lives now gladly. May we be worthy of you, and may you be worthy of us, and may all be worthy of this great day.'

The voice does not soothe them, but it does reassure them. It has a certainty that wraps around them. They are no better off, no worse off. They exchange glances, shrugs; they do not understand, but that does not matter. Some run to friends and embrace them, but not for long,

165

for the embraces feel like farewells. They sit soon dumb, waiting to be told what to do, where they are, who they are now.

The day we took power in the east was a quiet day. There was a sudden jump of adrenalin as the decision was taken, and then everything moved into place precisely as we had planned it. We struck clinically and cauterised the wounds. We had no casualties.

I was realised at last. That day I became a God, with the power of a God over men and women. I felt clear and pure. I had attained human perfection, the complete self-sufficiency that was beyond contamination. At that moment I became, as I had always wanted to be, utterly alone. I glowed with the intoxication of magnificence.

There was to be a time, although I could not at that moment imagine it, when I would again be as other men, when you came to me, Rachel. Life is finite: I might have learnt that from Gorham. At that time, and for a long time afterwards, I felt that life was infinite; but it was not, and when I began to move back down within reach of my mortality again, there you were, ready with your blessing and your affirmation of me. Oh Rachel, things have always worked out for the best.

THE INEXORABLE

Whilst Mark First, by multiple acts of murder, established his leadership, Rachel, in the quiet of the far woodland, tended by her husband, gave birth to a daughter, Rebecca.

It was an easy birth, though protracted, her swollen body urging and urging for a day and a night, at last opening to the great giving of which she had always dreamed.

Ben wept, and when she asked him why, he said that he did not feel it was right to be doing this, to be bringing children into the world at this time.

'We're safe here,' she told him. 'Be happy for me. Trust me. I am strong enough here for both of us, for all of us.'

When she had settled, he walked out into the woods, which were hung with a cold mist, crackling and dead. He sought calm here, but the further he went from her, the greater his unease. There was a vast silence over the land, as if they were truly alone, as if he was alone. He turned and, although he knew these woods intimately now, he felt that he would not somehow be able to find his way back to her. The child was so beautiful, she was so beautiful, that he could not in his cold solitude believe in them. Something would come from these woods, some malevolence would break cover and destroy him.

Jacob Catton had spent three grim years as chief security officer, asserting military authority in the capital. It was a bleak and hopeless time, in which he felt only that he was ministering to a terminal illness, lancing malignancies with sterile violence. He dreamed of a time when he could shed his uniform and step out anonymous into a clear world again, but as the months and years passed, he began to know that the authority he exercised, the repression and violence, had become a way of life, self-perpetuating, and that he was a part of that life. When it ended, if it ever could end, he would end with it. He avoided the company of others, avoided any sociability, avoided alcohol, any of which he knew could break his resolve and turn his violence inward. He lived always with the shadow of despair behind him: he never looked back.

He came into the barracks yard shortly after dawn, to be faced with the night's trawl of the streets: thirty items of human refuse – drug-peddlers and fanatics, pathetic terrorists, lunatics. That morning there were eleven women, not the highest number there had been, but confirmation of a depressing trend. He hated dealing with the women; something intimate within him rose against it. He had not touched a woman in years, could not bear to think of doing so now; but the presence of them, of their defiance and their fear, opened a desire in him. They seemed to embody a potential that had gone awry, the potential of the world perhaps. He lifted one of their faces with his gloved hand. The eyes were glassy, neutralised, did not register him at all. He let the head fall back in disgust.

A sergeant handed him a clipboard and he flicked through the sheets, looking for anything new. A couple of the names were characters they had been seeking for weeks. He asked for them to be pointed out. They were nothing after all; it relieved and depressed him.

'That's one's new, sir,' the sergeant said.

There was no name, which was not unusual. He had been distributing leaflets; nothing new there. One of the leaflets was attached, and he skimmed it for something significant, but it was the usual load of apocalyptic cant; better written and presented than usual perhaps, but hardly a serious revolutionary tract. *Purity is the only truth*, he read. *Purity is only possible when the individual has been purged of his weakness and made one with the cause.* A new religion, perhaps.

'All right,' he said. 'We'll deal with this one first.'

Seated behind his desk, with the suspect hauled in before him, he began in his usual way:

'You have been in breach of the martial codes. You have five minutes to give me a good reason why I should not have you shot at once.'

'My blood will shame you,' the man said clearly. 'And it will glorify me. I am the first ray of light from the east. Remember me.'

He looked up at the man and registered his face. It was a clean, strong face which met his with a surprising confidence, a brightness almost.

'Well,' Catton said, 'that's not much of a start. Four and a half minutes.'

But the man did not speak again.

He did remember the man, however, the next day when

he was summoned to Commander Fox. Something had happened in the eastern region. The usual channels of communication closed suddenly and completely. Then came rumours that Gorham and most of his senior officers had been murdered by fanatics, that there was some sort of outbreak, some sort of serious insurrection in progress amongst the wheatfields and dairy pastures. Fox instructed Catton to take a couple of trusted officers and drive out there to see what was going on.

They drove east in a fast car, Catton and two intelligence officers, with a sergeant driver. They arrived at an efficient road block. A polite young man in a suit, unarmed, wearing a white scarf thrown over his shoulder raffishly, approached their car. He greeted them and told them that they were expected, that transport was arranged for them the other side of the block, that their driver would not be required. They were walked through. The barricade was manned by a mixture of soldiers and civilians. Catton noted that they were relaxed but not undisciplined, and comprehensively well-armed. The security precautions were professional. He had assumed, as had Fox, that these were amateurs; he was becoming uneasy.

They were driven in a car with darkened windows very fast along empty roads by a soldier who refused to answer any questions put to him. They arrived an hour later at the information centre that had been Gorham's command post. There were no security checks on the way in. The car stopped before a low building and a man came out to greet them, an elegant civilian in his mid-thirties, dressed formally but with the scarf Catton had already come to identify as the local badge of belonging.

'Anthony Standing,' he said, shaking Catton firmly by

170

the hand as he emerged from the car. 'Welcome, Colonel Catton.'

They were led into a dingy room that smelt of vomit and which showed signs of recent violence. The filing cabinets had been broken open and their contents were arranged in piles on the floor. There was an oppressive neatness over the filth.

Catton and his men sat on low chairs. The man, Standing, sat behind the desk. There were three other men in the shadows about the room. Standing introduced them as Gary Garman, Jeffrey Lester and Mark First, all civilians. Garman was large, shock-haired and narrow-eyed; Lester was young and neat, with a precision that Catton recognised soon enough as military; First was short, stocky and dark-eyed, the image of an assistant bank-manager.

'May we ask,' Catton said, 'exactly what has happened here?'

'We have taken over from the army,' Standing said.

'And who are you?'

'We are a political movement based on brotherhood and integrity.'

'And where is Commander Gorham?'

'Commander Gorham is dead.'

'You murdered him, in other words?'

'He was assassinated, yes, as were others of his command.'

'May we know what others?'

Standing paused, looked at each of them clearly.

'For obvious reasons, we would not be prepared to publish lists of names, Colonel.'

'Were they all military? May we know that?'

'They were all military. Seventy-eight in all.'

'Seventy-eight? Good God!'

'You shot eighty-three last month in the capital,' the man Garman said suddenly.

'May I ask if Henry Radcliff was amongst your . . . assassinations?' Catton said quietly.

There was a pause, then First spoke.

'He was.'

'Fairly obviously, Radcliff would have been on our list,' Standing continued. 'We knew of his connections with Commander Fox. You will appreciate, I am sure, our need to be thorough.'

Catton began to feel nervous. The whole operation reeked of fanaticism. These were dangerous men, possibly immediately dangerous. And he knew who was in charge.

'And what, may we ask, are your ambitions, Mr First?'

First held his look directly, but it was Standing who answered.

'Beyond our command we have no direct ambitions, except to be left to run things here as we wish to without any interference. If Commander Fox has any thoughts of reimposing a military command here, I beg you, gentlemen, to dissuade him from it. The cost, in military and human terms, would be very high, very high indeed.'

'Well. You've made yourselves clear,' Catton said. 'I am not Commander Fox's spokesman, merely his messenger-boy. I am bound to tell you, however, that the murder of army officers is a crime of the utmost seriousness.'

'You had Archer and Clifton shot last year, with a whole clutch of their junior officers,' Garman said.

'I would not be prepared to discuss that allegation, even if it were true.'

Garman snorted.

Standing continued. 'We are really not prepared to

172

trade hypocrisies with you, gentlemen. What we have done is to change the landscape here beyond any attempt to change it back again.'

'And we are not answerable to Commander Fox,' Garman said. 'He would have been quite prepared to support Radcliff if he'd done what we did.'

'That is absolutely untrue,' Catton said.

'Do you want to see a file of their communications, Colonel Catton?' Garman said. 'I knew we'd get this shit from you lot.'

'Well,' Catton said. 'I'll convey what you have said to Commander Fox.'

'Please,' Standing said, 'try to convince him of the reality of the situation here. There is really no need for conflict. It would not be in his interest any more than it would be in ours.'

'I'll certainly pass the point of view on to him, Mr Standing.'

'There's one other thing,' First said quietly.

'And what is that, Mr First?'

'We are, as Anthony has told you, a political movement. We deal in ideals and we deal in faith. Now, there are a number of our friends in the capital. It is possible that you have identified them already.'

'It is possible, Mr First,' Catton said, eyeing him precisely.

First smiled.

'Those who embrace what we stand for,' he continued, 'are men of the highest integrity and, insofar as they adhere to the orders of your command, they deserve to have their integrity respected. We would consider it an act of aggression against us if they were in any way to be restricted in the freedoms they have as law-abiding members of your community, Colonel Catton.'

'I have no idea what you are implying by this, Mr First.'

'Nevertheless, please convey my sentiments precisely to Commander Fox. They are of the utmost importance. We are prepared to protect our brothers, wherever they might be.'

Catton looked at First, who returned his look steadfastly. There was a long minute of silence as the two men attempted to outface one another.

'Well?' First said when Standing returned from seeing their guests to their car.

'Predictable,' Standing said, going to the whiskey. 'And easy.'

'Who were the other two?'

'Er, the little one was a man called Leman, a basic thug. The tall one was Richards. No information on him yet.'

'He interested me, Anthony.'

'Which one? Richards?'

'Yes . . . Richards. There was an openness in his eyes, a flicker of the fire. I have come to recognise it, Anthony. It is an animal reaction, hardly even conscious, the opening of the senses, the intrigue. It is like the reaction in a woman who is sexually moved. You know that.'

'Yes.'

'He's not a strong man, I think, but we might make him strong. Have him approached.'

'With pleasure. What about Colonel Catton?'

'Now he is a strong man, with a real inner violence. He would be a catch indeed, but I don't think he's ready for us yet. Come, Anthony. Embrace me. We have had a good day, and I must return you to your wife.'

Catton reported forcibly to Fox, who was disturbed but loath to make any drastic moves.

'What do you suggest?' he asked.

'I would suggest a bullet for Mr Mark First,' he said, 'as a first priority.'

Fox shuffled around this. 'We have enough of our own problems,' he said, 'without going to search for others out of our territory.'

'And if we catch any of them wandering about the streets, sir?'

'You have the usual procedures for dealing with these people, Catton?'

'Very good, sir.'

They were hard, but not impossible, to catch; hard because they were careful, because they did not move amongst the dispossessed and the criminals. There was a similarity about the ones they did catch, however, a type set by the first of them. There was the same pride, the same clarity that not even the most practised brutality could ever quite subdue. Catton began to loathe them, to rise with pleasure when there were two or three in the morning's haul; he also began to become afraid of them. He issued precise, revised instructions to his men to seek them out specifically.

Then Fox summoned him again.

'Catton, I've been thinking about these madmen in the east.'

'So have I, sir.'

'I've been thinking . . . that perhaps we ought to license them in some way.'

Catton was speechless.

'Apart from passing round their dreary little pamphlets, what actually have you caught them doing?'

'Sir, I beg of you . . .'

'Well? I think you have them out of proportion, Colonel. I think pursuing them is a waste of our time and energy. If we let them loose, firstly we can see who they are and watch them more effectively, and secondly, I think they might even be useful to us. I've been impressed with some of the things they've done in the east.'

'Sir, I would like to register in the strongest terms, my opposition to this. I believe that they are the most serious threat we have ever had against us.'

'Yes, yes. Your opposition is registered, Colonel. Now go and do something useful for a change, rather than pursuing people who ought really to be on our side.'

Like some perverse springtime, they blossomed on the streets of the capital. In offices and shops, in factories and schools and hospitals, and amongst the shiftless mass of the gleaners and vagrants who made up almost half of the city's population, white scarves were now sported by scores of strong young white men. They greeted each other on the streets like long-lost friends, embraced and smiled, exchanged names and addresses. They laughed and congratulated one another like victors of a great and enduring struggle, walking with a pride of belonging. Those who were not of this fraternity watched warily, began to pale beside them, felt themselves pushed to one side by this strange bonhomie.

They began to congregate, to take over pubs on certain evenings, to hire halls and hold rallies. They were never rowdy, never aggressive, but always exclusive. They began to colonise derelict buildings, to repair and decorate them. They were careful to keep to themselves, careful at first to identify no specific enemies.

Their first active excursions were against readily identifiable social enemies – the criminal gangs and the drug-peddlers, the pimps and rent boys who operated in the shadows of the military authorities. They moved in a mass against such groups, in actions that were precisely organised, rounding up the masters of vice for general public execration, and for the authorities, who were embarrassed by this sudden thoroughness and who did not really want it. The military did not really mind what the civilians did to each other, provided the tight structure of their security was never threatened; the civil law had become increasingly impotent.

So they began to take the law into their own hands, and in their carefully limited spheres were allowed to do so. There were public committees of justice. There were makeshift gallows on which were hanged the mafiosi, the racketeers, the obese old men who collected children for trade in sexual gratification. They were exemplary in their selection of those who suffered thus, and little sympathy was roused for the squirming bodies who died at the end of the slip-wires, with the quiet crowd of serious young men watching them, noting their degradations and taking them to heart.

They were relentless, cut a wider and wider circle amongst the moral decay of the city, began to patrol, to set up vigilante forces. Their targets were always and only those who broke the established law; they enforced no regulations of their own, and their policing began to gather a substantial support amongst those who yearned for normality, for security, for some sense of ordinariness to return to their lives. They offered a set of brutal certainties that might be accepted as justice, and were so accepted by a tired and long-suffering populace.

Within a year large areas of the city organisation were under their control, and life seemed to be improving. The queers and the blacks might be having a hard time of it, but it was not hard to redress them in the prejudices

177

they had borne not so long ago. They were still minori-
ties, and the minority can serve to bolster the self-esteem
of the majority. We are white and we are normal, and
therefore we'll be all right. And, by and large, they were.

Commander Fox watched all this and became, as the
months passed, quite pleased with the way things were
turning out. He had not made Gorham's mistake of
letting them get too close to him. His command seemed a
clearer, cleaner place under their administration.

Catton however they appalled, filled him with a dread
that seemed like a waking nightmare, the confrontation
of a monster that appeared dormant but which emanated
a violence and power that chilled him. The monster
would wake, the monster would turn, any day now. And
when he tried to rationalise these terrors, he always came
back to the man First. He was never mentioned in any of
their propaganda, never even intimated; but Catton had
seen the man, knew him, felt his presence everywhere.
Without First, they would have been another sect of
thugs who could be corrupted, annexed, neutralised in
time; but First was absolute. From him Catton had
caught the cold, high reek of fanaticism that terrified
him.

The fanatic believed that he was right with an absolute
murdering certainty. Catton had known the breed
before, and had always wondered how ignorance could
become so monumental; for the fanatic was ignorant,
wilfully ignorant of the nature of humanity, blinding
himself to any edge of reality that snagged against his
certainty, piling up his bloody hypocrisies into barriers
against the world. As a psychological type the fanatic
was, he supposed, comprehensible. The paradox was
their ability to co-opt others into their fanaticism; that

Catton had never been able to comprehend, attributing it to the communal stupidity of human beings, the herd instinct. But, although he had a firm conviction of the natural rapacity of human beings, who disgusted him as a species with very few, fewer and fewer, exceptions, he knew that he had not survived by treating people as essentially stupid; on the contrary, the limitlessly cruel cunning of men was one of the absolutes of his world. What was it about the fanatics, then, that deprived men of their cunning, that drove their intelligence down, often below the level of their own survival?

The more he thought about First, remembered those cold little eyes caught upon him, the cold delivery of his conditions, the more Catton began to unravel his paradox. Behind the beliefs, the dogmas, the certainties, lay the power, the pure, limitless eroticism of power. The beliefs were finally irrelevant, constructs of words, ideas, shadows thrown behind the particular men who had turned to that ultimate narcotic, who like First had learnt the obscene secret of gripping men by the heart, of sucking their loyalty and obedience into his bloodstream, pumping their energy into the great priapism of his ego. He had not before believed in evil as a force in the real world any more than he had believed in truth, or love, or God, but, in the contemplation of the man First, he came to believe. The monster of his nightmares was First, the total, consuming megalomania, and it was inescapably and absolutely evil, inimical to everything that made life worth living on any level, to laughter and tenderness, to trust and hope, to the continuing survival of humanity; and there was nothing he could do about it.

Their leader in the capital was Michael Wilks, a genial, fair-haired man who seemed the reverse of menacing

179

when met casually. He came to see Fox regularly, to keep him informed of what was happening. Catton he avoided.

Then, late one evening, he presented himself at Catton's office in the company of two silent young men. Catton was alone, and immediately became afraid. Wilks was as ever disarmingly casual, chatting for a while, then presenting for the colonel's perusal a list of fifty-three names of those he denounced as undesirables in senior positions in the army.

Catton ran his eye down the list quickly to check that he was not on it, then put it down and promised Wilks he'd give it his earliest attention.

'You don't want to know in what way they are undesirable, Colonel?'

'What are you going to tell me?' he said, 'that they are homosexual, that they are fiddling the accounts, that they take a little cocaine, that some of them are not of clean indigenous descent? What?'

'Oh well, Colonel, it's your outfit they are corrupting, not ours.'

'Oh, I know what's corrupting the army all right, Wilks. A list of the members of your organisation who wear army uniform in their spare time, that would be a far more interesting list.'

Wilks laughed as if at a jolly joke and took his thugs off with him.

Catton copied the list and sent, by civilian mail, a copy to all those on it, with a note explaining what it was. Then he made his way to the quarters of Captain Richards. Richards was not pleased to see him. Catton at first thought he had a sexual partner, but he was alone. He admitted Catton warily, offered him no drink, not even a place to sit down.

'Brother Wilks came to see me this evening, Dick,' Catton said, seating himself anyway, lighting a cigarette which he knew would irritate the fastidious Richards. 'He showed me a list of names of those he called "undesirables" within the army.'

'Really?' Richards said, sitting down to play along. 'Anyone of significance?'

'Your name was on the list.'

Catton watched Richards's reaction, his stiffening, his rapid but visible mental calculation of how to respond.

'I don't believe you, Colonel,' he said quietly.

'Why should I lie to you?'

'I have nothing to be ashamed of, sir. They have the integrity not to include me in any denunciation.'

'You've already seen that list, haven't you, Dick? You helped compile it. You're one of them, aren't you?'

Richards went very still, held Catton's eyes.

'If you've nothing further to accuse me of, sir, I would be grateful to be allowed to go to bed now.'

'Who else is a part of this, Dick?'

Richards was silent, set into a posture of closed righteousness.

'You've betrayed us, Dick. I'm going to have you shot.'

'You wouldn't understand,' Richards said coldly.

'Oh, I understand betrayal very well. I understand hypocrisy and subterfuge. And what sickens me beyond anything is your superiority. You really believe that you are superior to poor old Justin Jackley, whose only indulgence is to have a little boy come and pull his cock for him once a month. Your lot are way below him on any human scale. You're part of a cancer that is eating out the heart of this city.'

'This city was dead when we came here,' Richards

181

said, looking up, out in the open at last. 'You, Fox and all the rest of you, have done nothing here but feed off the corpse. Loyalty to you is to be a part of the corruption. We are going to set this city free.'

'Free? Do you really think that when you lot have taken over here, there will be freedom? Do you know about the camps they have in the east? Do you know about the repression, the racism, the violence? Have you watched them hanging some old pimp, watched the glow in their eyes as he chokes and shits and dies?'

'There must be cruelty. It is necessary. We look at what we do with open eyes. We harden ourselves. We make ourselves free of the compromises and weaknesses that bred the corruption we destroy. We are all capable of that sort of corruption, and we must scour it out of ourselves as we scour it out of the world about us. That is the true freedom. It is the freedom from self. You know the truth of this, and if only you were honest with yourself, Jacob, you would not oppose us. You would join us.'

Catton stood, a piling violence lifting him; the use of his first name was the final insult. Richards rose too, held himself up, lifted his head. Catton turned and went to the door. Richards followed him, as if to see him out, polite and certain. Catton turned to speak, wanted to say something, to leave Richards with something stinging in his ears, to frighten him, diminish him, but nothing came to him, his mind clotted with rage.

Richards stood before him, his hand on the door, smiling. Then he reached over and took Catton in an embrace, a tight fraternal clasp about the shoulders. This stunned Catton beyond response. Richards released him and looked seriously into his eyes. Then Catton knew what to do. He reached forward as if to return the

182

embrace, grabbed Richards's head, pulled it to his and kissed him open-mouthed, forcing his tongue over Richards's, sucking the breath out of him.

He let him go, stepped back and regarded him. Richards was pale, his eyes wide, trembling. Catton laughed.

'Enjoy that, did you, Dick? Turn you on?'

Richards did not move. Catton was overcome by an infinite contempt for this man. He punched his head hard, broke his face, sent him sprawling back into a sideboard and down on to the floor. He stepped over and kicked his crotch, and when he doubled over, Catton kicked his head, stood on the small of his back and put all his weight down until he felt something give. The violence made him hard, filled him with certainty. He was not angry any more. What he had done was justified by every instinct within him. He had the monster out in the open now, and he fought it.

Richards lay still. He was not unconscious, for, as Catton moved around him, he could see the eyes following him.

'Get up,' he said.

He tried to rise but could not. I'm going to have to finish this, Catton said to himself. He looked around him, then had the perfect idea. He went quickly into Richards's bedroom and there, on the bed where he knew it would be, was the scarf, laid out neatly as if it was some part of Richards's night attire. Snatching it up, Catton returned to his victim, saw that he had turned onto his side and was reaching up for a drawer in the sideboard.

Catton stepped across, kicked Richards down and over on to his stomach again and then looped the scarf around his neck, twisting it, putting his knee on the man's back and wrenching until there was a crack and it was done.

He assumed that he was being followed, that they would find Richards very soon, that he had at the most half an hour's start. He went down to his car, checked that his pistol was in the glove compartment and was loaded, then drove off, out of the city, along the western motorways, off onto the side roads he knew would not be guarded.

I only met Jacob Catton once, when he came on an emissary from the capital. He had a certain strength, but he was essentially closed; another dull soldier, one whom we might colonise in time, or one whom, more probably, we might have to neutralise. He had a sharp, superficial intelligence, but this was never an ability I rated highly; the scientist's intelligence, the power to see minutely into whatever was in front of him, but never to understand its truth. He didn't interest me then. With hindsight, of course, I ought to have reached across and strangled him where he sat, squeezed his neck until his head burst. I ought to have known what he would be capable of, but I did not know, had other visions then that needed to be satisfied.

We moved into the capital, spread there like molten metal filling the cavities, burning out the rot. And from the capital we moved onwards, onwards.

I often imagine your quiet married life that was making its way up there in the dead lands whilst we were taking over the world. It pleases me to think of that, to think that it was possible, even in the swirling maelstroms amongst which we thrived in those years. I used to imagine such lives as yours out there, silent and uneventful. When the action became tumultuous, I supposed that my imaginings were fanciful, that surely no-one could be living like that now, not for the time being. When I knew of you, knew that you had lived and loved, and brought your children into the world whilst our energy was at its most dynamic, I was proud.

FULFILMENT

THE DARK HEART

They moved their headquarters to a large company house set in broad parkland: a central block of large rooms, with two sweeping wings about a gravel drive; and behind the frontage, a complex of old stables and store rooms converted to offices and living quarters; and out on the estate, lodges and cottages, and farm buildings turned to barracks and, about a mile from the house, a work camp from where the tillage and maintenance of the outlaying land was done.

Anthony and Muriel Standing were master and mistress of the place, had under their authority the hundred and twenty officers, secretaries, guards, workmen, cooks, maids. The men were all members of the Brotherhood and the women all married to one of the Brothers. There were a growing number of infants about the place, by whom both Anthony and Muriel, who were failing to produce children, were privately irritated. But they did their duty as the family of the house on the social, practical and political levels, which were hardly distinct. They supervised and inspected, advised and led discussion groups, he amongst the men, she amongst the

189

wives. Lunch was eaten communally in a large converted barn which served not only as refectory, but as the meeting house as well. Standing would begin the meal with a little speech, mentioning any complications that had arisen, commending what had been done, and offering a few sentences of the calm rhetoric of the Brotherhood.

There was a universal seriousness of intent in this community, a sense that everything done, from the most trivial to the most significant, from the raking of the gravel to the taking of decisions, all was part of the movement, answerable in integrity to the final purpose. It was not oppressive. Standing had read the old fictions about the individual soul's struggle against the monolithic state, had once assumed that they embodied a simple truism; but they were wrong – naïve, testaments not to the strength of humanity but to its weakness. Submission to the final purpose gave every aspect of life a cleanliness and direction that he had not believed himself capable of. Here, amongst the committed, there was respect and order, and in that, joy. He watched his men and their wives for signs of disaffection; he knew his position put him at risk of wishful illusion, but he felt no unease here. The faces met him clearly, seriously, intently, and he knew they felt as he did.

Certainly the house and its grounds were an ideal state. Beyond it, he knew, the struggle and the cruelty existed. He had seen that, had partaken of it, and he never forgot that it would go on, for years yet, perhaps until long after his own final release, until the world was brought into line with the truth they lived here. And he knew that there would be trials for him still to come. He welcomed them, imagined them vividly in his waking and his dreaming, lived here meanwhile in peace and harmony, grateful, but ready at a moment's notice to go back into battle.

Although there were still shadows, still things within her unresolved, Muriel too fell into the seductive fulfilments of their new life. Before her marriage, before her commitment to Anthony, she had been restless, struggling amongst the conflicts and compromises of a life that had worn her down with its hopeless, broken dreams. She listened to her husband's rhetoric as it denounced the corruptions of individualism, as it offered freedom in submission to the cause, and she applied this rhetoric flatly to her own life. She imagined a time when all would be finally achieved, when the women would be equal to the men; but, for the forseeable future, she agreed that the men must fight and unify their strengths beyond the emotional claims of their sexuality, and the women must wait, open to the needs of the cause and those who strove for it. And if this was a denial of what she had been brought up to believe, then she had been brought up in error. She disciplined herself with these thoughts rigorously.

Only in the evenings, when Anthony came to her and they were alone, did she feel something of the tensions of her old life – the anger and the dark self-disgust, the remembrance of the killings and the lurch of the paradoxes that had possessed her then. The dignity that she inhabited moving through the public glare of her days was compromised here in the intimate, knowing presence of her husband. There was something, like the stench of something decaying deep in the structure of the house, that caught her at times, that perplexed her. In the mirror she began to see lines digging into the flesh about and between her eyes, the markings of some faint permanent headache that she could never quite feel clearly enough to confront.

The tensions which rose in her were resoluble in the exercise of their sexuality. She trained herself to sustain and direct her various rages in the grim copulations into which she and Anthony locked themselves night after night, and which seemed to her not acts of pleasure, nor even acts of obsession, but which, in the gasping moments when at last they were released from each other, seemed a duty; a duty to herself, and to her husband, and to the community to which they belonged. That there was pleasure, that there was a turmoil of emotions to be confronted, were finally incidental. She imagined the other women of the community, sometimes in general, sometimes specific women who had come to her for advice and understanding; she imagined them out there in the night, turning under the touch of their husbands. She felt her community with them then, at her slow, post-coital ease. She was proud of them then as sisters, as fellow silent sufferers.

And at night, as at last he left Muriel to her dreams, Standing's thoughts also wandered out. From the moment of gripping personal intensity from which he ebbed, he could think most clearly of the man who lived above him, who had colonised the high attic of the big house. Anthony Standing was its possessor, the director of its manifold life, but above him Mark First lived and worked, was the quiet source of the energy that drove the whole enterprise.

First had, in the attics, a bedroom which contained a bed, a chair, and a wardrobe. Standing had seen this room and, had he not known that First slept there, he would have assumed it unoccupied. Connected to the

192

bedroom was First's office. There were four identical telephones with lights not bells to indicate they were active. There was a large map of the entire country on one wall, an old map without any of the new features upon it, a blank map. There were bookshelves and filing cabinets. And there was the growing rank of large hardback notebooks that First filled with his small, untidy writing.

First spent most of his days up in his rooms, moving quietly about, sitting at his desk, standing at the dormer windows and looking down. He would attend the communal lunch, the general meetings, although he never spoke at these. He emanated, though, an authority that was supreme; no-one was in any doubt of this. Occasionally, he came down to the Standings' apartments, chatted to Anthony and Muriel. Anthony welcomed him like a privileged guest: Muriel, however, was at her most formal in his presence. Occasionally he moved about the environs of the house and grounds, watching the work in progress, listening in on the edges of conversations in which he never joined, nor was ever asked to join. He seemed to inhabit a higher plane of existence, one to which they were all answerable, but which none of them might approach directly. In the discussions and complexities of their life, all problems were referred to Standing, but, if he said he needed time to think on a problem, they all knew that he would go and discuss it with First.

Standing, when he needed his mentor's advice, would go up the narrow staircase and knock on the door. He was never called in; First always came and answered the door, admitted him personally. Sometimes Standing's knock was not answered and, after a minute, he went away, knowing that First would know that he was

193

needed and would call down when he was ready. First would use the internal telephone to summon Standing, who always came the moment he was called.

The advice Standing received was immediate and unequivocal.

'I've been worrying about the work camps, Mark. Their productivity is still appalling.'

'Yes. We must rationalise the camps. They are growing too large and could become a danger, festering places that will lead us to pursue programmes of extermination if we are not in control of the situation soon. I don't want exterminations. When we use our power, we must use it cleanly and hotly, openly, to assert ourselves, not merely to rid ourselves of inconvenience. That path has been trodden before, and it leads to the degradation of those who have to walk it, to the progressive degradation of the whole state. As more and more comes under our control, we must beware of this. To take human life is easy, and there is as much pleasure to be had in the acts that end human life as there is in the acts which begin it. So, no death camps. Make an order, Anthony. I want this absolutely clear.'

Then there were the telephones through which First was in contact with the world beyond the house. Standing found himself to be, in effect, commander of the eastern region, but there were other regions and, through the telephones, First had a wider view of the world, spread himself out into hostile areas.

'The capital is going well. We are achieving control, although it is hard for them there: they have to fight far more than we did. Fox is no Gorham. Williamson tells me good things about the west. We are still proscribed there, heavily – there have been executions. Happily, they are not very accurate in their purges. It is likely that

194

they will mount some military operation against the capital in the spring, which will be marvellous. Garman will have his great battle at last. The western command will fall apart in a matter of weeks. Williamson has our knife at every vital point. We must try and arrange it so that Fox's regulars take a good beating first. The north is very slow. There is still the residue of the chaos up there. They are so numbed after all these years, they have come to oppose anything that tries to coordinate them. Any power up there immediately becomes repression. We must send our most persuasive and careful brothers into the north.'

'May I go, Mark?'

First smiled. 'No. I couldn't spare you, Anthony. Your company is my indulgence, my comfort. Here is our heart, our centre, free of all the struggle, and here you must build for the future. We must perfect ourselves here so that when the other regions fall into our control, we are fit to take up all that belongs to us.'

The world was opening before First like a blossom. It was as he knew it would be. He had found the truth, and every success confirmed it. In a few months they would be at war, and within a year they would have the whole country. There were hours when he did nothing but stride his rooms on an impulse of certainty so strong that he did not seem able to contain it. He was not large enough. He ought to have been a giant, a man of limitless physical prowess. At times he felt that he was, that he had changed in the night into the embodiment of his dreams. He longed for the day when the door would open and Standing would fall back in amazement. In his failure to do this, Standing was growing less in his leader's esti- mation; not dramatically less, but First began to become

195

aware of Standing's limitations, his essential ordinariness which, in the fulfilment of the dream, would not perhaps be enough. But then he himself would be enough, more than enough.

There was only one report that troubled him, that caught him as a thing unresolved and complex. This was the murder of the man Richards, strangled in his scarf as if in ritual desecration of the Brotherhood. First did not mourn Richards, whom he knew had been a man with developed homosexual tendencies, but in a way this made it worse, for the killer, Jacob Catton, had caught them in a potential hypocrisy, had struck them at a vulnerable point. First began to personify in Catton an opposition to him that was formidable. Those who fell before them were insects, caught in the light and squirming: in Catton, First began to imagine an enemy of their own stature who understood them but who had turned against them, who ought to have belonged to them; a renegade, therefore, a rogue. Having killed, he had vanished into the west. First had sent detailed instructions to all Brothers to be aware of him, to locate and neutralise him instantly. But he had submerged, and this only confirmed his cunning. He was waiting, dormant; and in the knowledge of this, although he confided in no-one, First had moments of fierce, secret apprehension.

Sometimes First articulated his growing vision to Standing, sitting behind his desk with the window behind him, Standing sitting before him, leaning back on his chair, his eyes half-closed, his hands in his lap, listening to the flow of words that became part of the dream. First would speak of God, of nature, history, evolution, a swirl of ideas that came with a quiet logic, like music, his voice quiet, his tone even, but just behind the voice, the tremble of excitement, inaudible but driving, the hum of the motor. Sometimes Standing did not listen to the words, bathed merely in the flow of them that touched him intimately, liberating him from all the complexities of life below.

One evening, however, Standing came up troubled. Muriel had spent the evening silent, and the silence had begun to defeat him. She often went into these silences, and he waited them out patiently. They did not usually last for long, but this silence had lasted, an hour, two hours, and Standing had become concerned. He went up at last to talk to First, was admitted. He sat in his chair and began to attempt to explain his trouble, but First hushed him, sat silent for some minutes and then began to talk about the problems of the movement in peacetime, after the final victory; how they might keep the Brothers on fire when there were no more enemies, no more struggles. Standing followed this but could not settle to it, could not forget the unresolved silence he had left below, wanted only his leader's advice, or even his sympathy, a word of consolation; he knew after half an hour that he was not going to get it.

For the first time, then, the magic failed to work, the seduction failed and, Standing realised, First did not notice at all, was winding through his own spirals, quite oblivious to anything Standing might be. The ordinary problems of life are beneath him, Standing thought, and felt as he thought it unworthy. He wanted to slip quietly away, but he did not have the courage. He waited and watched, and he began then to imagine that First might be a man in the same way that he was a man. It was a wild hypothesis, heretical, bred of his own frailty. He loved Mark First, but the inequality of that love seemed then to be in some way unjust. He had a squalid need for response, for some recognition of equality, out of simple shared humanity if nothing else. But First was incapable of this, quite incapable; it was, after all, his immaculacy tht made him what he was. Standing could not admit it to be a limitation in First, the limitation was entirely his; but, from that night onwards, he grew sad, heavy, began to catch himself in loose thoughts of a time when all this would be over, when he could go back to being something else, anything else so long as this weight was no longer his to carry.

Standing spent much time touring his region. He began to take Muriel with him. They would travel in a darkened car with motorcycle escorts. They would visit schools and hospitals, offices and factories. They were treated with the utmost deference, shown the best, sampled the best of everything. Standing watched minutely for anything that lay below the obsequiousness, usually found time to break schedule and talk to some of the real workers, those not in the Brotherhood. He made a speciality of talking to the ethnics. The more perfectly things seemed to work, the more sceptical he was. He generated an increasing power about his visits, supported as they often were within days by some central directive, some replacement of senior staff, some commission of investigation. He came to these places and opened them up before him with his intelligence and with the innate appreciation of human weakness that was, perhaps, his first strength to the movement.

Muriel kept mutely beside him throughout. He touched and kissed her in the darkness of the car. They had curtains drawn to protect them from the driver and, within this privacy, he could usually evoke a physical response from her that reassured him somewhat.

'Are you happy, my love?' he would ask her.

'Oh yes,' she would say. 'It's all working so very well, isn't it?'

He allowed himself to be reassured by this, but was nostalgic sometimes for the intelligent, frightened, fighting woman he had first gone to seek; but she had been a virgin then in all sorts of ways, all of which he had claimed from her.

Eventually he steeled himself and took her to one of the work camps; one of the camps for women. He took the precaution of having first removed from the camp any woman who might conceivably have known Muriel from before.

The camp guards were all Brothers now, first quality men who gained privilege and rank by their tours of duty in the camps. The inmates looked universally doped and featureless. Their hair was cropped close and they all wore brown sack-like garments within which their bodies seemed to have become neutralised. They worked without pride or purpose in a cold silence that seemed to preclude meaning of any sort. They were like animals, domestic cattle inhabiting a timeless vacancy. Standing squatted down before a couple who were weeding a field by hand.

'Are you treated justly?' he asked them. 'You are fed properly? You are not abused?'

They stopped their work and looked up at him, puzzled, distantly apprehensive. They did not understand. He realised that they were losing their hold on language. He studied them closely and thought, yes, this is what must be done.

In the car, Muriel was more monumental than ever. He sat in the corner and watched her sitting straight, holding herself against the jolts of the car over the uneven road surfaces.

199

'Well?' he asked eventually, Then, after her silence, 'My love?'

'Do they . . .? Do the guards ever . . .?'

'Ever what?'

She turned to face him. 'Ever fuck them?'

'Certainly not. Absolutely forbidden.'

'Poor dumb bitches,' she said, 'poor dumb, dead bitches. Not even that.'

He experienced then an inexplicable moment of panic. She had missed the point. He had thought that she understood, but she did not understand, not at all. A rhetorical rage possessed him. He wanted to stop the car, wanted to walk her out into the fields and explain it to her again, go over it, win her back, bring her to the light again where he thought he had had her secure. He did not have her secure. He had lost her. He knew this, falling back from his certainties. He took her hand, which was cold and heavy. He had lost her, and the hurt of that turned in him like poison.

'My love,' he said flatly. 'My love.'

She did not seem to hear.

Rachel came down the track. She had been with the Christians and, whilst there, the hurt had been eased; the old rubrics had calmed her. Returning now to the cottage, she felt herself coming into the pain again. She wanted to hurry but slowed herself, trying to bring some of the peace with her, feeling it leak from her as she approached. The day was cold, March, spring seeming loath to break.

Ben was standing out on the path watching for her, and for a moment she was glad, simply glad that he was there for her to run to. She did not run. She halted, felt the wave of the inevitable moving towards her and, if by

200

turning and running away, running away forever, she would have been able to avoid it, she would have run. He came to her. She could not look at him; knowing what he was bringing her, she felt alone, felt tiny, insignificant, stupid. He put his arms around her, and she shrivelled in his embrace.

'Come on, love,' he said.

Becky seemed to be asleep, at rest, certainly at rest now. The fever was gone of course, could do no more. For a moment she wanted to pick the child up, to clasp her and give in to her grief; but thinking this she grew self-conscious, and she knew it would be futile, an affectation. She did not feel large enough to have that sort of grief in her. In a while, she simply turned away and wandered across the stairhead into the other bedroom.

They buried Becky deep in the woodland, in a deep pit that Ben had hewn with the energy of his anger. They wrapped her in a clean white sheet and covered her with soil. They did not mark the grave, wanted her to become a part of the wood where she had been conceived and had lived out the brief year of her existence. They would need no mark to remind them of her and wanted no-one else to know she was there; she had not belonged to anyone else. These things they had agreed before, performed them now without speaking, without looking at one another.

That night, in the closeness of their bed, they began their grieving, the pain pouring from them, twisting them against one another, clasping and fighting to let it out, until it exhausted them and they slept. In the morning they woke cleansed and aching, pale and dry with hurt. They made love then with a quick greed that afterwards embarrassed them, caught them up in guilt. They could not face one another then, went through the routines of the day averted, quiet; but in the quietness, in the shadow of their loss, the longings grew again. They felt in the striving of their pleasure that they were fighting it, fighting the darkness, fighting the pain, burying themselves in one another and coming through.

Jacob Catton had driven deep into the west, had abandoned his car a hundred miles from the capital and had trudged overland to a large city.

He had planned to offer himself to one of the commands, but as he moved about the city he found himself amongst a degenerating chaos that was far worse than he had anticipated. He saw starvation and crime on streets dominated by military authorities who were corrupt and brutal beyond any depth they had reached in the capital. He also, as he moved carefully on the edges of the mess, another drifter amongst the thousands, began to mark unmistakable signs of his enemies. He overheard conversations in drinking halls and in ration queues, found occasionally pamphlets, recognised with a cold shudder a certain type of superior young man, watching with narrow eyes which he quickly avoided. He heard official pronouncements that proscribed them with a futile aggression that only defined their growing influence. Moving close to the military bases, he noted also the preparations for war. There would be battle soon, and he did not give these petty tyrants more than a month. He was in the business, he decided, of survival, not of climbing aboard sinking ships.

So he went into the countryside, trying to work out how the war would develop, placing himself as far out of its path as he could, moving himself deeper and deeper into territory that seemed to be under no effective command. He grew his hair and his beard and could pass easily for a mental invalid, taking odd labouring jobs, listening in to conversations and to radio broadcasts that told him more than the broadcasters knew themselves.

He despised these petty rural communities which had contracted into selfish insularity as the world without faded. The farmers were grabbing abandoned land, feuding with their neighbours, amassing as much as they could, oblivious to the storms that were gathering and which would soon sweep through them, cancelling everything they had hoarded in a matter of hours. Amongst the workers there was no community; treated as slaves they behaved as slaves, obeying their masters out of fear and greed; becoming indistinguishable, reduced to a uniformity of need and response that disgusted him.

As the months passed, he grew more and more isolated, a bleak lunatic whom the others avoided. They were at least without any curiosity in him. He had none of the greeds that they exercised, and that put him out of reach of their interest; and certainly he wanted to touch nothing that they touched. He hardly spoke to any of them, became externally like some animal; but he knew that they were the animals, that hard within him lay the humanity with which they were losing touch, which humanity he defined simply as the ability to feel a sick outrage at the condition of the world and its possessors. The repression of this humanity made him angry; there were times when he wanted to turn upon the others, to assert himself. He had mad visions of taking command of them, of shaking them into a recognition of him, of leading them out into battle; but to do so would have been to put himself on the map, to identify himself and to bring rapid destruction upon him.

For over everything he felt the eyes of the man First, scouring the country, looking for him. The moment he broke cover the predator would drop out of the sky. It was not that he was afraid for himself; he felt simply that he was the last link, the last hope, that if they got him they would have everything. He could see nothing around him that they would not digest at once. He was the only one who knew First as he really was, and therefore he was the last human being left; and it was this that made him afraid.

It happened in time, later than he had thought it would. He heard them talking of war, of battles. He saw the farmers begin to panic, torn between complacency and fight, wrangling to try to find the right side to be on, trying to appeal to the loyalty of their workers, who sniggered at them, who asked insolently what was in it for them.

A commission arrived at the farmstead where he worked, to conscript all able-bodied men. The dumb brutality which he wore then made him most suitable and he allowed himself to be taken, to be driven to a crude training camp, given weapons and uniform, scrupulously careful not to reveal the skills he retained deep within him. He waited for the moment to desert, had no intention of going into battle. He had no idea, nor did the officers who ran the place, to whom he was supposed to be loyal; he imagined that when they moved out they would be more like gangsters than any army unit.

He was approached one night in his bunk by a secret Brother, sounded out for his opinions. He listened to the seduction, which seemed to caress and lick him intimately. He played dumb, massively dumb to resist the monumental urge to take the man by the throat and serve him as he had served Richards.

In the event, there was no battle for the men in his

camp. They woke one day to find the officers fled, to find the place infested with rumour that the war was over, that the victorious armies were coming to kill everyone. The men began to loot everything they could find and disappear into the countryside.

Catton did not run at once, wandered around the deserted camp for a while, into the officers' quarters where he found a television powered by a small battery. It had been left on, but it broadcast only static. He rifled the place but found nothing of any real use. He found a pornographic magazine and was detained a while by the images, the impossible girls proud in the offering of their thick flesh, inviting him to rouse at the substance of their breasts and buttocks, to dream his way into the stretched clefts of arse and vagina. The distance between what they offered, between the response he gladly gave them, and where he now was brought a lump of hard emotion to his throat.

Suddenly from behind him something changed. He turned with a white shoot of fear rushing up him. It was the television screen. The static had evaporated and, against a background of red silk, the clear, full face of Mark First appeared, staring into him. After a while came the voice, quiet and authoritative, the words clearly enunciated.

'The war is over and the armies have gone home. We will begin again. We have already begun. My name is First. I am your leader. I welcome you to your birthright . . . I am your leader. I will never betray you.'

After the voice went silent, the face remained, staring out at the nation; not a frozen image, but a man looking silently into a lens for long minutes, becoming a force, an icon, a reality that grew and grew as the minutes passed. Catton stood before it unable to move.

★　　★　　★

I could not resist going into battle. I was too old to fight, of course; and anyway, the sort of fighting that I knew was in the quickness of dark alleys, not in the sweep of battalions, but I kept as close to the action as I could. I loved the danger, the exhaustion and exhilaration, the volatility of landscape under the billowing smoke, the sing and rip of bullets, the explosions that upturned horizons and obliterated the senses, coming back slowly to the thrill of having survived; it was like leaping into deep water, going down and down until you lost all sense of yourself, gradually feeling the pull of the surface again, coming up and gasping with the delight of the air. It is the intoxication of youth. There is a terrible ecstasy in battle. All life should be lived on that intensity. But it is too easy. Even if the killing is face to face, the blood hot, you are reduced to a unit, beyond individual motivation. Too easy. The secret would be to encapsulate the energy of battle into the stillness of ordinary life: it is an impossible, magnificent paradox.

I made sure also that I spent time amongst the debris, familiarised myself with the carnage we had made. I gave instructions that all our Brothers should meditate amongst the ruins. We needed to confront the notion that all the dead were our dead, and we needed to honour them; not in the sentimental way that has been the traditional military hypocrisy; not for us the monuments and solemn days of slow marches. There is nothing noble or romantic about a corpse. It is a lump of corruption out of which the flame has been blown. It has the sick weight of its own uselessness, the stench of its collapsing metabolism, turned in upon itself, devouring only itself where once, a little while ago, it had the possibility of devouring the world. Sometimes the dead looked as if they had fallen into a sleep, as if they had covered their faces and gone away for a while; these I found the most distasteful, as if they had shrunk away from death, too small for its majesty. Better to see upon them the fury of the destruction which had torn them apart, ripped off their limbs, sheared open their skulls; to see them thrown back by the force of something so much greater than they were; there was no taint of shame in this. Truly, I did not feel differently for the corpses of our Brothers than I felt for the corpses of our enemies; they had been spent in the same purpose, were equal now. At times, when I thought of the enormity of what we were about, I envied the dead, but not for long, never for more than a moment.

We eliminated most over the rank of major. I gave instructions for the executions to be supervised at the highest level, attended as many as I could myself. I am curious of the ways people face death, and I am struck, more often than not, by the nobility of men at that moment. If only all life could be lived with the intensity of the moment when the eyes rise to the sky for the last time, when each breath is infinitely precious, when the senses are tightened absolutely and the heart pounds with its desperate final assertions; if only we could bind our lives to this intensity.

Soon now, it will be my turn. I wish only, Rachel, that you might be with me at that moment.

THE STATE OF THE NATION

At dusk when Ben came into the cottage, Rachel was sitting in the gloom, nursing the baby. She smiled up at him then turned her concentration back to the sucking cheeks, the throbbing fontanelle, the clawing fingers. Ben pulled out a chair, sat and watched, leaning forward, elbows on knees. He watched with silent intensity the maternal transaction. They did not speak.

Eventually she sighed and eased the mouth away, wiping her breast, then laid the child on her shoulder, a small weight with its tense belly, the limbs flexing as if trying to gain a purchase. She smoothed the soft back and the child broke wind fluently.

'Take her for a moment, would you,' she said.

He obeyed, carried her to the window whilst Rachel eased back in her chair, put a hand to the small of her back.

'Where's Matt?' he asked.

'Upstairs. He came in filthy. I had to bath him. He went for a rest. Did you catch anything?'

'A couple of rabbits.'

Ben handed the child back to Rachel and went to light a

lamp. Rachel, rocking the somnolent child on her shoulder, took her upstairs.

When she came down again, he was standing by the window, looking out into the shadows. She moved behind him, stood close, watching his preoccupation.

'There's someone up at the Hall,' he said.

'Who?'

'I don't know. Some men. They look like they're going to open it up again, live in it or something.'

'Soldiers?'

'No. Not renegades either. They could be some sort of religious sect. I'll wander over tomorrow. Keep inside and keep Matt with you, just in case.'

Next morning he found things to do around the house, chopping wood, mending a gate. Rachel watched and saw that he was concerned about something, about the men up at the house probably, that he was putting off going up there.

Then, as she watched, he suddenly looked up, straightened himself. Two young men came into their yard, neatly dressed. She remembered what he had said about their being a religious sect: they were neatly groomed and smartly dressed in black trousers, black jumpers with loose blue jackets. Around their necks each had a silky white scarf.

She looked quickly back at Matt, who was sitting on the floor playing with some wooden animals. She went to the bottom of the stairs and listened for Mary. Hearing nothing, she went quietly to the door, slipped out into the yard and came into the attention of the young men.

'This is my wife,' Ben said.

'Greetings,' the men said, one after the other.

Rachel stretched a smile across her face, went and stood beside Ben, took his hand.

'My name's David Marker,' one of them said. 'We're looking at Darrington Hall with a view to setting up the regional administration centre there.'

'It's a dreadful mess,' Rachel said.

The men smiled.

'We're used to clearing up other people's mess,' Marker said.

'If you do . . . set up at the Hall, what will become of us?' Ben asked.

'Nothing. Certainly for the moment.'

Then the other man spoke. 'We will have to give you security clearance'.

'Se we can issue you with identity papers,' Marker added reassuringly.

His less reassuring companion had drawn out a notebook.

'I'm Rachel . . . Darrington, or I was. Lord Darrington was my father, is for all I know.'

They exchanged glances.

'And I'm Ben . . . Carr. You'll not find much trace of me on the records.'

'I was wondering how you'd missed out on the conscription,' the notebook scribbler said.

'I came down from the north, what, about ten years ago now.'

'And what were you doing in the north?'

'Trying to stay alive.'

'You appear to have made a reasonable job of that,' the scribbler said.

'And we have two children,' Rachel said. 'Matthew is six, and Mary is five weeks.'

'What do you do for a living, Ben?' Marker asked.

'We've a garden,' Ben said. 'I catch birds and rabbits round the estate. I help some of the smallholders now and then.'

'And we've been living on what's in the Hall,' Rachel said.

'Is that so?' the note-scribbler said.

'If it belongs to anyone, it belongs to me,' Rachel said.

'Everything belongs to the state now,' the scribbler said. 'Everything.'

'And everyone,' Marker added, as if trying to weaken the implications of this pronouncement by expanding it into the abstract, 'everyone and everything are part of the great new beginning.'

'We're a long way from all that here,' Ben said. 'We just live our lives quietly. We've no interest in what goes on anywhere else.'

'That's a very reactionary attitude, Ben,' Marker said. 'Great things are happening now. You are a part of them, even if you don't know it yet.'

'Can I still use the woods?' Ben asked, after a silence.

Again, they exchanged glances.

'I don't see why not,' Marker said, 'for the time being. If you get stopped, mention my name. Perhaps there will be work for you up at the Hall in time.'

'Oh, and if you see anyone strange in the woods, you let us know. All right?' the scribbler said. 'And keep away from the Hall. Keep out of sight of it at all times. If we want you, we'll call you.'

They turned to go.

Rachel and Ben watched them from the window as they walked out and around the house, looking, pointing at things, muttering together before they disappeared along the track that led to the main drive.

'We should've asked them in,' Rachel said.

She noticed that Ben was trembling, his teeth gritted, his hands balled. She had not seen this reaction in him in years, not clearly. Something had come to the surface in him, and it frightened her.

'What is it?' she asked. 'Ben?'

'We've got to get out of here.'

'They'll leave us alone. They're only officials. They had no guns.'

He reacted only by shaking his head, as if she did not understand.

'Where could we go?' she asked.

He did not answer, subsided and went to sit on a chair. Matt, who had watched closely, rose now from his toys and came to lean against his father's knee. He lay back, tipped his head up, then brought his eyes into her watching, looked at her as if he had never seen her before, as if everything had suddenly become very strange again, as if she too frightened him. She wanted to move across to him, but did not know how to.

Out on the street morning comes, the blackness of the unlit night released into a dull grey. Faces come to windows, peer down on to deserted, broken pavements. Perhaps, in places, there is still hope that something will have changed in the night, that the dawn will be a real dawn; but what that change will be, few can imagine. Most have some secret dream of the good life, the free life, the hour of release; but few can imagine how that could come to them here. The dream of a different world is soon stilled by the waking knowledge of what must happen to bring about that dream, the chaos and the violence that has been at the edge of their lives for so many years now. They live in a moral and emotional ice-age, but the thaw, if ever it were to come, would animate monsters. The dawn brings only a perpetual ache that is neither accepted not struggled against; it is the

212

condition of the world, a part of the new condition of humanity to which all are bound and by which all are defined.

There is little work. There are rations to be queued for. There are the petty injustices of those who distribute the rations. There are the petty triumphs of those who manage to outwit the system over little things. There are long hours of nothing, of sitting and waiting, for food, for the hour when one might go out and see someone, for the time when someone who has gone out might return. There are still books, although there is to be a census soon of all literature, which will mean a control, an impounding; but even the most dangerous books, those that celebrate beauty and true sexuality, the assertion of man and women against a dark world, even these are dull now, fairy stories from a world that no longer exists.

There is still sex to fill in the time; but if you want a partner of your own gender, or if you want to play about in the other bourgeois taboos, you run dire risks – there are rewards for good informants, but otherwise you can fuck whom you will. Pregnancy must be avoided, unless officially sanctioned, and to transmit a sexual disease will also incur your disappearance. Otherwise, fuck whom you will. It is discovered, however, that, in this world where so much has been drained of its significance, sex has lost its savour. Somehow the ability to fantasise has been stunted, the interplay of relationships become marginalised. The uselessness of life is enervating, exhausting. Copulation is finally pretty pointless. Better, safer, quicker, to run your energy off on your own; like blowing your nose.

This is the world of the Brotherhood, the young men who move through the city freely in bands of half a dozen, driving at speed in substantial black vehicles with

213

fat wheels with antennae that quiver, with powerful headlights that are always blazing. They are not armed. They retain their appearance of smart executives, cold, aloof and efficient. They have access to everywhere, to everything; there are no rights any more. They search continuously, knocking on doors, coming into rooms, opening bags and packages, inspecting passes, looking through belongings. They never tell what they are looking for; perhaps they are just looking, continuously looking, satisfying some need within them, creating some force around them. There are many things forbidden, and sometimes they find them: an old weapon, a radio transmitter, drugs, hoarded supplies. Sometimes they take away things that are not officially proscribed: books, tapes, piles of personal papers, old army uniforms, objects of religious significance, objects of no perceptible significance to anyone. They have the right to everything; they are answerable to nothing outside their own monolithic command.

Sometimes they take away people, not too many, certainly fewer than the army took away in their time. There are stories of execution sheds and torture rooms, of death camps. The official line is that those who are taken are put into programmes of re-education, but no-one believes that. No-one has the capacity to believe anything anymore, neither their stern official optimism, nor the horror stories of those who still have the energy to hate them actively. No-one who disappears ever returns, is ever heard of again; so beware of whom you love, and beware of loving anyone or anything too much. Everything is provisional, every possession, every relationship, every movement is to be seen as a privilege that might be withdrawn without warning and without right of contest. They do not respond to questioning; they do not say, 'We're sorry, but our orders are . . .' They have set themselves to behave as if everything they do is a personal action, a personal action of the movement with which they are totally at one. They are not individuals.

There is little resistance to their power. They are over–whelmingly well-informed, and to foment resistance is a sure ticket to disappearance. They have apparently excised the spirit of resistance. They are too large to hate as a body, and too unified to hate as individuals. Their power is mostly concealed, implied. They are careful not to foster martyrdoms. And they do, as time passes, seem to be making the world work again, slowly and painfully.

There is more work. Men, and women too, white and black, are conscripted into factories and offices, building sites, storerooms and depots, even out into the country to the farms and mills. The workers are, if capable, if tractable, taught trades and skills. The workplaces are run efficiently and fairly. The work is monotonous, but the hours are not punitive and the rewards for those in work are significant. It is better to work than to hang idly about the streets.

The years pass slowly, hardly marked, and the new world seems to accrue a steady permanence. The greyness still dominates, the emptiness still clouds everything; but perhaps this is, after all, the only practical reality, only what's left after everything else has failed. You were taught once that you were unique, precious, individual; this was a cruel illusion, and the emptiness you feel now is only the withdrawal symptom of that illusion. You can become useful, but you will never again be valuable. You can acquire a place in the new world, but you no longer have the right to a share in it; you belong to it, it no longer belongs to you. Did it ever, really?

Leader First watches you and knows you, weighs you and apportions you your space, the area in which you may live and by which you are determined. It happened before like this, but before, those who controlled you were hidden, or pretended that they gave you what you wanted, fulfilled your needs and desires. There is no hypocrisy now. The power of the state is claimed clearly, exercised absolutely. You are significant only in so far as you are recalcitrant or productive; and there are systems which deal with you either way. This is how it was always meant to be, finally: it is easier and easier to accept this, to live within it, to accept the drowning greyness of it, to feel even that as some sort of swaddling protection.

The Brothers stood about in the hall in loose clusters. There were several hundred of them, waiting. No-one spoke. There was the small rustle of movement, the creaking of bone and leather, the stretch of cloth across taut flesh, but the waiting consumed them all. There was no sign of impatience; none of them had anywhere they would rather have been than here at this moment. At one end of the hall was an empty dais, high and well-lit, and it was upon this that their waiting was focused.

In a small room behind the dais, Leader First waited also. He was alone and sat on a high-backed chair with armrests upon which his elbows rested, the hands clasped in his lap. He breathed evenly, closed his eyes for a few seconds then flicked them open again. He was waiting for the moment to rise and go to his Brothers. He did not know when the moment would come, but he would know it when it came. He was at one with them. His heart beat with their hearts, his desires rose with theirs. The world was perfect.

Before he had decided to do it, he had risen and was

striding through the double doors and up onto the waiting dais, into the silent tumult that filled the hall before him. He spoke.

'My Brothers. What we have achieved will be a testament to mankind long after the pain of it has drifted into dust and been forgotten. Civilisations are judged by their monuments, not their detritus. Suffering is eternal, ubiquitous and trivial, for it only concerns the individual, and individuals have never mattered for more than the merest blink of time. Our monument is not in stone or artefact, but in the hearts of all men. The truth we have generated will live for ever . . .'

His voice was slow, rhythmic, expressionless; the power lay in the images which gathered them up in their certainty, which made each one of them yearn with a deep passion to belong, to be perfected within that certainty. Everything that clogged or cloyed them was purged by his voice. Only this moment existed and only this moment mattered. Doubt was a betrayal, an assertion of individualism that, in its difference, was always wrong. To belong was to be, defined and purified and immaculate. Nothing else was necessary, for within it everything was possible, everything was justified.

When he had spoken he stood and surveyed them in slow silence. They stood straight under his penetration, held themselves tight for his knowledge of them to find no flaw. Then he turned and went, and they turned and went out to resume the active possession of the world which he had given them.

There were, it turned out, ten girls invited. Each showed her invitation at the gate of the Hall. A young Brother came forward, introduced himself politely and ushered the girl up the steps. There was a rest room for the girls,

217

and they clustered in there. Four of them were students, three typists, two laboratory technicians, and one a stores clerk. One or two of them knew each other, lived near each other, worked in the same building. All were either nineteen or twenty. All had received their invitations privately, had reacted to them with very much the same mixture of apprehension and curiosity. All were slim, large-breasted, long-haired, and dressed in the nearest thing to party finery that they could have achieved. From beyond the rest room a thump of music could be heard. They compared descriptions of the men who had escorted them in, wondered if these were to be their partners all night.

'Oh well,' said the boldest of them, 'if I'm going to get pissed and screwed it may as well be with and by one of the Brothers.'

They emerged together from the rest room to find their escorts waiting, were led through to the hall, which was decorated with banners. There was a band which was playing quiet, sentimental brass music. There were tables laid formally for dinner, and about sixty Brothers, some of whom had girlfriends or perhaps wives with them.

The girls were led to tables. Two girls on every table with six young men, including their escorts, who were not, it appeared, to have exclusive rights to their company. They were introduced to the men, engaged in a banter of conversation round the table about their work and their lives. They were all girls who could cope with this sort of social formality, and they were all girls who were sensible enough not to try and turn the conversation upon their hosts with any serious intentions.

The meal, they learned, was a celebration dinner. On this day fifteen years before, the Brotherhood had taken control of the eastern region, had opened their new world. There was one of the Brothers present who had actually participated in this great event, Brother Danmore, who had been with Leader First at the actual moment of power.

'Were any of the Brothers killed?' one of the girls asked.

'Not that day. Leader First was in complete control. They fell before us like overripe fruit shaken from the tree.'

'Why don't you make it a day of national celebration?' another of the girls asked.

'Because the nation is not yet with us. It is happening slowly, but who would understand it outside the Brotherhood? It is our celebration.'

The dinner was more than any of the girls had ever seen set on a table at one time: roast meat, three vegetables, fruit and cream, cheese, wine or beer, as much as you wanted of anything. In spite of the bravado in the rest room, all the girls were careful how much they drank.

After the dinner, Brother Danmore made a speech. He remembered the great day, the dawn of the new age. He spoke of killing in strange, rhapsodic terms that made the girls uncomfortable. He raised a glass to Leader First, to the movement, to the future. The toasts were drunk by the Brothers standing, answering the toasts with loud unity but not with any raucousness. The girls had been signalled to remain seated during the toasts. They felt intimidated and excluded, but noticed that none of the other women rose either. Then the men sat and the band played a solemn, stirring, slow tune, which was received in complete silence, each of the men sitting with their heads down in silent contemplation.

After this the formalities were over, the band played dance tunes, and the girls danced with all the men at their tables, and with some who came from other tables. There was more drink, quite a lot more. They sneaked back into the rest room and gathered there in twos and threes, comparing notes.

Then, as the night grew late, the girls found themselves monopolised by one partner. None of them was quite sure how this had happened, whether they had shown a preference, or whether it had all been decided beforehand; certainly none of them was displeased with her partner. The unattached Brothers began to drift off, the band played slower, easy music, and the girls pressed close to their men.

In the early hours, each was asked by her partner if she would like to be taken home now. Three of them said yes, were escorted to waiting cars and driven back, given a tender kiss and offered the possibility of further social contacts. The seven who stayed danced on a little, then were asked again if they would like to go home, but given this time an alternative. They accepted the alternative and were escorted from the hall across a courtyard and up into the Brothers' quarters, neat little rooms with neat little beds, into which they slipped with a lover who was considerate and careful and thorough. In the morning they were woken with coffee and with a set of working clothes, and were driven promptly back to their places of work. They did not discuss what had happened with their workmates, having been asked not to.

Within six weeks, all but one of the girls were married to their partners of that night. It all happened so fast that they had little time for any reaction beyond bewilderment, beyond a gratitude that they had been so selected, so included, so promoted with such deftness and certainty. None of them seriously questioned what had happened to them; none of them felt the manipulation of this pairing as an imposition. But then none of them was that sort of girl to begin with.

I do not know how long I have been here. Years. The seasons change, have changed. I do not mark them, but I remember when it was stifling hot, when it was bitter cold before, as it is now. I am dying. I began my dying the day they brought me here. My greatest fear is not knowing when I have died. Perhaps I have died already. Perhaps there will be no end to this, ever. I can't bear that.

I remembered my name again this morning. Lizzie Ford. There are days when I do not remember. I remember my name, and it is like breaking the surface of water in which I am drowning. I want to shout it out. Lizzie Ford! What would they do if I did? Nothing. They never do anything. And anyway I cannot. I haven't the strength. It is hard enough to bring the name into my mind. It would be impossible to bring it to my tongue.

I am carrying sacks of roots. There is a field. The wind slices across the field and flaps our coats around us. We picked the roots and put them into sacks. Now we must carry the sacks one by one from the fields into the barn. There is a long line of us, a loop of us, linking the pile of sacks with the barn. I can count up to two thousand footsteps on each journey. It is better to be carrying a sack than walking back to pick up another sack. The weight of the sack on your back gives you a purpose, a desire to get to the barn and let the weight down. That is the best moment of all, the release of the weight, the moment of completion. Then you have to turn and go back. It is hard at times to remember where you are going. Without the

221

sack you are lightheaded, purposeless. You might even drift off into the field. They do not shout at you. They do not beat you. They let you wander for a while, until you stumble and fall. Then they come and pick you up and redirect you back to the mountain of sacks. It never seems to get any smaller. Perhaps there is another team bringing the sacks back to the pile.

I cannot now clearly remember a time when I was not carrying sacks. The days we spent picking the roots do not seem to be real any more; no more real than sitting on the barn floor spooning food into my mouth; no more real than lying down to sleep, waking up. I remember these things not as realities, but as things that must have happened, that I must have done, that I must have seen, but which are pressed out by the immediacy of the sacks, the carrying, the pile, the barn, the stumbling back over the rutted earth.

I do not know any of the others. We do not talk to each other. Sometimes someone says something, perhaps I say something, but the words do not have meaning any more. This is an unusual moment of clarity for me. I know who I am again. I could stop one of them, one of the stooping, stumbling loop of figures. I could say to her, 'My name's Lizzie. Lizzie Ford.' But what would that mean?

It's stupid to remember things. It hurts. To know who you are is to grab hold of things that no longer exist – joy, pain, dreams, lovers, friends – a mess of things that were once all gathered about something that was called Lizzie Ford, that was unique, mysterious, striving through a life with light in its eyes. To remember is to suffer. I must not remember.

I must reach the barn with this sack, I must turn round and walk back over the rutted earth to the pile of sacks. I must bend down and lift another on to my back. I must take the strain. I must feel the strain in my shoulders, the wrench at the base of my spine, the weakness in my thighs, the sores between my toes, the numb cramp in my fingers, the wind that blows into my eyes and knots the nerves in my forehead. The pain is easy. It is a kindness of them to keep us in pain. They are not cruel any more than the wind is cruel, any more than the sacks are cruel, than the earth, than my own body is cruel.

Remembering is cruel. I must not remember. I must not remember who I am. Only when I have truly forgotten, totally forgotten, will I be free at last. I must set myself to perfect myself for that one great freedom.

Jacob Catton had taken to the woods and fields. He kept clear of towns and made his way slowly northwards, foraging carefully and moving on quickly after he had struck.

His only impulse was survival. He was determined to outrun First as long as he could. He became therefore nomadic, sensitive to any curiosity, ready to grab at anything that he needed, to kill anyone who came too close to him. In time he avoided all active human habitation.

He established a network of small supply dumps across a wide range of country, storing weapons, rations, rope, changes of clothing, all in waterproof sheeting, buried in caches in the woodland, on the moors, at the edges of abandoned fields. He based his operations on the northern edge of the central region, keeping south of the anarchy, but within reach of it should he ever need to lose himself there. He learnt his territory very well, fifty miles square. He became seasonal in his habits, wintering in deserted buildings and in burrows in the wood, coming out to forage in spring, at all times keeping out of the company of people, at first through caution, but soon for preference. His suspicions set into a deep psychological misanthropy. What began as distrust grew into disgust. He began to loathe the thought of other people, felt himself the only survivor in a world taken over by corruption and degradation, peopled by disgusting zombies. He was the last man alive.

He knew that he was probably mad by now, that he had buried himself so successfully that he could never again come to the surface. He slept with momentous dreams of slaughter and horror from which he woke gasping, aroused and terrible with the need to slake his dreams with reality. It required a stronger and stronger mental discipline for him to resist these cravings.

He became afraid in his more lucid moments, sensing that he must either embrace his extinction or take up an armed struggle against First, against the world. His whole psychology moved him towards the latter course, but he was still vestigially rational enough to sense the futility of this, to realise that by hurling himself against the world, he would not be its saviour but another of its scourges. He lamented the humanity that had deserted him.

When Rachel and Mary returned from Communion, David Marker was sitting in the cottage talking to Ben. They were drinking beer and smoking their pipes. The big pot of stew was bubbling on the stove. When Rachel entered, Marker rose as he always did. Rachel sent Mary upstairs to change out of her dress, went and greeted Marker with a kiss whilst Ben poured her a mug of beer. She did not really like the heavy beer that Ben brewed, but she was thirsty and sociable, and she liked to tease

David Marker, who didn't think women should drink beer.

'And how are things in the movement, David?' she asked.

'As splendid as ever.'

'As ever. Have you some work for Ben?'

'The roof's leaking again,' Ben said.

'I thought you'd fixed that,' Rachel said.

'It's an old roof, Rachel,' Marker said.

Mary came down. 'Where's Matt, Dad?'

'Out in the wood, I expect.'

'Go and fetch him in for his lunch,' Rachel called as Mary ran off.

'David's been talking about Matt,' Ben said.

'Oh?'

'He's becoming quite interested in the movement,' Marker said.

'He's only seventeen,' Rachel said, looking at Ben, alarmed.

'Oh yes,' Marker said, 'he's young yet. But there could be a great future for him. He's a wonderful boy.'

'Don't take him away from us, David,' Rachel said.

Marker laughed. 'You can't keep him from his destiny,' he said.

There was a pause then. Rachel went and stirred the stew.

'Will you eat with us, David?'

'No. Thank you. I must get back. Thank you for the beer, Ben.' And he left.

'He's right about Matt,' Ben said, having given Marker enough time to be out of earshot.

'I know. I know he is. They won't take him yet, will they?'

'In a couple of years.'

225

She returned to the table and sat with her hands around her mug, looking down. His tense proximity filled her with complexity, as it always did now.

'Why have you never joined the movement, my love?'

'You don't join. You're invited in, if they think you're suitable.'

'Why aren't you suitable?'

'Because,' he said, 'I still hate them and everything they stand for.'

'Why?'

'I don't know. I suppose it's their certainty, that light that seems to glow from them. It's a sickness, like radiation. Something within me turns at that. There's something in them that's not quite human.'

'David Marker? He's a bit stuffy, but he's hardly subhuman.'

'He comes here, drinks beer, shares a pipe, brings us things, plays with Matt, but he's not a friend, not really.'

'Of course he's a friend.'

'Rachel, if he was told to come here and shoot us, he'd do it without ruffling a hair of his fucking immaculacy.'

'And you're going to let Matt join them?'

'If I could stop Matt joining them, I'd do anything. They'll take him away from us, and he won't even remember who we are in five years. Rachel, listen to me. I get depressed at times, so depressed I can hardly stand up straight. There are times when I've wanted to go to Matt and slit his throat, because I know that's the only way I'll keep him from them. I'm a madman, Rachel, a madman. I saw too much. I did too much. It's burnt something out of me, some facility to put up with them and all those like them. They scald me like acid. I want to tear them down, tear them off me, tear my own flesh off to rid myself of them.'

She watched him and feared for him. She believed what he had told her absolutely and, closing her eyes, she prayed and prayed for the strength of solitude if she should ever lose him now.

A shadow came into the doorway, and Matt was home with Mary piggy-backed and laughing.

Did I know what was done in the name of my ideal? Of course I knew. I knew and approved of everything. I instigated everything, motivated it, liberated men that they might perform it. There is no triumph without pain, no assertion without cruelty. You cannot build a city without tearing open mountains, ripping up forests, and you cannot build a society without tearing and ripping your way through the unformed, random and contradictory nature of human beings. What we did had to be done. Our uniqueness was in our belief that what we did was always the end itself. How we behaved was what we were. They will never understand this. They have no courage to understand it.

I regret nothing. Nothing. No, not even that it is now, in its present form, over. Better, perhaps, that I have lived to see it finished, to have followed it through from beginning to end, at least in this manifestation. I am not defeated. I knew that I was finite, and I accept my ending as I have accepted every other stage of my life.

I have nothing more to say to them. These pages are not for them, they are for you, Rachel. I seek only to give myself to you. I only want you to know me as well as I know myself; I want only to be alive in you a little longer. It is an indulgence, but I have earned that indulgence.

227

BREAKING CIRCLES

Leader First, on the fulfilment of his final victory, had bidden farewell to Anthony and Muriel Standing. He had outgrown them. Muriel was becoming neurotic as she progressed into middle age, and Anthony doggedly followed her. He had lost his spirit, the fight and fury dulled in domesticity. It must be so, First thought: I sent him into that particular thicket. He was sad, but had seen it coming from a long distance. Standing did not belong with him now. He had his immaculacy to inhabit, and it was better that there should be no intimacies there.

He chose as the hub of his new universe a barracks in the central region, nondescript buildings with a substantial underground labyrinth of offices and sleeping quarters. He did not, however, live underground, but in the top storey of a three storey office block, the tallest building in the barracks apart from the air traffic control tower which on clear days marked his western horizon.

Around him he gathered an élite, about whom an aura of sinister authority was established, young and strong and handsome. They bore his messages and instructions. They attended to the small needs of his

228

personal domesticity. A couple of them always slept in the room next to his. He would discuss with them what was happening in the country, in other countries, his plans for the future, his visions. He would laugh with them at times, put his arms around their shoulders, look into their clear eyes. They were his bodyguards and his executives. They were his disciples, and he was their father.

He took great comfort from them, loved to be amongst their moving, their arrogance, their beauty. He had them all soberly dressed and obedient to innumerable formalities, but he liked to imagine the naked strength of them constrained beneath all that, felt the lift and strain of their many desires, their hunger for life. He loved, silently, as they stood attendant and nameless about him, to imagine them unleashed in action, mouths and fists and genitals. He knew that his pleasure in them was at heart erotic, but it was a clean eroticism, abstract, removed from any possibility of fulfilment. They were like living statues.

Close by First's new headquarters was a large camp, or 'neutralising complex' as the official euphemism now was, the most important of all the camps, for it was here that the active politicals were processed. The turnover of prisoners was high in this camp, and there was only one way out.

The prisoners were woken before dawn, were taken individually out of their small cells to find themselves in a room full of senior Brothers, ranked and watching them with a close seriousness that made them at once afraid.

One of them said their name. Perhaps they answered to their name, perhaps not; it did not matter. They were identified.

'You are to be immediately put to death,' one of them said.

'Your crime is opposition to the state,' said another. 'In the few moments left to you, settle yourself to the certainty of death, and to the absolute power of the state which you have defied.'

'We are here to witness your death, and in that, you will have significance. Do you understand?'

He could not understand. Five minutes ago he had been turning in a labyrinth of dreams and aching, waking through the nights and days, striking his head against the wall of his cell to keep himself aware, to keep his fragile sense of himself alive, telling himself that there would be an end, that the sky would open above him, that this was finite. Now, suddenly, barely awake, he had been thrown into a black space, and they stood watching him fall, watching him turn about, watching him gasp for air, watching his legs begin to quiver, his eyes fill with tears of shame as his watery shit dribbled out. They did not move upon him for some minutes. They waited and watched him bleached of dignity and meaning, confronted him with a prurience that was beyond cruelty: cruelty was individual, this was infinite.

Two at last came and took his arms, pulled him through double doors into what appeared to be an old squash court. A stretcher waited, before which he was placed. He faced a wall and thought briefly of rushing at it, of smashing himself into it, or through it. A hand took the hair at the back of his head and tilted it up. There on a gallery above stood Leader First, waiting to meet his eyes, to know him, to consume him personally.

Then the arms pulled him down to kneel at the end of the stretcher. Then the cold tip of the pistol probed for the nodule at the base of his spine. Then came the explosion that filled his head but was bigger than his head.

His young men noted with amusement that Leader First often returned from his morning meditation with an erection. And as, with the routines of day, this stimulation faded, First always thought of Jacob Catton, wanted to see him like that, wondered if it would be more interesting to have the condemned naked.

One day in the woods, Catton came upon two women. They wore loose grey dresses and heavy shoes, had cropped hair. They were fleeing from something, stumbling and stifling cries of terror. He watched carefully and saw that they were not pursued, assumed their terrors to be imaginary. He tracked them for two days until, in the depths of a wood in which they had been blundering around in circles, they came to a halt, exhausted. They had snatched things from the ground to eat and had made themselves ill. They were wasted and dying, abandoning themselves to death.

When he first decided to move in on them, his thought had been to put them out of their misery. When he was within reach of them, however, he paused. He stepped out of his cover two feet from one of them who sat listlessly on the earth, gnawing at the sleeve of her dress.

'Hello', he said, the first word he had spoken aloud in months, years.

The woman turned and looked in his direction, but incuriously, her eyes vague. The other woman, some three feet away, shrieked and fell back, scrambling to try to burrow herself into a bush.

He reached in his pack, and pulled out a haunch of roasted lamb that he had wrapped in cloth. He hacked off a slab of the flesh and handed it to the first woman. She had difficulty holding it, dropped it and couldn't find it. He picked it up, brushed the leaf mould off it and put it back into her hands, closing them round it, lifting it to her mouth. She began to eat, to slobber and tear at the meat, swallowing it down unchewed.

He left her and went to the bush, where the other woman's eyes burned with terror as he approached. He reached out a piece of meat towards her.

'Eat,' he said. 'I'll do you no harm.'

At which point the woman behind him began to retch and vomit. He looked back and, as he did so, the meat was grabbed from his hands. The bush woman ate, but more carefully than her companion, sniffing the food, chewing it. Catton moved across to the other, who was now lying on the ground, curled up, clutching her stomach, the sickness dribbling from her mouth and nose. Catton placed a hand on her shoulder, but she did not react. He moved back to the bush, into which the woman had embedded herself even further. He left her there.

In the centre of the clearing he lit a fire, fetched kindling and built it up. The sick woman was sleeping now. He lifted her and placed her carefully within range of the heat. He took a blanket from his pack and draped it over her. Dusk was coming into the wood. The bush woman was still eating, still watching, still pushing herself further and further into the thicket. He put down a water bottle and the rest of the meat by the fire, then he left them.

He made a wide circuit of the clearing, listening and watching and waiting for any movement. He unearthed one of his supply dumps, fetched another blanket, more food, a flask of brandy. He ate and then made his way carefully back to the fire which glinted dangerously through the undergrowth.

When he arrived back at the clearing, the woman had extricated herself from the bush, had taken the blanket off her companion and was sitting close to the fire. He came out of cover suddenly, and the woman rose to flee again.

'I won't harm you,' he said. 'If I had meant you harm, I wouldn't've wasted my time.'

The woman curled her lips, clenched herself, but accepted his intentions at last, sat down again, shuffled the blanket around her and stared into the fire. He took the second blanket and went to drape it over the sick woman, who was still unconscious, breathing unevenly, her grimy face gleaming with sweat.

'Leave her,' the other woman said, her voice rasped and emotionless. 'Leave her. She's dying.'

He covered her anyway, returned to the fire.

'Who are you?' he asked.

The woman did not reply, her mouth in a tight line, her eyes wide as if the terror had set into her face. He asked again and she raised her face to him, but did not seem to understand the question. He offered her the brandy flask, from which she drank greedily, allowing it to shudder through her, submitting to the palsy of it. He studied her. She was young, in her twenties probably, but had been subject to some catastrophe, struck down from within or without.

'We're from the camp,' she said suddenly.

'What camp?'

'The camp. Give me some of that.'

He gave her the flask which she drained, then she shuddered and groaned.

He waited a while, then said, 'I'm going to leave you now. I'll come back in the morning. If you're still here, I'll try to help.'

233

'Tell them . . .' she said, finding the words with difficulty, 'tell them it's better to die out here. If they leave us,
we'll die and they won't have to bother with us
anymore.'

'Tell who?'

'Just tell them.'

He waited and watched her for a few minutes more,
then he carefully retreated into the darkness, made his
circuit of the fire once more, then settled himself in a
hollow to sleep.

In the morning he returned. The fire was out, but
the girl still sat where she had been last night. She had
both blankets around her. Her companion was dead.
He rekindled the fire and put a skilly of water on, then
he dragged the body off into a bank of wild garlic at
the edge of the clearing and began to dig a grave. The
body stank as if it was already advanced in its decomposition.

As he worked, the other girl wandered over to watch
him.

'You don't need to bury her,' she said.

'If they come after you, they'll come with dogs.'

She shrugged.

'Give me her dress,' she said.

He stopped and looked up at her. She looked tired
beyond anything.

'I'll find you something warm to wear,' he said.

She wandered back to the fire.

He took her to an abandoned cottage nearby, where
the woods thinned and the moors began. It was a tedious
journey; she walked slowly, painfully, and she kept losing concentration, wandering off, stopping. He was
patient with her. She was beginning to interest him. She
had been so broken down that he was intrigued to see

how much of her he could recover; he wanted to learn who she was and what had been done to her. She was simply too negative at the moment to arouse his suspicion or fear.

The cottage had a well and he drew water for her to wash, for she stank fearsomely. There were some old trunks of clothes there. She would not help herself at all. He cut away her dress and, sitting her down on the bare boards of the floor, he worked soap into the grime of her skin, doused her down. She shuddered at the cold water as if to shake it off her. She was pitifully thin, but not suffering real malnutrition. There were old sores on her hands and feet and back, but no signs of active brutality. She did not react to his exposure of her. He rubbed her dry, pulled an old dress over her, and found her an old jacket. He fed her and then began to wonder what he was going to do with her.

He could hardly let her travel with him, nor could he leave her on some doorstep to be returned to them. If he set her up and let her fend for herself, she wouldn't last a week. He didn't think, even if they caught her and brought her to any sort of coherence, that she would be of danger to him. She had hardly even looked at him. He determined eventually to take her north and try and find somewhere for her to bolt. It was not a definite plan; he mostly wanted to shift her out of his territory and hoped that, on the way, she might somehow find something to grip on to and fend for herself.

He put her under a pile of blankets and left her to sleep whilst he prowled about, took another lamb, collected some roots from an abandoned field and went to one of his caches for more brandy. He returned to the clearing and checked to see that nothing had been disturbed, rekindling the fire and roasting the lamb's flesh and edible entrails in the embers. It was nightfall when he returned; she was still asleep.

He took a short sleep himself then roused her, told her that they must eat and move on. The food drew her from her lethargy. She ate enormously. He fed her and she ate, and he needn't have been there for all the recognition she gave him. She was completely locked into herself. It was as if they had found some way of imprisoning people within their own minds; the ultimate security. It made him angry to think of it, made his hatred for them glow and find direction. But then it couldn't have worked entirely, for she had broken out, had fled into the woods, and this was at least a germ of hope.

After the food, they left the cottage and made their way over the moor. The night was still and the moon bright, so he kept to the valleys, had to subject her to blundering about in marshes. Occasional lights could be seen on the roads which made her tense and emit small frightened cries; but he kept well away from the roads.

At dawn they found some old shooting butts to settle in on a slope of moorland that gave them clear and wide views all about them. He gave her food, told her to rest whilst he surveyed the landscape and tried to work out the way he would take if there was any sign of trouble. There was a gully that he could slip into and scramble along, but only if the trouble were coming from the south. He realised that he was at risk here, wondered what he would do if it came to it: leave her certainly; give her food, tell her to keep low and break out after dark. It was only surprising that he was having to think it out at all.

They ate, and he gave her brandy, not too much this time.

'Light a fire,' she said irritably.

'Not here.'

He had some tobacco, and they shared a pipe. He began to put questions to her: how long had she been in the camp? What had she done? She did not answer any of his questions, and he realised that she did not know the answers.

'Tell me about the camp, anything you remember,' he said.

She sucked on the pipe, inhaled the smoke.

'We . . . we had to work,' she said. 'We had to work in the fields.' She had no more to say.

'How did you get away?'

'I . . . I don't know. They weren't watching. It was night. I just went into the night.'

'Who was the other woman?'

'Which one?'

'The one who died.'

She seemed then to remember something. 'I don't know. She was with me.' Then she began to cry. 'I couldn't have made it alone. She said, Let's go. Let's get out of here. It doesn't matter. Anything's better than this. Death is better than this. I'm going to die too.'

'We've got a chance,' he said. 'Just keep going. There are places in the north where they don't go.'

'You fucking liar. Don't fucking lie to me. They don't lie. They tell you, you're here forever. You're as good as dead. So don't you fucking lie to me.'

Her wretchedness affected him profoundly. I am not alone, he thought. There are others. There must be others like her who could be set free, who could gather and fight.

She slept and he kept watch, dozing but never submitting to any depth of sleep. He was used to this, and anyway she had caught him, got his mind working

237

again. He did not want to sleep. He wanted to watch over her, to guide her to safety, although he had no idea how he might achieve that.

They travelled on at nightfall. It was a cloudy, windy night, and they could use the uplands and travel faster. She was travelling better now too, plodding on beside him steadily, not drifting or stopping any more. By dawn they had entered another belt of woodland. Here, after his usual circumspection, he lit a fire. She sat before it, bared her legs and basked in the warmth. He noticed that she was watching him today, following his movements, curious. He enjoyed her watching, smiled at her now and then, was pleased to be able to demonstrate his woodcraft.

'What's your name?' she asked.

'Will,' he said. 'What's your name?'

'Jen.' She laughed. 'Well, that was somebody's name once, probably not mine, but that doesn't matter.'

They ate, drank some more brandy and smoked a pipe. The clouds had disappeared and above the trees a wide blue canopy opened. The sun rose above them and poured down warmth into the clearing. She lay back on the turf and spread herself out.

'I'm just going to look around,' he said. 'You'll be all right. I'll be within earshot.'

But she didn't seem concerned. He watched her stretched out there and saw her for the first time as a woman, as someone he might desire. He watched her and it made him feel good; whole sections of his mind that had been closed down for so long seemed to open in the sunlight as it glowed off her.

When he returned, she had undone her dress and lay with her breasts open to the sunlight. He thought she was asleep, so he squatted down before her and watched her,

238

taking pleasure in her nakedness. She opened her eyes, saw him there before her and smiled. She moved her hands over her body. She sat up and began to examine herself, squeezing her flesh, smoothing it, recovering it with her conscious mind.

He moved away and put dirt on the last of the fire. He usually urinated on the embers of his fires, but was shy of that now.

'What do you do for sex out here in the woods?' she asked.

'I do without it,' he said quickly.

He heard her stand up, but did not look back, heard her move towards him. He tensed himself to listen to the woods, sensed danger all around him. He could hear nothing beyond her slow approach, drowning out all other apprehensions.

When he turned she was naked, a foot away from him.

'No, no,' he said gently.

She took his hand and placed it on her breast, held it there, leant back and closed her eyes. He pulled his hand, but she gripped it with a strength that surprised him.

'I need . . . I need to be touched,' she said.

He sighed and concurred, smoothing her breasts and flanks. She moved closer and put her arms about his neck, her face against his. He caressed her carefully, trying to master the desire that was beginning to press him, for behind it he began to imagine their imminent discovery, their killers breaking cover, engulfing them in a storm of pain and humiliation. She took his hand and placed it between her legs, urged herself over his fingers. She was trembling violently, trying to order the surges of her desire about this trembling. He thought of animals he had snared and netted, the trembling of animal fear as he extricated them from the traps.

239

She slipped from him suddenly, went down on her knees and fumbled at his belt, at his fly, her twisting fingers hardly able to close about their task. He helped her and his heavy trousers, with all their pockets and flaps loaded with the keys to his survival, fell solidly about his boots. She held him to her, felt around his thighs and buttocks, nuzzled her face against him, took his penis into her mouth. He drew her shoulders back from him and she looked up, her face streaming with tears.

'It's been so long,' she said. 'I dreamt of you night after night, tasted you, smelt you, felt you night after night inside me; but they found out; they took that away from me; even that, even that. I couldn't bear it.'

He stooped down and kissed her open-mouthed, salty, the taste of her tears and his sex clearly on her tongue. He remembered the last kiss he had given, to Richards just before he had killed him. The disgust of that rose in him and the need to exorcise that memory became the only importance.

He hunched himself over her, her buttocks on a rise of turf, her legs locked around him. He drove into her an accumulation of sexual energy that he had never imagined existed within him. She twisted and clawed at him, jerking her body up against his, banging her head back on the earth behind her. His desire was long in its fulfilment, rising in slow surges into the numb tension of his genitals. When at last he came to his completion, she went still, held her breath as he came into her.

He lay for a moment in complete blankness upon her, then withdrew quickly, stood and dressed as fast as he could, trying to attune his senses again to the woods, although his pulse was beating too loudly for him to hear clearly above it. She lay spread at his feet, just as he had left her, her eyes open with, it seemed, the blank terror he had first seen in them returned.

He felt a sudden tenderness for her, a shame at what he had done. He knelt and gathered her in his arms, drew her up against him. She was limp and watery and silent. She began to tremble, and he held her tightly. After a while he settled her, fetched a blanket and covered her.

'Sleep now,' he said. 'I must go and check that we're still safe. If you need me, call. Right?'

As before, she did not seem to hear him. He left her there and went off into the woods. He circled their campsite and returned, checked that she was as he had left her and set off again, certain that they must have been heard, certain that something was moving in upon them.

He found that he was exhausted, tireder than he had been for years. The urge to curl up somewhere and sleep was enormous, and eventually he could not resist it. He found shelter, covered himself in bracken and was pitched into dark sleep.

He awoke abruptly, held himself still. Something was out there. He had slept too long. He had abandoned her. He peered from his shelter but could see nothing, could hear nothing; but he could sense it out there. Carefully he pulled aside the ferns that covered him, brought the grip back into his aching thighs, began to move out.

Alert to anything, stopping, dropping, listening, he made his way back to the clearing. She had gone. The blanket was left as if she'd risen from it and wandered off. There was no sign of a struggle. Her dress had gone but the jacket was still there, her boots were still there. He examined the ground and picked up her trail out of the clearing, broken grass stems, a bare footprint in the soft mud. She had just wandered off for a bit. He tried to be reassured.

He found her in a hollow about two hundred yards away. When he first saw her, he thought she was standing naked, her head oddly to one side; two paces further on, he saw how the ground fell steeply, saw that there was no ground under her feet. He sprinted down to her, grabbed her legs and took her weight, but it was a dead weight. She had made a cord of the dress, had shinned up an oak tree, had dropped herself into the air. He fell below her, looked up, saw the body he had taken in love now turning, open, doll-like, the head tilted under the wrench of the cloth; he saw the face with the eyes open, the mouth dropped, the empty expression now stamped into her eternity, waiting only for the decomposition to peel it off.

He could not bear to look at her any more. He could not bear to touch her again. He left her there, went back to the campsite and covered all traces of his occupation. He drank the remains of the brandy and set off south, back the way he had come.

Crossing the moor at dusk, he saw on one of the roads a car moving, then stopping. Keeping to the gullies, he came close and saw that the car was a patrol car. They had a puncture. Two of them were at the wheel, whilst one was sitting on the bank smoking. He edged in closer and nearly stumbled across a fourth who was squatted behind a stone wall, defecating.

Catton appeared suddenly before him, a long blade at his throat.

'Call,' he said. 'Call the others.'

He curled his lip and moved his hand down to his trousers, so Catton slashed open his cheek.

'Call,' he said.

'Maxwell!' he yelled. 'We've got company.'

Catton slit his throat and dodged back to see what was

242

happening. The wheel changers had risen and were talking with the smoker. All three were peering down to where their comrade had called. At last, the smoker took a rifle out of the van and began to slide carefully down the bank.

Catton waited behind the wall, heard the man come down, register his dead comrade, come slowly forward to where he lay; Catton vaulted and rolled over the wall, landing on him and running the knife deep under his ribs.

He did not know whether the others had seen him cross the wall. Collecting the rifle, he moved fast to be clear of the bodies, slithering along a ditch, up the stony bed of a little stream. When he surfaced he could see the other two, both now armed, moving down, one either side of the wall. He had outflanked them. He clambered up to the road and hid behind their vehicle.

He took one when he came running back to radio for help, leaning into the vehicle through the open door; all Catton had to do was reach over and cut back. He found a pistol in the car and waited across the road behind a tree for the last one. Up he came eventually, ducking and dodging, good boy, no static target, covered from as many angles as possible, until he came round the van and saw his dead comrade. As he reached across to him, Catton stepped out and shot him dead, the hard sound of the gun like an exclamation.

Thus Jacob Catton came to justify Leader First's intuition. Up here amongst the moors and woods, on the furthest reaches of their command, he became deadly. He used his knife when he could get close enough. He used a rifle when he had to kill from a distance. He would kill once and then disappear whilst the others reoriented themselves to the direction of his

243

attack. He was scrupulously careful, never striking unless he could see his escape clearly, never killing within ten miles or within ten days of his last kill. He took them on roads, in farmyards where they had come prying, in quiet village streets where they had come for a night in the pub, at their command centres, which were conveniently placed away from other habitations, often in old country houses with rambling, overgrown parks. If they were properly guarded, he killed the guards. If they were left open, he came in close. Once he caught one in the back of a patrol car humping a village girl; he had to kill her too, which he didn't like.

They never came near to catching him. He was solitary and absolute. His anonymity and his self-sufficiency were impregnable. He was a dark god, striking them down wherever they stopped. He imagined them afraid of him, not knowing him, unable to predict him, building up legends about him, waking up in cold sweats having dreamt of his coming into their rooms and slitting their throats in the darkness. He did not think of them as individuals, rather as insects, part of a great seething colony. He imagined himself a cramp in Leader First that woke him in the night, that would not let him rest. He had no policy, no strategy beyond finding them wherever he could and killing them. He soon came to love the killing; it was sufficient in itself. It entered him like a drug. It was like sex; it roused him and it completed him. It was all he needed.

The winters were cold and bitter, and he began to feel them penetrate his bones. There were months when he had to abandon his desires and to curl down in the struggle for simple survival. He felt at these times weak and mortal, began to be weary of his mission, weary of himself. He began to plan spectacular ends for himself. If he could have taken a hundred with him, he would have done it; he did not think he was worth less than a hundred of them. When the spring came and he made his first kills of the season, he felt better again, felt himself reconnected to the driving force of life, beyond caring when the end came.

They began to come into the woods to search for him, which was perfect. On his own territory he was limitlessly efficient; he could take out whole patrols at a time. They were well-trained and, he came grudgingly to admit, of considerable courage; but he never developed any real respect for them. They were never a match for him.

One autumn day, he had been tracking a platoon of them through a belt of thin scrub and pine woods. They were well spread out and were, he could see, waiting for him to strike at one of them so that the others could wheel and face him; not that they knew he was there for certain. Perhaps he would have to let them off, perhaps just pick off one on the end. Then two things happened to his advantage: there was a blinding hailstorm that poured an opaque white obliteration through the woods, and one of them stumbled and hurt his leg. They were forced then to group, to huddle, forming a ring about the wounded man and the officer who attended to him. Catton circled to make sure that they were alone, then settled himself with his rifle to wait for the hail to lift enough for him to cut down as many of them as he could. His first shot caused chaos, and he took at least six of them, four certainly fatally, before they could find cover. As he dodged back through the woods, their returning fire rattling blindly into the trees behind and above him, he heard one of them yell out, 'You bastard, Catton! You nasty little cancer! Catton! Can you hear me?'

He halted, turned, was about to shout back. He was appalled that they should know who he was. A coldness, a fear and rage gripped him. How did they know? It had been years, years since . . . his whole fantasy of dark anonymity fell at his feet. He crawled away numb and stupid. Had they pursued him with any real vigilance, they might well have taken him that day.

That they knew who he was obviously altered everything. The edge of his pleasure was blunted. He spent days sitting alone, moving from place to place blindly, wondering what he should do. At last he decided that, although he knew it would be the beginning of the end, he must find others, he must form a body of men who could fight with him. It was all he could do, the only opportunity he would have, now they knew him, to make a significant mark against them.

There were parties of renegades here and there in the woods. Catton avoided them, and, more often than not, they were rounded up by the patrols. They were stupid and clumsy and, although he kept a careful eye on them, none of them lasted long. Now he began to watch them more carefully, apprising them. They were, he knew, the worst sort of trash, but he searched for some elements of courage that he could command and direct.

One night, therefore, having watched and waited, he stepped out of his cover and stood before a campfire around which five ragged men huddled, cold and hungry. Two of them were awake, one of whom grabbed a knife, their only weapon, whilst the other yelled out and grabbed at the others. Catton stood before them as they came to consciousness, as they struggled with their terrors and aggression. He placed a large haunch of meat down before them, at which a couple of them started forward, to be dragged back by the others.

'Don't touch it, it's poisoned,' one of them said.

'D'you think I would waste good meat poisoning you?' Catton said.

'Who are you? What do you want?'

'I am Jacob Catton, and I want you to come and kill with me. Share out the meat and, as you eat it, think. If you come with me, I will feed you and train you. If you do not want to come, when you have eaten, go. You can go to them and tell them you have seen me, but that won't stop them from killing you. You can try and live on your own here, but you won't last long. They're out looking for me, and when they find you instead, they'll kill you. I have seen groups like you before. It's always the same. If you come with me, you must obey me absolutely. If I suspect one of you of an intention to betray or disobey me, I will kill you without hesitation. We will fight and we will kill. Our chances of survival beyond the end of the year are very slight, but at least we will have made our mark. I am offering you the chance to die with a little dignity, with a little fight in your spines. Now eat.'

He stayed and watched them eat, did not want to give them a chance to take any corporate decision, or to wrangle and disunite. When they had eaten, he asked each of them two questions. 'What is your name? . . . Are you with me?' They were all with him.

He spent a month teaching them the rudiments of survival, the rudiments of killing. They were better than he had anticipated. Two of them at least, both the blacks, had real potential, and the other three were stupid enough not to make trouble; all were in reasonable physical shape. He did not ask, nor did he care, where they were from or what they had done.

They went into action first against one of the patrols, a

dozen sleek young men who were butchered efficiently before they were aware of what had hit them. They fell upon a fishing lodge which was used as a recreation camp; twenty they took here, slitting throats in the corridors, bedrooms and out in the guard houses, then bursting into the bar and spraying bullets until the chaos stilled. There were girls here and Catton allowed his men to rape them, a reward for their fidelity and a compensation for the absolute ban on alcohol he imposed. He had intended that the girls should be killed also, but after the rape he felt a disgust. It didn't matter. This was open war. They could tell them little that they didn't know already.

After this, the stakes were raised. The patrols were larger, the security tightened. They were no longer digging into the soft parts of the movement, they were cutting deep, and the response was commensurate with their success. They came across a group of them drinking at a deserted pub, and his men leapt at the prospect; Catton was suspicious, but they were randy for killing. He kept himself behind them, kept his eyes open. He saw the trap but not quite in time; one of his sergeants was shot dead, and another of the men had his arm shattered.

They withdrew deep into the woods, and Catton watched them become broody and frightened. They talked of finding more recruits, but Catton suspected what had in fact occurred: the whole area had been put under strict martial law and they were shooting anyone on the loose.

He determined, therefore, on one last throw. They would move fifty miles south and go for one of the command centres. The men were alarmed by this, but Catton drew them close and inspired them with the glory of it, the slaughter, wholesale, hundreds of the little insects caught squirming in their nest.

He moved them slowly and circuitously south, keeping them alert, refusing them any killing, storing their powers ready for the great day. It was November when they finally came within reach of their target, a large country house set in rambling woods and parkland in an area where neither they nor he had ever operated before. The nights were dark and rainy. Everything seemed propitious. 'They have their women here too,' Catton told his men, a pure speculation, but one which had the desired effect.

They would attack at the dead of night. At dusk they moved into the park, keeping together, coiled and tight. They made their first kill unexpectedly, a solitary man wandering along one of the paths. The man who slit him nearly took his head completely off, which roused and pleased them all. He was not one of them, they discovered when they had turned him over, which was a disappointment, but, Catton promised them, there were lots and lots of them just through those trees, fat and as unsuspecting as this poor bastard.

They came upon a cottage in the woods, about a mile from the house, lit brightly. They could see at least one woman in it, but Catton didn't want them blunted with that yet. They grew surly at this, so Catton circled the house and noted that it had no electricity, no telephone wires. They had been living on tight rations, and it would do them good to have something solid to eat. And there was something else: the more he circled the little cottage, saw the woman moving in there, the more it affected him. There was a child in there too. They were preparing a meal. The small domesticity of this gripped him with a strange sentimentality. He knew that, whatever happened, this would be the last fight, that he would be dead within twenty-four hours. It was reckless and pointless, but he wanted to go and stand before a warm hearth, to watch a woman at her work, for the last time. It had been so long, so very long.

'All right,' he told them. 'We'll go down there and wait. No-one touches the woman. You two on guard, there and there. We'll bring you food out.'

So Catton with Barker and Maclennie, the two he put least reliance on, slipped down, dodged through the yard, then walked straight through the unlocked door of the cottage.

Inside they found a woman and a girl, the girl about fourteen, the woman in her late thirties. They greeted their intruders with surprise, but not panic.

'Hello?' the woman said.

Catton looked at her, could not help himself, saw her shapely, strong, desirable. And as he looked, he saw her begin to grow afraid, to reach for the child's hand.

'What do you want?'

'I am Jacob Catton,' he said.

'Oh God.' She grabbed the girl to her and closed her eyes. 'Oh sweet Jesus.'

'It's all right,' Catton told her. 'We have no quarrel with women and children. Send the girl upstairs. Go on. Go on, child.'

'Mary,' the woman said. 'Go.'

The child let go of her mother, looked at the three men with a face full of spite and contempt, spat with a dry mouth at them. Maclennie sniggered and went towards her, but Catton jabbed him in his bad arm and he gasped and fell back. The girl ran upstairs, closed and locked a door.

'What if there's a weapon up there?' Barker said. 'A husband?'

'Well? Is there?' Catton asked the woman. 'Shall I send him up to have a look?'

250

She shook her head.

'I trust you then. I've said you'll not be harmed, but if you break your trust with me, I will break mine with you. We need food. For us and for the others outside. And drink. Water or milk.'

He drew aside a chair and placed it strategically out of range of the windows, signalled Barker and Maclennie back. She brought bread and bowls which she filled with stew.

'There are ten of us,' Catton said.

She put six bowls down and filled them with all the stew she had. She did not look at him, did not sit down, moved about restlessly, finding things to do. He watched the breasts shifting about under her apron, watched her lean flanks under the loose trousers. She fascinated him in every movement, in every caught breath, in every glint he got of her large, frightened eyes. It was not desire, not simply; he found himself delighted with her as she was, moving, alive, her emotions large and tight just below her surface. He had forgotten people could be like that.

'Take four bowls out,' he said to Barker. 'Turn those lamps down,' he said to the woman.

They waited. Maclennie ate like a dog; Catton was ashamed of him, wanted to send him out too, but did not think that would be politic. As he ate, he asked the woman questions to which she did not respond, although he could see by the way that she reacted that his words caught her.

'This is not their house, is it? . . . Where's your husband? . . . Where's the man? . . . Is she your only child? . . . What have you heard about me? . . . Am I the devil himself? . . . Wouldn't you like to be free of them? . . . Why don't you look at me? . . . I'm real. I'm as real as you are, woman . . . go on, look at me.'

251

He didn't mind that she did not reply, enjoyed pushing the questions out at her as if he was teasing her with them, winding her up, egging her to turn and open her emotions all over him. He began almost to forget why he was here, only Maclennie slobbering there at his elbow kept him in contact with his reality.

'You cook good stew,' he said, looking at his watch.

There was a burst of automatic fire outside. Catton went down on to the floor, reached up and opened the door, Maclennie scurrying across beside him. There was no more shooting. Barker appeared, breathless, grinning.

'Only one, but we got him. We got him dead.'

'Who fired?'

'I did.'

'If they don't kill you, Barker, I will. Get out there before they have us pinned in here like dogs. You too, Maclennie.'

They scuttled out. Catton turned to see, at last, the woman's eyes upon him. He smiled at her and she rushed forward, fell against him, sobbing. He put his arms softly around her, so glad of her at this moment that he hardly felt the knife that she slid into him. He could hardly believe it until she backed away from him, pushing things down around her. He looked round to see the haft sticking out of his side. He touched it and as he moved the pain struck, the damage opened up a chasm within him. He had his back against the door and he went down, slid down, pushing himself to try and stay up, but the world slipped from under him. He reached the floor with a jar that swallowed him, but he came up again, gasping, his eyes filled with water that felt like tears. He was glad that they might be tears.

'Not my child,' she was pleading. 'Kill me, but not my child.'

'No point,' he said. 'No point, woman. Get me a drink.'

She brought him a mug of water. He tried to raise his arms, but there was no strength in them. He looked up at her and tried to smile. She knelt down and brought the water to his lips. It made him cough, burnt in his throat like spirit, seemed to open a tunnel through him as it went down.

She withdrew, sat watching him. Through the closing mist of his pain he struggled to hold her watching.

'Darrington Hall,' he said. 'I came here, twenty years ago . . . Lord Darrington's Charity Ball . . . thank you . . . thank you . . . I came back here to die. I . . . I am grateful that it is you . . . who have killed me, and not . . . not one of the insects. You are beautiful. I . . . perhaps . . . probably I have brought you something . . . something terrible. Once I . . . once I am dead, they . . . I'm sorry, truly sorry, for . . . for what that's worth. Nothing . . . nothing to you . . . nothing, but I am sorry.'

The darkness flooded through him, choked and blinded him, roared in his ears, but there was something else that he had to say. He struggled to put his mind to it, to cling on with his last strength.

'Do . . do something for me . . . will you? . . . Do something . . . First . . . the man First . . . look, you have . . . have killed me and that's all right. I have to die, but he has to die too. He is a . . . a monster. Go to him. Find him out. Kill him. Kill him. Kill him. Can you hear me? Can you hear what I'm saying? Kill him.'

Rachel sat with the dead man for what seemed like hours. He had not bled much. The knife still jutted from his side, but it was like a joke knife blade she had seen at a party once. She remembered the Ball, the cruel young officers from whom she had hidden in a lavatory, afraid to trust her sexuality to them. She wanted Ben to come back, wanted him to hold her and love her; and then she remembered what he would have to come through to reach her now, and she grew afraid, dared not think about that.

She concentrated upon the man she had killed, tried to imagine him as one of the young officers on that night so long ago, tried to believe in him as something human, comprehensible, capable of love and of forgiveness, of her forgiveness. She did not think of what he had said to her; it did not have any meaning for her. She did not seem to be able to do anything. She looked at the vicious array of weapons that clung to him like parasities. She had no idea how to use any of them. It occurred to her to go up and be with Mary, but then, if they came through, she would rather be down here. She would throw herself against them, try to block them, try to spend her death usefully. She had killed, and her life was forfeit. She accepted that; she wanted to die now, and she didn't want Mary near her for that. There was hope for Mary, perhaps. She knew there was none for her.

When it happened, it came too fast for her to follow clearly. The door was wrenched, the man came in, looked at Catton, looked at her, fired his gun at her. She fell dead on the floor. She lay in a black space, heard Mary screaming, heard the furniture falling, heard something being beaten down rhythmically on to the floor, heard Mary screaming and screaming, heard her silence which came down like a blow into her. She knew then that she was still alive, and the knowledge of that was the worst of all.

There were shots outside. Then the room was full of

men and lights, and there was shooting in here. She tried to pull herself up, tried to pull herself into the line of bullets, but it was over, they were lifting her, helping her.

Outside the cottage they wrapped a blanket around her. She had not a mark upon her, and she hated herself for that. In a circle of harsh torchlight, they had three bodies laid out including the man she had killed and two prisoners, who were kneeling naked on the earth, their hands manacled behind their backs. One was wounded, bleeding from his thigh and head.

David Marker was beside her, telling her what she already knew – Mary, Matt, Ben. She hated him for telling her, wanted him gone. She looked at the naked men and thought of the Passion of Jesus Christ, wanted to go and release them, take them into her home and feed them, tend them.

Marker was offering her a gun.

'Would you like to do it, Rachel?'

'No . . . please . . . no.'

'That's all right. I understand.' He nodded and a man stepped forward and shot them one after the other. The second had begun to whimper and was trying to say something when he fell.

Rachel turned away and walked back towards the cottage.

'Rachel,' Marker said, holding on to her arm. 'You can't go back in there. You must come to the Hall now.'

'Why? What have I done?'

First had hoped that they would catch Catton up in their sweep west, but he was nowhere. It was possible that he was dead, but to assume that was a complacency First could not permit. Catton had the stamp of a survivor, and until First had personally triumphed over his corpse, he could not be easy. When the reports came of someone striking blindly and efficiently at them in the north, one individual driving himself into them, cutting at them with a random but precise fury, with no other purpose but to do them damage, he had known instinctively that it was Catton.

First knew that they would have to destroy Catton as soon as they caught him, but that did not stop him from longing to meet and argue with him. Everyone who came near him was by now committed to him. He began to need someone from outside to whom he might justify himself. He imagined long conversations with Catton, turning and testing what they were under the light of his antagonism. He dreamed of converting him, of reaching a moment when he would open his arms and Catton would come into his embrace.

When they brought the news of his death, First demanded that his body be brought to him. He wanted to be sure of him, to see him at last, to confront him. First went down to view him, laid naked on a slab. He had thought that it would be a moment of triumph, but it was sad; something dynamic had gone, something had escaped them that they ought to have claimed. First had expected something beautiful, a young god: he saw a white bulk covered by a thick tangle of hair that seemed not to belong to him, as if they had not cleaned the undergrowth from him. First saw the white rent in his side, the lips of an empty envelope that had once contained his secret. The face was nothing, the flesh had sagged and sunk; he was long gone from there. First found himself intrigued by his genitals, that most animal part of him, the least affected by death, the only part of him that he could find beautiful. First wondered if he had fathered a child, a son, in all his fury, thought that it would be a fine thing to have done, imagined in this fantasy the possibility of him opening up again.

Then they told him that he had been killed by a woman. He was appalled. He had imagined a brotherly embrace, the knife sliding up at the moment of his recognition. First had not known that this was what he had thought until they told him that a woman had done it, and then he thought of another sort of embrace. First imagined him naked at the moment of his death, in the embrace of love, the hot blood gushing from him in a way that he had never imagined. Whole new complexities of life opened up within him.

I had come to think that the shadow behind me was Catton, but he was only the mask, behind which was you.

There was something missing. I knew that I had everything, was everything, but there was still something more, something in the corner of my eye that I could never quite catch clearly. It was not a lack that I felt, but simply that there was something small and irritating that I had not yet encompassed.

It had become personal between Catton and me. He was my closest enemy. He understood me. He ought to have loved me, and, because he could not love me, he fought me. When he was dead, I mourned for the lost opportunity of proving myself to him; but I thought that it was over then, that whatever it was it would not matter any more.

When they told me that Catton had not been killed by one of my Brothers, in my name, but by a woman, by you, I knew that the problem had not been resolved; it had entered another dimension. At that moment, although I resisted you for years afterwards, Rachel, you became essential.

257

RETRIBUTION

THE DARKNESS OF WOMEN

One afternoon, Anthony Standing was driven out to see Leader First. He watched from the comfort of leather and carpet, through the tinted glass of his car, the poor landscape streaked with snow: broken hedgerows, neglected fields with their straggling, weedy crops left to die in the furrows. He looked at the towns, the crumbling boroughs with dark houses, the smoke rising here and there listlessly, weakly, the occasional huddled figure moving over broken streets, loaded with a bundle of something too large to be of any value. So much had been simply abandoned, no longer of use, no longer significant, no longer capable of generating purpose. Such places, he knew, were the abode of the weak, the stupid, the failures. The movement was growing yearly stronger and stronger; the rest of the world was atrophying inexorably, crumbling down to make room for the new power. He saw it, and it should have burnished his sense of fulfilment. It was the consequence of thirty years' struggle, the working out of the vision that he had been the first to share, to which he was still utterly committed. He must not look away from it; he must not hide the

261

consequences from himself; he must confront and rejoice in them. Today, however, he could not avoid melancholy. Today he was going to see Mark First as a friend, as a fellow human being. He did not know whether such a being still existed. He believed it had existed once, and he was bound now to go and seek it.

The young men, 'my young gods' as First called them, greeted Standing with absolute deference, their faces set, their bodies held straight as he passed, a tall man, now stooped in late middle age, who caught himself in the mirrors with which Leader First had covered the walls of his headquarters. He saw himself stumbling and shambling amongst these oppressive young men.

First lived still in the barracks, but he had now added a higher storey, a glass turret, a large rotunda with a conical roof of triangular glass panels supported by a thin red pillar. Here he had his great desk. Here he sat and wrote in fat leather ledgers. The practical lives of command and of domestic necessity were on the floor below. Here, open to the sky, floored with marble and finished with oak and leather, was his private Valhalla.

Standing climbed the spiral staircase with difficulty, his hips shunting lumps of pain up into his back. First sat with a young god at his shoulder, and three more standing by the window, four more accompanying Standing. A chair was brought and placed before First; Standing sat and watched him writing, the slit of his mouth straight, but the echo of a smile, a satisfaction, in the lines about the mouth.

There were a lot of lines on the face of the leader now. They swept up from his forehead and the hair had receded dramatically from them. The eyes were buried in nests of tiny creases, the flesh was sagging a little and, as it gave, it fell into layer upon layer of tiny folds. It was as if age was trying to assert itself upon the strength within that head, but was being shattered in the attempt.

First finished writing, handed the pen to the young man who took it, sheathed it, reached across and collected the tome, First leaning back to allow him to do this, a practised move.

'Anthony,' First said, smiling at him at last, welcoming him.

'Are you well, Mark?'

'Of course. Below, there are always complications, always intricacies to be unravelled, but up here I am impregnable.'

'I need to talk to you. . .'

'A difficulty? The east is our heartland. Surely you have no cause for concern.'

'A personal difficulty.'

First waited, curious, detached.

'If . . . if we might speak alone, Mark.'

First frowned at this, disapproved, drew breath, took a decision.

'Of course, Anthony, if that is what you wish.'

The young men did not need to be told. They left quickly and orderly. But when they were alone, Standing could not bring himself to it, sat looking down, feeling weak and vulnerable, foolish to be wasting the time of the leader.

'What is troubling you, Anthony? You are not ill, surely?'

'Feeling a little old, perhaps. I. . .'

'Age is not to be regretted. I feel its claims upon me, but they do not depress me, do not diminish me. As nature slows down within me I can feel its processes more clearly. This is to be savoured, Anthony.'

'Muriel is unwell, Mark.'

First studied him hard, looked into him, tested the quality of his soul.

'Of course, every consideration must be given to Muriel,' First said at last. 'She is the pride of her sex, Anthony, and I would not have her degraded for anything. You have good doctors in the east, surely. What do they say?'

'It is . . . it is not a physical problem, Mark.'

'All medical problems are physical problems, Anthony.'

'May I tell you about her?'

First sighed a little, looked beyond Standing at the cold day outside.

'I need to tell you. It is a weight upon me, a terrible weight, and I need to have your knowledge of it. You are my life, Mark, and in this darkness I now need your light more than I have ever needed it.'

'You are a great man, Anthony. Never let yourself be turned away from your greatness. You must not compromise your freedom.'

'I find . . . I find that there is a weakness in me, Mark, and I need to have your understanding of it so that I can resolve it. It has perplexed and troubled me. I am weak because I cannot see my way through it.'

'Then tell me, but remember who I am and what I am, and beware that I have never sought to bring comfort to weakness.'

'I am aware only of your certainty. I place myself before that.'

'So be it.'

Standing suddenly needed to drink, but could not face the ministrations of the young gods. He swallowed, and a knot of dryness was pushed down his throat.

'She . . . it began . . . a while ago. She had not been

264

sleeping, not properly. To begin with she was just rest-less, then I would wake in the night to find her awake, always awake, staring up at the ceiling, tensed as if she was waiting for something terrible to happen. Then, later, I would wake and she was gone from the bed. I found her wandering naked about the house, lost and looking for something, desperate. At first when I reached her she was embarrassed, confused, afraid. She came back to bed, and I comforted her. In the mornings I wanted to talk about these incidents, but she had no recollection of them, or said she had none, although she was certainly troubled, very troubled by something. I talked with Doctor Lewis. He suggested some pills, but she would not take them. I had them ground up and put in her food, but they had no effect. It got worse. When she went on her night walks, she began to hide from me, and when I found her, huddled in corners or cupboards, terrified, she resisted my comforts. Sometimes I could not get her back to bed. I had to bring a blanket and cover her where she was hiding. I had to sit and watch over her, talking to her, trying to call her back to me, Mark. Then she became aggressive. When I found her she would spring out at me, beat me with her fists, and I had to restrain her. I did not want to hurt her, and sometimes we struggled and struggled for hours, she trying to destroy me, me trying to contain her, to reach her with some sort of comfort. I could not understand it; this beautiful woman who had given herself to me and to everything I believed in, now writhing against me like an animal, hitting and biting and clawing at me. During the days, it was as if she was not there. She ate little, drank brandy, sat and looked out of windows, wrote letters to friends she had had before we married, to dead women, in which she said we had lots of children, I was a . . . a poet, we

265

lived alone in a cottage, she spent her days helping with mental cases. It went on and on. I was desperate, Mark. I didn't know what to do, where to find her anymore.

'Then, two days ago, she suddenly came out of it. She came into my office and said she was all right now. I was for one moment very happy. I went to touch her, to kiss her, but she shook me away. She said she was going to leave me, was going to leave and tell the world what was going on here. She called me a murderer, depraved, disgusting, a monster in a world of monsters. She reeled off a list of names of people I had murdered, women I had raped and then had sent to death camps. She said she had a disease, a sexual disease that I had given her, that she was dying from it. She was not hysterical, not emotional; everything was calm and clear and settled. I told her that she had not been well, that she must rest. She agreed. She said she had been mad but that she had come through it now, now at last she saw things as they were, that as far as she was concerned I was dead.

'Mark, for twenty years she has been with me in everything. I have hidden nothing from her. I have loved her as a man loves a woman in all things. I am not like you. I was never self-sufficient. I needed the warmth and tenderness of another. I needed to make love, to build up a life of touching and knowing and intimacy, to have a foundation to my life, the support of it. I know it has been a weakness, but it is a weakness that is of nature itself; surely it is, and I thought in Muriel I had found someone who understood, who fitted perfectly with me, with everything we were doing. I feel at times that she has betrayed me, that it is the greatest betrayal of my life. But I cannot hate her, Mark. I can only feel a terrible pity for her, and a pity for myself.'

He stopped at last, drained of it, collapsed, waiting to be lifted up again.

'You have made her secure, Anthony?'

'Yes.'

'She is dead, Anthony. You know that.'

'Yes.'

'She fed her strength into the movement, poured her beauty into the heart of our power. She was the first lady of our state. Mourn for her, grieve for her, allow the pain to sharpen you, to make you strong for her absence. We will celebrate her passing with ceremony and reverence.'

And he rose, and Standing rose. They came together by the thin red pillar that held up the glass roof, and they embraced. Standing's eyes were full of tears, and Leader First waited for him to master the emotion before he called down for the young gods to come and lead him away.

Standing came at last to the door of their bedroom, told the guard to give him the key and go. When he opened the door, Muriel was sitting up straight on the edge of the bed, looking at him as he appeared, waiting for him. He had imagined her like this, exactly like this, and it frightened him a little to see her so. He closed the door behind him.

'How are you, Muriel?' he asked.

'Fuck off.'

'I . . . I've been to see Mark.'

'Of course you have.'

'Who else could I have turned to?'

'I'm only grateful we have no children.'

'If we had had children, I don't think it would have come to this, Muriel.'

'This is freedom. This is what I have betrayed all those years and years and years. I have woken up now. I went mad and it cured me. You drove me mad in the end and I came through. I broke free of you.'

'You have lost your faith, that is all. You have grown inward over all these years. I should have given you friends, given you something of your own.'

'You raped all my friends. You had them all murdered. Now what? My turn for the death camp now? For the bullet in the back of the head? I won't mind them raping me. After being fucked by you for twenty years, rape has no terrors for me. I . . . I don't want to die, though. I'll fight and scream all the way. I'll denounce you with every breath I breathe.'

'I want you to come down and have dinner with me.'

'Is that reptile First in the house?'

'Please, Muriel. Please try to be brave.'

'Am I to be killed?'

'You are to die, yes.'

She faced him to see if he was being serious. Then she put her hand to her mouth, bit her knuckles, curled over, whimpered. He stepped forward and stood before her, then crouched down and looked up at her.

'And I am to die with you,' he said.

She saw him there, drew back, did not believe him, grabbed at a hope that it was some profound metaphor.

'You? Why?'

'Because I love you.'

'Because you love me, they will kill you?'

'Because I love you, I must die.'

'First will have you killed?'

'No. I will die because I want to die. I do not want to live anymore, not in a world from which you are absent.'

'I . . . I hate you. I despise you.'

'That you should feel that is a source of infinite pain to me, Muriel, but I accept it. I have no choice.'

268

'If you love me, get me out of here. If you love me, come with me.'

'That is not an option. I will not be disloyal to the movement.'

'Your movement is an organisation of thugs and perverts.'

'I will not argue with you. I thought you understood. If you don't understand any more, if you have lost your faith, then I am sad for you and sad for myself. You have broken my loyalties in two. You have opposed my loyalty to you and my loyalty to the movement, and I no longer want to live with that conflict.'

'Anthony, I don't want to die.'

'There is no way out, Muriel, no way at all. I promise you. I have never in my life lied to you, and I would not do so now.'

He reached forward and took her hands. She did not reject his touch, allowed him to take her hands and to bury his face in them.

'When?' she said.

'Tonight.'

'How will it be done?'

'I have some pills. We will go down and have dinner. We will come up to bed. We will bring a bottle of brandy with us. We will lie down together. That is what I want to happen.'

'Anthony, I don't want to die. I don't want to die. Please.'

'Death is nothing. It is a resolution of life. It is only terrible if we shrink away from it. Together we will welcome it like a lover. We will lie together in each other's arms, we will feel the life beating strongly in us, our life, and we will let go of it as if it was a bird we were letting out of a cage. It will be an affirmation of life, not a denial of it. Death is not the opposite of life; it is its consummation. Muriel, trust me in this. Give yourself to it. Forget everything else. Perfect yourself for this one last, liberating act of will. Come now. Let us go down.'

'Hold me for a little while before we go down.'

The young god brought Leader First the news of the deaths of Anthony and Muriel Standing printed out across two lines on a sheet of paper. He stood beside his leader and waited for recognition. At last the writing stopped, the pen was laid in the furrow of the open book, and the hand came up. Into it the young god placed the message.

Leader First looked at it and his face shadowed, as if someone had made a move in a chess game that he had not expected, that he needed to assess scrupulously.

It did not take him long. He called an amanuensis who waited across the room, and gave detailed instructions for a double state funeral. All brothers not on active duty to attend, all commanders required. He appointed a man to take detailed charge of the arrangements, sketching out broadly the ceremonials that were required. A mausoleum to be constructed in the grounds of their house, an architect appointed. A statement to be broadcast to all regions at once: 'The deaths are announced of Commander and Lady Standing. They had suffered personal illness and chose to terminate their lives simultaneously. We are to rejoice in the perfection of their loyalty and their courage, and to mourn that their active presence amongst us has come to its natural conclusion. Leader First.'

Then he sent them away, remained alone in his glass turret. He could not write; he could not think. He rose and paced the icy floor, snapping his heels upon it like

270

shots. He stood at the window and looked out into an ocean of mist that clung close to the world.

Something had fallen out of him, something physical that it required all his strength to contain. It had been out of his reckoning. He had not conceived that she would have that power over him. His first instinct was anger. Standing had betrayed him. He hated him, and her, for what she had brought him to. But this was too simple, too personal. He calmed and criticised himself for this individualism. But he needed to have an understanding of it, for he knew clearly, with all the honesty that he possessed, that there was something he had missed, that had escaped him, he who was everything and knew everything.

He had known Standing's limitations, but he had never to this moment doubted the perfection of his loyalty. Had he simply been deceived? Had they been incubating something inimical all those years? If so, why then did she break as she did? Why did he not seek to protect her from the movement? What was it? What was it?

It was the darkness of sexuality, the darkness of women; and he had to know that darkness at last, face to face, as he had known fear and death and cruelty, face to face. And like a key into a deep lock, sliding and turning with perfect precision, Rachel came into his heart.

Rachel's grief was an amputation into which the nerves strove for purchase and purpose. They had taken her to the Hall and subjected her to prolonged sedation, but she did not need that; it delayed the grief which she needed to have clearly out for her clearly to come to terms with. It was a black abyss in which she was hung suspended by a tangle of choking threads of which she yearned to be free. Everything she had in human terms had been ripped

271

from her, every root of love in her torn out, but that, hypothetically, might have been borne: she had a faith that was strong enough to sustain and give shape to this simple grief, however monumental. What could not be borne was her own part in it.

That she had taken human life was a source of the most terrible, intimate pain to her. She knew bluntly that, had she not killed Catton, Mary might still be alive. She had violated her deepest beliefs, had responded with an animal rage that disgusted her. She was appalled that she had been capable of this, and knew that she had been punished terribly for it, would go on being punished for the rest of her maimed life. She did not believe in a God who took the life of a child to punish her mother; but she knew that, before she had killed him, she had a moral strength, an integrity. By the act of murder she had lost her right to grieve cleanly for her daughter or for her son or for her husband, because she had become an active part of the violence that had consumed them; in her awareness of this was her punishment. She no longer knew herself. At times she despaired, felt herself to be nothing any more, a cypher, a shadow, something that not even death would alter.

This had been her home for the first seventeen years of her life, and yet she hardly recognised it. They had rebuilt it, reshaped it, taken out everything they could take out that had not already been plundered and ruined. Only the views across the park, into the woods, and the seasons of the skies, were familiar, and they were all outside, in a wild world where as a child she had filled her imagination, and where as a young woman she had brought up her children. All that was gone now; the recognition she felt when she looked out of the windows brought only a bleak nostalgia. She lived in a small space, and the small space was not hers; it was given to her by them, defined and sustained by them. She was Rachel Carr, the wife of Ben who used to fix things, the mother of Matt, dead hero of the movement; and she was now Lady Carr, the honoured woman who had slain the arch-enemy, Catton. She was a symbol, a husk, moving through her days with as little of herself as she was able to engage, with a solid deadness of heart that had nothing more to give to anyone. She did not want anything, not solitude, not companionship; she did not finally mind what they did to her, what they made of her.

Only one thought, as the months, as the years passed, troubled her vacancy. Painfully, she set her mind to recover the man she had killed, the man they hated. It was necessary, she felt, only to come to terms with him, then she would be able to rest. Her own dead were beyond her now, beyond even her emotions: Catton was still with her as if he had possessed her, lay bleeding and unfinished within her heart. She went through the moments of her killing, but there was nothing there for her. She had taken no decision, had blundered forward, had taken up the knife and become a part of it. It was watching him die, those slow minutes when the life had struggled out of him, spilling that tumble of words upon her; this was what was left. Once she had struck, everything was cancelled: after she had struck, in the misery of her survival, there was a new obligation.

She had hardly heard what he had said then, remembered vaguely that he had come to the Hall as a young officer, but perhaps she had imagined that; perhaps she wanted him to belong to her past; this was not what it was. There was something else he had said that she had forgotten, had obscured within her. She could not remember what it had been, and the more she worried at it, the more important it became to remember. He had laid an obligation upon her; with his dying breath he had asked her to do something, to see someone, to deliver a message. Only when she recovered that, only when she had fulfilled it would she be free of him, would she be able to return in some way to what she had been before. She would be reunited then with Mary, with Matt, with Ben, even with little Becky. She imagined them reaching out to her in the dark, unable to come to her. Catton lay between them, shutting her out.

There was not a day, hardly an hour, when she did not think about this. She lived in a small apartment high in the house, ministered to by the polite young men. She came down when they required her, moved through the house, a tall woman, greying, dignified, Lady Carr, the dark widow in a sheath of silence. They bowed their heads when she passed. She did not look at them, met their dignitaries, sat at their tables; rising to leave, they all rose with her, opened the doors, let her go up the broad stairways to her solitude. What was it? What was it Catton had said to her?

Then one day she had turned to the man next to her at table and had asked, 'Who is that?' indicating a large portrait of a man's head on the wall adjacent.

'That is our leader, Lady Carr: Leader First.'

'Ah yes. Of course. Thank you.'

She had seen the portrait often before; there were prints of it, she now noted, in almost every room apart from hers. She asked if this omission might be rectified, and they were pleased to rectify it, came the next day, polite and discreet, tacked the face to the wall of her sitting room between the windows.

It was not a distinguished face at all, and certainly not handsome. The eyes had a staring, mad look to them, and she suspected that they had been touched up on the photograph, made to look as if they followed you around. It was a cheap trick, a cheap image; the man they worshipped was a dreary little confidence man.

She remembered then, quite casually, what Catton had said to her. He had said that this man, First, was a monster. He had told her to find him and kill him. The remembrance came quite flatly, and its impossibility made it, after all her worrying, a melodramatic absurdity. She would have nothing more to do with killing.

She wanted them to take away the image. She had achieved all she needed to achieve from it. She had come through Catton, and there was no revelation on the other side of him. She had been overwrought, suffered some sort of breakdown perhaps, but she had come through that now. She felt relief, the relief of waking from a complex, inescapable nightmare; she felt she must do something, make herself busy again.

She asked Marker if he might come and talk to her one evening. He came dutifully, laid his scarf across the back of a vacant chair and smiled at her.

'I need to be useful here, David,' she said. 'I am beginning to grow lightheaded with so little to do.'

He frowned.

'There must be something for me to do. I'm completely adaptable. I will try anything, anything at all. Come now, you have women here, don't you?'

'Yes, we do have women, Rachel. Many of the Brothers are married, and their wives live with them here.'

'Ah,' she said, 'but surely that's not essential?'

'Rachel?' he said, taking a deep breath.

'Yes, David.'

'You could become my wife.'

After a moment of complete blank, of a surprise so total that it winded her, she felt outraged. She felt as if she had been tricked into this, wanted to tell him to get out, that she was a married woman . . . and as this assertion rose and died and crumbled within her, she began to cry.

'It's been a long time,' he was saying softly, leaning forward, reaching out to touch her, but losing the courage to make contact. 'Rachel, it's been such a long, long time. I have been in love with you from the day we came here, from the day I first saw you at the cottage with Ben. I was consumed with jealousy. So many times I was tempted to have him sent away, so many times; but I could not do it, I could not win you on those terms.'

The scene had lurched now into farce, and she choked as the tears were jammed in surges of laughter that blundered up her throat.

'Please. . .' she managed to say at last, 'please, David. Go now. I . . . I'm sorry.'

'May I come and see you tomorrow?'

'Yes, yes. Tomorrow. Please . . .'

He rose, collected his scarf, bowed to her and left her.

She rocked backwards and forwards on her hips, numb in the wake of the emotions that had broken loose, too many all of a sudden bursting out of her in all directions. For hours she sat, until the darkness fell about her and she could not find stillness.

At last she found a practicality to grapple. She turned on the light, went to a table and wrote a note to Marker, a formal rejection of his offer penned with as much gentleness and humility as she could muster. It was a difficult letter, and took her a long time. She did not think about Marker as she wrote it; she struggled only with a tone, objectified herself into a voice making a public announcement. When it was done and sealed, she wanted it delivered, did not want to have it sitting there unexploded through the night. There were things that were waiting in her solitude, and the letter was an impediment to them. She went out on to the landing, went down the stairs, surprising a sleepy night guard, who agreed to deliver the letter to Brother Marker first thing in the morning. Rachel returned swiftly to bed.

Now that the letter was on its way, she wanted it back again. The phrases she had used seemed, now they were sent, pompous and hurtful; and anyway, why had she refused him so finally, so abruptly? She had wanted a purpose here, and he was kind and sensitive. Marriage to him would be an easy thing for her to give. It was logical.

Then came the long slide down into the things she had been dreading, the close imaginings of an intimacy with him; then, with a shudder, she knew why she could not marry him; then came the surprise that such things should still involve her. What would it matter if, once or twice a week, he climbed on top of her if it pleased him to? She could lie there dreaming of Ben. But, lying there and dreaming of Ben, she writhed and turned at the thought of Marker, shook wih disgust at the idea of his seeing her, touching her. Why? He was not physically repulsive, was hardly likely, given all their puritanism, to require complex degradations from her.

There. There it was. She could not be touched by one of them, no, never. She could never belong to them, she did not belong here. She sat up in bed, turned on her light and felt afraid, felt them all around her, moving, plotting, bowing and bobbing to her, opening doors, pulling out chairs for her. Lady Carr. What had she been doing here? To what had she given herself?

She knew at once what Ben had hated in them, saw

suddenly, below the silky mask of their humility and deference, the violence, the violence. She remembered Catton. She remembered the men she had seen executed. The violence rose round her like a smog. She choked and retched, clawed at her flesh.

Then she met the cold watching eyes of Leader First and she became still. She imagined for a moment that he could actually see her, that he would know everything she thought. She turned out the light quickly and lay in the darkness, buried herself under the blankets, longed for her husband, longed for the comfort of his touch, the arousal and oblivion of pleasure, longed for it with a sudden physical desperation that appalled her.

She was old now, beyond all that, surely. She grew, in the darkness, aware of her body as something that would never again be shared, never again be of any value except as the vehicle for her diminishing individual significance. Give in, she told herself, go to Marker, go now, go to his bed; then the repulsion gripped her again, the terror; and she knew that to give in would be to become a part of the violence again, that sex without love was only violence, that they had no love, no, not in the sense of opening themselves in all their frailty and need to the love of another in the way that she had offered herself to Ben, her shame, her delight, the strange beauty of his sex sleeved within hers, the miracle of conception, birth, their children nurtured and loved in the crucible of that love; and then had come the violence, always at the end of everything came the violence; stronger than love because it did not recognise love; and love is always tender and fragile and provisional, and violence is certain and final and absolute; and she needed love again, she needed a touch upon her old body that was uncertain, clogged with its own desires but afraid of hurting her with them. She was alive again, aching and twisting with life that would never be fulfilled. She cried out in the darkness, strangling in her solitude.

And the face of Leader First watched her and apprised her from the terrible distance of his certainty, turned her with the curiosity of his psychosis, wondering how he might most interestingly pick her to pieces to find out all about her. And Catton's curse made sense. She could no more have struck First down than she could have flapped her arms and flown away, but she understood now his evil, and knew that he would have to be destroyed if the world was not to become bleached of its humanity.

She sat in her room through cold days, waiting and trembling, knowing that something was coming for her. She assumed that it would be death, and, for the first time in her life, she was not ready for death.

Eventually Marker came. He was accompanied by two immaculate young men whom she had never seen before. He greeted her with a smile that turned in her like a knife. She braced herself against the fear that rose steeply within her.

'What is it, David?'

'You are to leave us, Rachel,' he said.

'Why?'

'Because you are required elsewhere.'

'Where?'

'Leader First wants to meet you. You are to go to central command.'

Seven years I resisted you, Rachel, but there was not a day during all those years when I did not think of you, when I did not know that eventually I would call you.

279

At times I even wanted you to die, because this was the only way that I could keep you from me. You were a conclusion I fought day after day to avoid.

As I grew older, I began to become aware of my flesh in a way that I had never been before. As my bodily functions began to slow, I found that I could sense precisely the various operations of my metabolism: the push of my heart, the little lethargies that slowed my joints, the shifting of my guts, the queasiness at the edge of my liver, the gathering of the mucus in my nose and throat, the weight of the air I breathed. I grew secretly more inward, intrigued by my corporality. There was no disgust, nor even morbidity in these meditations. I was fascinated by the process, could easily project these awarenesses to the moment when the slowness would overcome me and I would cease to exist. I kept detailed notes on what I experienced, was proud of my strength of purpose, my clarity of mind and of body.

I became more acutely aware also of the needs of my body, of heat and cold, of the weight of tiredness in my eyes and temples, in the weight of my limbs. I examined my hungers and thirsts. I noted the stodginess in my bowels and the bloating of my bladder. And I found the leisure to note in detail the stirrings of sexuality that came to me, mostly at dawn when I came from my brief sleeping. I had always, as a young man, slept cleanly and blankly. Now there began to be a shadow time between sleep and waking, when a small swirl of desires and fancies possessed me before I came clear of them, rose and set to work.

They did not linger, these shadows, did not oppress me in the slightest; and certainly I was never moved to bring them to the surface of my life. There was never the time for that, nor was it ever appropriate that I should use the power I had been given to assert any physical need. The more my inward awareness intensified, the more ascetic I became, eating and sleeping less, setting myself against chills and sweats. I like to watch my young gods, to measure my own ageing strength against the selfishness of their youth.

The death of Anthony Standing made you at last essential. My own purity was no longer enough, because it could not explain the impurity of others, tainted by the darkness of active sexuality. The woman who had slain my dark brother Catton, who had embraced him like a lover and had cut open his life as she did so, this woman had the answers I needed.

The joy with which I anticipated your arrival, Rachel, was a new purpose in my life.

Let me be nothing, let me be so small that I do not matter, let me be nothing, she said to herself over and over again as the car tore her away, as the empty countryside, the vacant towns, a whole sterile world was revealed to her, the moral atmosphere of the Hall made palpable, the nightmare coming real as she was carried to the heart of the power. It was not a physical fear that she felt; she knew that she could let go of her life easily. It was the fear of being forced to confront something so monstrous that it would deprive her of meaning. Let me be nothing, so that it will not be able to touch me, she said.

She passed through the lower offices of the central command building and found their unexpected ordinariness frightening. She would have been reassured by grandeur. She would have been reassured by brutes, by thugs, but the sleek, superior young men broke down the images she had formed with which she might have found some bearing here. And then came the ascent of a tight iron spiral into a place of light at the top of the building where she did not expect to be able to breathe. And then she came into the presence of the Leader.

He stood waiting for her on a floor of glass-green marble, in a naked sea of light. He was short, balding and far older than she had expected, a small, stout, ageing man dressed in matt black. His hair was grey, but his eyebrows were still dark. She recognised the face from the pictures, but not the substance. It was an anticlimax that brought a nervous giggle to her throat. She looked back, but the young men had gone, and being alone with this man was not reassuring.

'Come,' he said kindly.

She approached him, not liking to come too close, not wanting to assert her height. She came close enough though to see the face, the mass of tiny lines, the dark hard eyes that held her, the reptilian nature confronting her with a smile that seemed to offer a terrifying complicity. She was afraid again, hot, felt absurdly that she should take off her clothes, that this was what he wanted of her. She began to tremble, began to feel her eyes pricking.

He took two sharp steps towards her and wrapped his arms around her in a tight embrace that made her clench. He released her, took her hands and led her to a leather bench that ran around the edge of the glass room. He sat and drew her down beside him, clasping her hands strongly.

'Lady Carr,' he said. 'Lady Wallis, perhaps. Rachel Darrington. I will call you – Rachel.'

'Yes, Leader,' she said as they had taught her.

'You put a knife into the man Catton, and you sat and watched him die.'

She had no response to this.

'You did us service, Rachel, although you do not even belong to us. You are a testament to the truth of what we are. You behaved instinctively as if you had been brought up faithful to our beliefs. And you are a woman. So firstly, I must thank you.' He patted her hands. 'I have wanted to meet you for a long time; but there is another reason for your being here. I have a perplexity, and I think perhaps you might be able to help me unravel it; especially perhaps as you are not formally committed to us. You are intelligent and independent. And you are no child. Now, Rachel, it occurs to me increasingly that somehow we do not do right by women. Things have gone wrong that ought not to have gone wrong. We have neglected something of importance. So I have called you here, Rachel, because I want you to tell me what it is.'

She knew that not only was it obvious what they had neglected, but that this man did not want to be told the obvious, that he would not accept it. It was like being asked by a man with a hideous deformity if there was anything unusual about him.

'Tell me, Rachel. What is it? Don't be afraid. I have been surrounded for too many years by people whose thoughts reflect my own. I need your independence.'

What could she say that would remotely reach him? A silence began to amass. He still had her hands clasped on the bench between them. She did not look at him, but knew that he was still looking at her.

'I think . . .' she began, without any real thought in her head.

'What do you think, Rachel?'

'I think that you have degraded love, Leader,' she began at last.

He considered this briefly, then replied, 'There is the love of the Brotherhood, the love of truth. There is love between men and women too, but that must surely come below the higher demands of love. It always has done. Love of the country, love of God, of integrity, of freedom. In all the higher societies that love always came first, and that love we have not demeaned. Oh no, Rachel, that is central to what we are. It binds us together.'

'Between men and women, Leader, you have degraded love between men and women.' She was crying now, hard stifling tears that hurt her to cry.

'It is interesting that you should say that. Tell me, is there something more that women need from that sort of love? From sexual love? Something that men do not need?'

'I don't know, Leader. I don't know.'

'Is it motherhood? Does that make the difference? You were a mother. When you lay with your husband, were you possessed by some secret procreative force?'

'I don't know, Leader.'

He released her hands, put his fingers to her face and touched her tears as if he needed to feel what they were like. He put his hand upon her thigh, stroked her experimentally, watching for her reactions. She had no reactions.

'They will take you down to your quarters now, Rachel. Come and see me again this evening. Think about what I have said to you. I need your understanding. You are my honoured guest here.'

She spent her days in a cell-like room with a bathroom attached. They brought her food and drink, the young gods, but they did not stay to talk. She was not locked in. She could go out and walk in the grounds along gravel paths by neat rectangles of lawn. She did not approach any of the buildings, far less the high fencing that loomed on every horizon. She knew she was watched whenever she came out, suspected that she was watched even in her room, knew she was a prisoner here.

Every day at dusk she was fetched and taken up into the glass turret. As the sun set in a majesty of cloud, or as the day simply drained out of the greyness, she sat with Leader First and was put through a progressive catechism. He was relentless, obsessed, too much for her; her head ached, and she was weary of the questions that could not be answered.

'I am told that the sexual pleasure of women is more profound than the sexual pleasure of men, Rachel. Is this so?'

'How can I answer that, Leader?'

'Do you have no opinion upon it?'

'I have never thought of it before now.'

'And yet men have more direct sexual energy than women. Would you agree with that?'

'I . . . I do not know how such a thing might be measured, Leader.'

'Perhaps men have more energy which, in the corrupt times, found its easiest expression in sexuality.'

'Perhaps that is true, Leader.'

'Perhaps women are the true sexual creatures. Perhaps the energy of women is most naturally expressed through sexuality and reproduction.'

'Yes, Leader.'

Frustrated by her refusal to generalise, his questions grew personal.

'Did you have lovers before your marriage, Rachel?'

'No, Leader.'

'Have you felt any desire for sexual intercourse since your husband's death?'

'No, Leader.' It was an unavoidable lie in this circumstance.

'You were sexually active throughout your marriage?'

'Yes, Leader.'

'Was he always the initiator of sexual intercourse?'

'I . . . I don't remember, Leader.'

'Come now. You must remember that.'

'I . . . I think when . . . when it happened we both wanted it to happen. I . . . I don't think either of us was . . . the initiator, Leader?'

'A spontaneous, mutual desire, then.'

'Yes, Leader.'

'The basis for a profound and fully satisfying relationship?'

'Yes, Leader.'

'And you believe that the relationships between men and women that exist within our organisation are in some way less than the relationship you had with your husband?'

'I have no opinion upon that, Leader.'

'But you said we had degraded the love between men and women. What did you mean by that?'

'I think . . . it was wrong of me to say that. I have no way of judging the love of other people.'

'No, no, Rachel. It was a direct challenge to us. You must not run away from it now.'

'Perhaps . . . perhaps then, because my husband and I were so close, that I cannot . . . cannot appreciate a relationship that is not like that was. Perhaps I was merely being idealistic, individualistic, Leader.'

During the days she thought of answer after answer to his questions, but faced with him, she could only deflect him, continuously push him away from her. It was not only that she was frightened of him, although she was

286

very frightened; and it was not only that she wanted to defy him, although she resisted him with all her conscious strength; it was just that, when he jabbed his careful questions into her, everything seemed to lock in her mind; no fear could release that lock, and the defiance that resulted from it was not conscious. Simply, she could not be drawn into this sort of dialogue. It did not mean anything.

But there was something further, something in this man himself that caused the locking of her mind. Certainly she hated him: she knew him clearly as the apotheosis of evil. She would have liked to believe that her resistance to him was some sort of struggle against evil, some metaphorical fulfilment of Catton's command; and perhaps it was. But as the days passed, the abstractions within which her conscious thoughts sought to contain him became less absolute, less certain. She felt increasingly that she was confronted with a man like other men, that his questioning was, on a level that he himself was quite unaware of, increasingly personal. He wanted to know her, to be able to imagine the world from her point of view, to control and possess her; and his obsession with this grew increasingly like prurience, like lust. And realising this frightened her even more, because it brought him into her reach, and her into his.

'You are resisting me, Rachel. Why are you doing this? What you say may be of help to all women. Surely you understand that.'

'I . . . I cannot find the answers to your questions, Leader. If I could, I would give them to you. I do not have the words to make you understand what I feel. I cannot put it into words. It was my life. It was simply my life, and I cannot turn it into words.'

'You are not trying. You are resisting me deliberately.'

He took hold of her shoulders, pulled her round on the bench to face him squarely. His mouth was open, and she could see the pink tip of his tongue as it moistened his lips. His breath was sickly sweet. She closed her eyes and imagined his touch on her breasts, his fingers slithering up her thigh. He was disgusting. The filthiness rose in her throat, and she had to gasp for air.

'Now,' he said. 'Now, Rachel, dear Rachel, tell me what it is. Set it free within you. Be strong now.'

She shut herself down, her nerves straining for the first intimation of his touch. He did not touch her. He was waiting for her to touch him. She ground her nails into her palms.

'Yes,' he said. 'Yes. You're nearly there, nearly there. You're fighting it, but it's too strong for you, too strong. Be brave now. Take the leap, Rachel, take the leap.'

She writhed in a sudden involuntary spasm, jerked aside and fell stupidly off the edge of the bench, tumbling in a disjointed tangle across the glassy floor, slithering away on a spurt of energy that quickly consumed all her strength.

Weak and trembling then, she could not find the co-ordination to lift herself. Now she was down, she had no motive, it seemed, to rise and face him again. She sank on to her side, curled her legs, moved a little way towards the centre of the floor. Perhaps if she gained some real distance from him she could turn to him, could lift herself. She was not afraid at this moment; she seemed to be drained of emotion, of memory, of everything. If he had asked her who she was, she would have had trouble finding an answer. She knew only who he was, and knew that she had to resist him.

She heard him rise, slowly, step across the marble until his shoes were by her face, black shoes, glassy and creaking, the black trousers with their perfect creases coming exactly down to rest upon the shoes. She twisted up her head to see only a black bulk.

'Give in to me, Rachel,' he said, almost tenderly.

She covered her face as he squatted down beside her. She heard his joints crack.

'I . . . I have no more strength,' she said.

'I know.'

'Whatever it is you want to do to me, do it if you must. I have no more strength. I only want to sleep now.'

He sighed, rose and walked away from her.

'You don't understand, do you? You still don't understand.'

She pulled herself in, curled her legs tightly in and, on the base they gave her, she was able to sit up. Around her the floor spread like a still sea. Rain fell heavily on to the glass, but no sound of it penetrated the double panes. She felt giddy, disorientated. The blank of the floor and the silence above it were too much for her; they seemed to crush her.

He stood by the window, his back to her, one hand grasped in the other.

'Tell me something, Rachel. Did Catton rape you?'

She tried to remember, thought now that he might have done but could not clearly remember it; surely she would have remembered.

'Well?'

'He did not . . . rape me.'

'I think he did, Rachel. I think he did.'

She came clear suddenly. She had resisted and she had brought him out of cover. An excitement took her, straightened her back, although she did not rise.

'Catton did not rape me,' she said clearly, 'even though it would please you if he had.'

He turned and, although she could not see his features, she knew that she had caught him.

'If you like, Leader, I'll pretend that he raped me. Would you like me to?'

'Why do you think I should like that, Rachel?'

'I suppose it might give you pleasure.'

'I have no use for pleasure.'

She rose steadily and crossed the floor towards him, stood by him, stood close, a clear but active space between their bodies. She stared hard into his eyes, looked deep into his head.

'It was when we were alone,' she said softly, 'when the killing had started outside. He turned to go, then suddenly he came towards me. He grabbed my wrist, and I thought he was going to drag me out with him. I tried to pull away from him, but he came with me as I pulled, would not let go of me. I hit the wall, jammed against it. He was fumbling at himself and I thought he was going to draw a knife, I thought I was going to die. I whimpered. I urinated with fear, Leader. He pulled my hand, and I was touching his cock. It was as hard as wood, a great root, Leader, naked and purple and gigantic, glistening, dripping, bloated with semen . . .'

He did not move as she spoke, set himself hard against her. She could sense him trying to turn himself into stone, into steel, but she was too close to him. She could feel the quiver of flesh below the tension.

She stepped back, looked down and saw the awkwardness in his groin, the tumour of his pleasure.

'There is no secret,' she said. 'I have nothing to tell you. There is only this. Only this. Why does it make you so afraid? Why has it made you so cruel?'

He did not speak, did not move. She expected him to strike her, to scream for his catamites, but he did not.

She turned and left him, went down the spiral, passed the attendant young men who were waiting below, who were surprised to see her come down alone, surprised at the silence above. She saw herself in the mirrors, and she seemed to burn. They took her back through the pouring rain to her room.

She lay on her back in the darkness, catching hold of the raw, thoughtless pleasure that rose in her triumphant. She had found herself again. She had prevailed against him. Catton could have asked no more of her.

She slept and woke in silence, to blackness; the lights outside which always burned through the night were strangely dark. At first she could hear only her own heartbeat, but then she heard the roar of aeroplanes coming in from a far distance, flying fast and low. Without the conscious decision to do so, she rolled suddenly from her bed and slithered beneath it as the rockets struck, as the darkness burst into flames and the glass shattered and the world came down around her.

OMEGA

I knew they were coming. I knew they would defeat us. I knew that we would all die.

When the first reports came of their intentions against us, I gathered my Brothers and we began to plan our defence. But as we planned, it became plain to me that in the final analysis we had no defence, not against a concerted attack. Within our own territory we were immaculate, but they were coming from beyond us with all the blind, bloody brutality of armies.

I could not openly admit the possibility of defeat in the face of the loyalty of those who had given themselves to me, but when Anthony died, I lost the will to sustain the fiction any longer. I felt a weariness. I spoke more to them in abstract terms, told them to trust me, told them that it would all be for the best if our hearts were prepared and strong. I sent them away with programmes of moral austerity rather than with battleplans. I was no longer interested in battle, only in the perfection of the will.

The crown of those last days, dear Rachel, was my

time with you, probing the secrets of your nature, pressing myself closer and closer upon you and watching how you were afraid, how you struggled to remain clothed in your dignity whilst the nakedness of your feelings quivered and liquefied. You thought that by refusing to answer my questions you were evading me. You did not evade me.

I had no clear idea what I wanted from you, but I did want something, something enormous, that I knew. I wanted perhaps only to know clearly what it was that I wanted. I thought that it would involve the physical act of love, but it could not have only been that. I could have taken that from you at any time. I wanted some act of giving from you, some recognition of me, not as Leader First, but as a man, a man of all men, whose power, whose sexual power you would recognise and rejoice in.

Was that what you gave me, that last day of my power? I cannot be sure. At the time I was alarmed by the energy you roused in me. I felt as if you had taken something from me that I had not wanted to give. When you left me, I was confused. I wanted to call for you to be dragged back to me. I wanted to submit you to the energies of my young gods, to stand and watch as they devoured you. But as I sat alone in the darkness, recovering myself, I felt a sweet purity of desire for you, as simple and complex as a bud. I imagined with a single intensity your coming back, moving through the darkness towards me on the certain spring of your desire, bringing me the joy of fulfilment. The imagination was so strong that I actually felt that it was happening.

When the sky fell upon me at that moment, I felt that I had experienced all that there was to experience, that I was complete.

* * *

The air strike lasted no more than fifteen minutes. Then the howling of the fighters was gone, the blast of their rockets ceased, and from below the numbness that followed, the roar of burning filled the night.

Again, wearily, unwillingly, Rachel found that she had survived. She pulled herself out from under her bed. The door and windows of her room had been blown in, and fumes of burning blew through on the cold, wet blackness, behind which the glow of destruction leapt and billowed. She pulled a blanket around her and went out into the night.

The building she lived in had not been struck directly and was not immediately threatened by fire. She stood twenty yards from her door on the lip of a raw crater, listening to the shouting, seeing figures running against the glow of the conflagration, perhaps even being caught up within it. She watched for a while the tornadoes of flame swirling up into the night. She heard the incessant crashing and blasting as everything was brought down. She felt cold and immensely tired. Once again everything had been cancelled. Once again she was nothing and no-one. She went back into her room and, dressed in all the clothes she had, huddled herself under her bed. There was a cut on her head that was bleeding profusely, but she felt no pain. She licked the salty blood off her hand; it felt cold and dead.

In the morning, she emerged from her shelter to find, as she had expected, a whole new landscape of desolation before her. She wandered out aimlessly, trying to find some bearing. The fires still burned, choking the air. There were bodies and sections of bodies scattered across the shattered ground. She did not have a reaction to them; neither pity nor horror. Even when she found a body that was still moving, she could not stoop to help. None of it was real.

Only when she recognised the remains of First's building, the glass turret blown completely away, did she begin to react. She knelt down on the broken ground before it and wept, although she could not have said for what she wept, nor for whom; for herself, probably.

They found her eventually, lifted her gently and led her down into one of the underground bunkers. She was surprised to find that down here nothing had been damaged, that there was still power, that there was warmth and food. She sat in a canteen and was brought soup which she could not drink, fighting against a rising sense of claustrophobia that filled her full of an aching restlessness, a longing to shrug this place off.

At one point she got up and went to find the way out, but they stopped her, brought her back to her soup.

'I have to get out of here,' she said.

'There's nowhere else to be now,' they said. 'Be brave now, Lady Rachel.'

She was surprised by their naming of her, wanted at first to deny herself, but submitted soon enough.

'Leader First . . .?' she asked.

'Leader First is well, and is planning our answer to this horror. Horror for horror. It will all be settled.'

She found herself in a substantial group of women. As at the Hall, they were young and, superficially at least, submissive and mute. She sensed, however, the shock and fear that had been stamped upon them overnight, and this made them more real to her, began to give her something to belong to. They did not talk about what had happened, as if it would have been disloyal to do so; but they were survivors, and quivering behind the masks of their obedience were images of loss and terror that individualised them.

She found that she could be useful amongst them,

going to the men and asking where they were to be quartered, leading them to a dormitory with bunk beds, making sure each of them had somewhere to rest. She went amongst them and asked their names, talked with them if they wanted to talk, which most of them did not. She watched them fold into their weariness, some sleeping, some weeping quietly, some just lying and looking into the nightmares by which they were all now possessed.

She slept herself at last, woke and, after a moment of disorientation, she dressed herself quickly in a sense of purpose. The girls were ragged and filthy, and she went to find someone who could tell them where to wash, where to find clean clothes. They told her to wait, told her there were more important things.

'If you want the women to be useful,' she said, 'then you must allow them their dignity.'

They conceded, and Rachel went back to rouse the women, to lead them down to a room of shower-heads, to arrange a pile of trousers and shirts and underwear for them – all male attire, but she was pleased by this. She returned to the shower room to find them listlessly waiting their turns, standing about bewildered, half-undressed, some embarrassed by their filth, some hardly aware of their nakedness. Rachel herded them all into the showers with her, clustering them together, finding the more listless and applying soap to them, scrubbing their backs, scratching at their scalps. Her busyness became infectious, and soon they were all helping one another, some laughing and playing even, some weeping and embracing; but in the strong jets of hot water they began to rouse, become aware of themselves, feel again the pleasures of their bodies, their youth beside Rachel's age, embarrassed perhaps at their limpness beside her wiry activity.

Back in the dormitory, Rachel called them all together and told them how they must all set to work, must pull their weight, must liberate the men for the work of war. As she delivered these platitudes, she felt herself strange, felt that these admonitions did not belong to her. She had so quickly and completely become the situation and she was not, somewhere within herself, happy with that. Gulfs of dark remembrance opened about her, and she shuddered. But what else could she do? What else could she be? And looking at their bright faces held upon her, their trust in her holding them against the pain and the sadness, against the fear, she felt fulfilled. At night she indulged in fantasies of showing them that women were as strong and sure as they were, even these women, even their hand-picked, docile little whores.

They took over the domestic regime of the bunker, marshalling the supplies, working the kitchen and the laundry and, although they were superficially reduced to a class of servants, the men began to depend upon them, to defer to them. And truly, the men had little to do. There were meetings and plans. There were, apparently, sorties out into the chaos above. But mostly the men sat about and waited, whilst the women ran things and, under Rachel, ran things well.

In the bunkers, the reality of the world above slipped away. There were rumours of battles, of a great barbarian army sweeping its way towards them, of counter-attacks and victories; but below ground, none of that was real. The daily cycle of meals and duties became everything here in the artificial light, amidst the omnipresent hum of the generators, in the warm, synthetic air, shut away from the turn of seasons, from the rise and fall of the days, from wind and rain and the vagaries of sunlight. The men grew tight-lipped and irritable, always aware of

297

the weight of ruins that was gathering above them, caught in the trap of their impotence, whilst the women entered a loud and functional sisterhood.

Rachel was proud of them, was proud of herself and, if no-one she had ever known would have been able to recognise her here, then there was no-one she had ever known left alive; and if, as she still somewhere believed, they were all waiting for her in a higher life, then she knew they would understand; her heart was clear. She would gather her women at night, address them, make them laugh, worry aloud over things that were not going right, rejoice in things done well. She would sometimes sing songs with them, children's songs and old, tired love songs that they crooned together, each articulating a personal ache, but in doing so together releasing and stretching their cramped emotions. None of them ever spoke about the future. She watched them become individuals again, and this seemed her greatest achievement.

One morning, waking first as she always did, walking quietly amongst the bunk beds and watching the sleeping women, she saw on the pillow of a woman called Sue a bunch of spring flowers. The sight of them affected her so strongly, their delicacy, the brilliant impulse of their colour, the sad, severed wilting of them, that she could at first draw no significance from them. When she did, she became angry. She sat on Sue's bed and shook her shoulder.

Sue stirred and, seeing who had woken her, blushed, grabbed for the flowers and crushed them in her hands.

'Well? What's it like up there, Sue?' Rachel said after a watching pause.

Sue struggled for words. Rachel saw her stupidity, wanted to slap her.

'Who was he?' she asked flatly.

'He was . . . he was one of the men. I couldn't sleep. I wandered out to the latrine. He . . . he was waiting for me. He . . . he's been watching me for a while.' She burst into tears.

Rachel put her arms around her, patted the shivering flesh.

'I'm sorry, Rachel, I'm sorry.'

'Was he . . . was he kind to you?'

'He was so . . . I didn't mind. I wanted . . . I wanted him to feel good again.'

'Will you . . . will you go with him again?'

'No. I promise I won't. I promise, Rachel.'

'It doesn't matter. If you want to, then go. You are free here.'

She watched the girl during that day, watched her confide secretly in a couple of the others, saw them react with alarm, but soon with fascination, with envy even. She knew that it would happen again, knew that Sue would draw others up with her, knew that to try and stop it would be futile. What could she expect? These were women trained in sexual subservience, bred up to it. Her dreams withered, and she felt her age and futility move out of the shadows.

A couple of nights later, Sue went again, took a friend with her; then others began to go. Rachel watched them, saw how it exhilarated them, intoxicated them. She noticed in the shower bruising, cuts, noticed how some of them were becoming modest, embarrassed by the bodies that had now become pieces in another game. She felt that something had come amongst them that was beginning to feed upon them. She lay awake on her bunk and could hear below her the whispers and shufflings of the women as they made their way to their assignations and, for a moment in the darkness, she envied them, became rapt in the sweet memory of copulation, the imagining of a submission to the energy of a hidden stranger. Then came the revulsion, with counterbalancing ferocity. She would stop it. She would go out there with them and denounce them all.

Articulating this, she suddenly wanted it more than anything. She wanted to break surface, to get her head into the air. She wanted to know that there was still a world up there, however devastated, however dangerous. Down in the bunkers she had found herself again for a little while; was losing herself again now: up in the night, the real night, the weight of that self-awareness would be lifted. She knew that they all felt this, that the danger, the blind exposure, the degradation, the simple nihilism of what they were about was, in part, what they all sought: the terrible freedom. And realising this, she realised the full terror of how the world had become, the full obscenity of what First had dreamed of and what had been done in pursuit of that dream, was still being done; for, even if he was dead, even if his rule only had days left to it, the force of what had been done at his will would remain, and the force of the counterforces that broke him would be tainted with what they destroyed; it had always been thus. She would rise up with them. She would find some way of taking a stand against them all, even if it meant her own destruction.

She cornered Sue the next morning.
   'Are you going up again tonight?'
   'I . . . I don't know.'
   'Wake me. I'm coming with you.'
   'No, Rachel, you can't, you can't. Please.'
   'Wake me.'

She had no need to be woken, was ready at Sue's touch, slipped from her bunk. She made her way past the sleepers and those who pretended to sleep. She was ablaze with righteous disgust, but also with excitement. The former had driven her all day, but the latter had always been there, and now, at the moment of it, it rose to the surface.

They passed through dark corridors and up the long steel throat of a vertical ladder. The bunkers were deep and the ladder was long; they were ranged up it like a column of toiling ants. The metal of the handrails was icy. There was a red night-light glow below them, but they were moving into darkness. They moved slowly, but did not pause. Rachel's head was level with the thighs of the girl above her, and she could feel the breath of the girl below her on her thighs; she was caught in this symmetry, felt herself part of a chain, deprived of her own volition, as if she was becoming subsumed in the general purpose, as if she was going up for a man. She clenched her teeth.

Suddenly the legs above her halted, and her momentum briefly pushed her face into the buttocks above, and below her a face pressed into her. The contacts alarmed her physically and she contracted, suppressed a cry, became afraid. There was a sliding of metal on metal above, and down the ladder-throat came a bolus of wet night air that made her gasp. They were moving again, up into a terrifying exposure.

The open night seemed to draw them up in a nervous scramble. They were out in a field, perhaps on the edge of the airfield. The night was dark and still, misty, and they huddled together, glancing back at the darkness where Rachel waited, looking about to see where these men were, mustering her thoughts, trying to find what she would say, afraid of having nothing to say, beginning to know that she was irrelevant up here, useless; that she would be ignored, that she would be raped, consumed. She had no authority here; her whole purpose shrivelled in the night.

They began a slow progress across the field. They had to move in single file over the ruts and mounds of earth, avoiding the craters, which glinted like lakes. It was easy to believe they were walking some high mountain ridge. The night air clung to them, made them wet, swirled slowly around their heads. Rachel began to lose the sense of where she began and ended. Beneath all the damp numbness a strong pulse was all she could clearly claim as her own.

Before them at last the ruins of the complex came out of the darkness. Rachel was surprised to recognise the shell of First's command building, thought for an alarming moment that this was to be their destination, but they passed it, and there before them was a low building in which an orange light glimmered. The ground was clear now, and they released each other, began to spread out and straggle as if, now they were approaching the place of assignation, a reluctance, a trepidation, began to reach them. But Rachel could see the entrance to the building and could see how they were going in one by one, some turning aside, squatting down to urinate or to adjust their clothing, to prepare themselves, to settle and steel themselves.

Rachel did not want to stop, could not have relied upon herself to continue if she had stopped. She steered herself at the glowing space and was in a low, large room, an old mess hall perhaps, now a great empty space. The men stood in a cluster in the middle of the room about a brazier that was the source of the glow and before which

302

they were silhouetted. She glanced about her, but could see none of the women apart from those who had come in just ahead of her, although figures were moving in the darkness at the edges of the room, shuffling, writhing. She stopped, stood as those before her stopped and stood. A man moved out of the cluster and came up to one of the others. Rachel could hear muttered voices, the exchanges of the bargain, offering and acceptance. What was she supposed to do? Tears of futility filled her. Any moment now one of them would come and claim her.

She moved away into the darkness. Her eyes were blurred, and she did not see the couple until she was within a pace of them. They did not see her. They struggled together in intense silence as if wrestling, the woman trying to claw her way up the man, and he trying to push her down. In irregular flickers, she could see the shadow outlines of their faces, both clenched shut, teeth bared. They did not seem to have removed any clothing, but she knew it was happening in the livid darkness between them. She could not see it but had a violent image of it, the engorged penis, the sucking and flowing and gripping of the vagina. She turned away. She couldn't bear it. It was too strong, too oblivious, a bestial coupling that meant nothing to anything she had any experience of. She was betrayed, but not by them, by life itself, by nature in all its repulsive simplicity.

She went quickly out into the night. She looked up at the ruins of First's building and felt her numbed spirits drift into memories of her attendance there, of the struggle she had endured there. She felt a strange yearning for those hours. She dreamed of moving across the night space, of climbing in the ruins there. When the end of all this came, which for the first time she clearly knew that it would soon, she would go and wait for it in

303

that building. She felt by some strange logic that she belonged in there. It puzzled her to feel this. Waiting in the unreality of the night to return down that long ladder to the sleep she needed, and which dragged at her now, she knew that this was why she was here; to come to an awareness of this place again. It excited her terribly, was the realisation of the excitement she had felt in setting out tonight. Over there was the reality, and over there she would have to go to find it.

She rose, sauntered a little forward and back so as not to draw attention to herself, then she moved across a pool of moonlight into the shadows, and entered the building through a great rent in its side.

First was alive in here somewhere, and she was going to find him and destroy him.

It was dangerous here. The air strike had reduced it to a card-house of leaning walls and fallen floors. She sensed rats, heard scurrying, shifting, scratching noises never loud or close enough to be clearly identified. The moonlight poured in from gaps and fractures, but there was nothing here she recognised, and any ascent to the higher levels was out of the question; whatever destiny she sought for herself here, she did not think it was to be crushed in an ice-floe of shifting masonry. Nevertheless, almost without thinking, she picked her way through the ruins until she was deep within the building, until she realised she would have a hard time of it picking her way back again. She moved on all fours, stretched out, clambering across the fallen concrete, seeking a place to rest, to feel safe, to take stock; but every move required another move; she never seemed to have both hands and both feet in places of security at any one time. The deeper she went, the darker it became. She seemed to be penetrating a cold shadowland that reeked of decay, that dripped and crumbled as she moved through it. She lost track of time.

She was desperately weary and moving almost without thought; but in time she began to be afraid; a sense of something haunting the place found her, and she shuddered. This was a place of death, a place of final sterility. There was no secret here, only oblivion, ugly, meaningless oblivion. She looked for a way out, for a glint of the outside, but the moon had become hidden, perhaps had set; only a faint, ubiquitous glow outlined things vaguely and seemed, not external, but rather the emanation of the place itself, some massive radioactive charge that was penetrating her, activating disgusting cancers within her. I am an old, mad woman, she said to herself, aloud, the sound of her voice frightening her. I am going to die here, she said.

She found at last a sloping shelf of fallen floor upon which she could stop, rest, spread herself out. She had to coil herself to stop herself from slipping down the slope. She was exhausted, wet, filthy and hopeless.

She began then to pray, to activate the words of her old faith. She prayed not for deliverance, but for peace. She confessed her frailties, her sins. She prayed for the souls of her dead. She recalled the moments of her happiness and expressed thanksgiving for them. She prayed for the peace of God and it came to her, drained her of her miseries, calmed her; but even as she received it, she felt that it was a deception, an avoidance of reality, a manifestation only of her weariness and despondency. It was not peace, but surrender. For true peace she had to be moving, to find peace in purpose not in submission.

She struggled herself up, and the slope shifted under her. She felt herself slipping down, had a sudden, awful premonition of falling into terrible wreckage, of the slabs of concrete sliding and crushing her. She clawed and turned, grabbing at an edge of torn steel which bit into her hand. She screamed, ripped the silence with her cry, made the dust shiver with its echoes, the ruin shudder. Then a terrible stillness came. The moment was suspended with her hanging by lacerated hands, her muscles wrenching, with the frailty of her humanity small in a tightening, strangling silence.

Then a light came on above her, a cold light that seemed to catch and freeze her. She heard a footstep, felt a small scatter of dust fall into her hair. Then there was silence.

'Help me,' she said. Then again, 'Help me.'

'Who are you?' said a man's voice, frighteningly close.

'Rachel,' she said. 'Lady Rachel. Help me.'

She heard him stepping down, placing strong, certain feet on the wreckage. She closed her eyes, the shame of her stupidity exposed now. Once again, as last night, she was reduced to a pathetic triviality. She felt his feet astride her, felt him stoop over her, catch her armpits and lift her up. She found herself fact to face once more with Leader First.

'You have found me, Rachel,' he said. 'Welcome.'

I had not expected to survive. The moment of assault was magnificent. My roof fell in a million stars about me. The night rushed in. The glory of destruction rose like a sea. But I was not touched. I had not even fallen to the ground. It was a dream, a fulfilment. I thought for one moment that I had died and that death was just a continuation of life, but that is too much to hope for.

306

I survived, Rachel, because you had survived, because you rose out of the rubble and made your way back to me. I was waiting for you, urgent for you; time was brief. I needed the seal of your affirmation to make it all complete.

CALLED TO ACCOUNT

I wanted you to come to me in triumph. I did not at
first understand the way it happened, did not like to
have to pull you from the wreckage like that. You
came to me defeated, degraded, and it was only later
that I understood that this was necessary. You were
nothing when you came to me, naked and empty. I
had to learn to be like that. It was a hard lesson for me.

He lifted her trembling and gasping from amongst the
rubble, and set her on a solid level, where she sagged
against him. He put his arm like a clamp about her and
bore her to a place at the centre of the ruin where he had
his lair: an office with a bedroom and a bathroom off it,
both doorless, all windowless, patched and hermetic
within the surrounding chaos. A fluorescent tube hung
from wires above her. She sat on a folding chair and
shuddered whilst he boiled water on a small electric ring.
She did not look at him. The room was no warmer than
the ruins outside. It was naked and bare.

He brought her a mug of soup. She clasped it scalding

to her stomach. He sat behind his desk, leant back on his chair and considered her. He was greatly pleased with her, smiled and resettled himself in contemplation of her.

'Did you think I was dead?' he asked her eventually.

'No, Leader,' she said. She had not thought about it at all, either way.

'I am going to die soon,' he said. 'We will all die. They are ruthless, and they cannot be stopped. I admire them. Are you ready to die, Rachel?'

'Yes, Leader.' She was.

'I have often considered calling you to me. We have unfinished business, you and I, but you have done so well down in the bunkers. It was indulgent of me to want you here. Now that you have come of your own accord, however, I cannot tell you how glad I am.'

She lifted the mug to her lips and sipped. The liquid was scalding and searing, gave her pain, brought hurting to her mouth and chest. Her raw hands could not hold the mug and it slipped into her lap, drenching the thick trousers and spreading an effusion of warmth. She watched as the mug rolled off her lap and spun on the floorboards at her feet. He studied her, unaffected by her condition, seeing her not as she was, wretched, hurting, filthy, but as something miraculous.

'May I . . . may I use your latrine, Leader?'

'Of course.'

In his bathroom she sat in the darkness before the doorway that had no door. He moved about in the office, talked quietly on a radio. There was a shower in there, a simple shower head over a steel tray. With thoughtless greed she shed her clothes and stepped on to the tray, turned on the water which was hot and delicious, bringing a flood of warm aching over her whole body. There was a nail brush in the soap tray, and with it she scrubbed herself raw. She cleaned her cut hands scrupulously; the damage was not as much as she had imagined.

In this recovery of herself, she did not consider him, was surprised when he was suddenly standing in the doorway regarding her nakedness with a pleasure that, in anyone else, she would have known to be sexual. She stood under the shower jet and turned from him, but made no attempt to cover herself from his watching. If he wanted to see her, she had nothing to hide from him, nothing physical at least.

She turned off the shower.

'May I have a towel, please, Leader?'

He stepped aside and returned immediately with a large, clean white robe which he reached out for her to take. She wrapped herself in it and stepped out into the office. He stood back to let her past.

'Can you call for someone to take me back?' she said.

'Stay here,' he said.

It was just enough of an offer for her to be able to refuse it; but she saw beyond him the neat little bed with its clean sheets, and she thought of the journey back down. She thought of her women, but remembered them not down in the bunkers, the purposeful sisters, but over there, clambering about like animals, smeared with sex. She submitted, closed her past down again behind her.

'May I . . . may I sleep in that bed?'

'Of course.'

'Are you to share it with me?'

'Oh no.'

She looked at him, at his smiling, round face, at his smug immaculacy, then she turned, stepped into his bedroom, shed the towel and slipped still damp into his delicious sheets. Sleep swallowed her at a gulp.

★ ★ ★

Her nakedness was strange. He had expected to be roused by it, but was not. It seemed so factual. He had imagined the nakedness of a whore, shapely and alluring. He pondered this and came to be glad of the looseness of her flesh about a frame that was stooped, whittled down. His first insight was that she had a body in the same way that he did.

She had no idea how long she had slept, for when she woke everything was quite unchanged. The fluorescent light glared in. He was sitting at his desk. She ached enormously. She writhed in the bed and he turned and looked in, rose and stepped to stand over her. She closed her eyes, waited until he had gone away, then struggled from the bed. She remembered the robe, but it had gone. She looked around for something to cover herself, but could find nothing. There was an open trunk, but in it were only his clothes folded in neat piles.

She knew that he was watching her, so she stood, naked as she was, and walked out past him into the bathroom. She was no longer careless of her nakedness before him, wondered if he was going to keep her naked and shivering here. She sat on his lavatory and opened her bowels noisily and shamefully. Looking up, he was there in the doorway watching her. Not even Ben had watched her like this.

'Please,' she said. 'Please.'

He stayed for a moment, then turned and went. When she had finished, had washed, she went back quickly through the office to the bedroom, an arm across her breasts, a hand over her pudendum. He sat at his desk and did not turn to watch her pass. On her bed was a warm, black dress, underwear, a hairbrush, toothbrush, night-wear. She dressed quickly. It was a long time since she

311

had worn a dress and she was glad to do so again, grateful to him, but suspicious too. She had been given back her surface dignity, but knew that she would have to trade it for something.

When she was ready, she came through and stood beside him, not too close. He was looking at a map, squinting down at it and marking it with a pencil. She could see that he needed glasses. He did not lift his face to her, so she sat on the chair she had sat on last night, straightened herself, knees together, hands in her lap.

At last he looked up, smiled at her.

'There will be food for you soon, Rachel,' he said.

'Thank you, Leader.'

'You slept well?'

'Thank you, Leader.'

He smiled and looked down at the map again.

'How long . . . how long did I sleep?'

He looked up. 'A long time, but that is not important. You are here now. Here, time is nothing, or rather it is merely a closing space, without separations. This map is the only clock. They are within reach of us. I am surprised they have not begun to soften us up with their artillery.'

'Will you . . . surrender, Leader?'

'Oh no.'

'Is there hope for us?'

'None whatsoever, but it is inconceivable for us to surrender. We have no alternative but to fight and to die. Anything less would be a betrayal. No, Rachel, don't look so downcast. We are ready for death. It is our fulfilment. Come now, you understand us well enough for that.'

'Is this . . . was this always a part of your plan, Leader?'

'Was what always a part of our plan?'

'Defeat?'

'Not defeat, no.' He considered this. 'But in some ways I let it happen. We have concentrated ourselves on the perfection of our lives, the power of our community. We have not looked beyond ourselves. And as it unfolded, as it has unfolded, it seemed to me increasingly right that we should face a force that is greater than us, that we should perfect ourselves with death as that force swept down. Only in this way, without compromise, without surrender, will we survive finally. What we have achieved here will outlast us. Those who destroy us will come to understand us. In our necessary death lies our certain resurrection. They slaughter us by the thousand, by the hundred thousand, Rachel, and not one, not one has betrayed the cause, not one has weakened. They have gone to meet death like your women go to meet their lovers down there.'

'I think . . .' she said, the hatred rising like vomit in her throat.

'What, Rachel? What do you think?'

'I think you are mad,' she said quietly.

He laughed quietly, from a distance, made her feel futile again.

'Of course I'm mad, Rachel. I found this fire in my heart when I was a boy. Perhaps all children have it, all boys certainly, but I kept it. I did not allow it to be softened, to be tainted. I kept it pure. I kept myself pure. I nurtured the fire and I let it fill me. It is madness. Of course it's madness. It's the madness of God.' He stared into her, the smile like a blade.

He rose then, went to the door, opened it, and took a tray that was handed to him from outside. She had heard no knock. He brought the tray, on which a plate of rich stew steamed, and placed it on her lap.

313

'Are you not eating?' she asked.

'No. That is for you. I eat little, have no need of food. You however must keep up your strength.'

She thought of resisting the food, but could see no point in that, spooned it into her mouth, wiped her chin with a slab of bread, washed it down with a tumbler of beer. He watched her, waited until she had finished then came, took the tray, handed it through the door.

'Good,' he said. 'Rest now, Rachel. Later I will take you out on to the roof, and we will see if we can see them coming.'

No, no, I am not mad, he thought. I have merely shorn away all the compromises and dishonesties of ordinary life. I am not mad, but real. In the intensity of this reality, men turned away as if afraid. They called him mad because they could not admit that such a one as he could exist.

And he sought her reality too, which is why he wanted her there just as she was, living so close to him that nothing she did could escape him. He loved to watch her sleep, eat, wash, defecate. She was an image of him, a shadow thrown from him, moving as he moved, intensely aware of him in everything. He began to know how beautiful she was, to mark the simple beauty of her being, from which the obviousness of youth and beauty would have been a distraction. He began actively to desire her.

From the roof, a field of broken glass, she could see the extent of the devastation. The day was pale and misty; it could have been any time. He stood beside her and raked the horizon with a pair of binoculars, but she looked only at the shattered buildings, the great pocks the rockets had made in the earth. She tried to work out where they had come up on to the field, tried to find the line of their progress to the place of assignation, but she could not. It could have been any number of places. She tried to imagine the honeycomb of the bunkers below this wreckage, but she could not. The whole landscape was still and deserted. They were perhaps the last people left alive.

'There!' he said at last. 'I can see them. Ha! They're keeping out of range. I will send the Brothers out after dark. It will be better for them to die in the open air, don't you think?'

'Yes,' she said blankly. She had stopped calling him Leader now.

'There are moments, Rachel,' he said, lowering the binoculars and looking at her, 'there are moments when it occurs to me that you may not die here. That you will survive me and bear my testimony to the world.'

'How can I possibly survive?'

'I don't know how. But I feel it is possible. I would like you to survive. I would like you to be my messenger.'

'But I don't believe in you.'

'What do you mean you don't believe in me? Am I a ghost? Are you imagining me?' He took her hand, squeezed it cruelly. 'Don't you believe in this?'

'Oh . . . ' she said, pulling free of him. 'That is always real. Pain is always real. Because you can cause pain proves only that you are as real as a bullet, as real as a piece of falling masonry, as real as a disease. I'll testify to that for you. I don't believe in you as a human being.'

Again the cold laugh, the high smile.

They returned. More food came. She ate. She felt the dragging of tiredness and realised it must be night, or what would have to stand for night. She performed her ablutions and went to bed. He sat poring over his map, his eyes glinting with excitement. Occasionally he talked into his radio, but never so that she could hear what he said. He spent long periods still, sitting in his chair and staring ahead, staring at her if she was there. He did not eat in her sight, nor sleep, nor use his bathroom. She felt that she was supposed to be impressed by this superhumanity, but she was not impressed. It did not seem to her like strength, rather a manic intensity, perverse and masochistic. She had no intention of competing with it.

She slept in indeterminate fragments that eventually began to leave her more tired at their release of her than she had been submitting to them, at which she deduced that it must have been morning. She struggled to rise, saw his black shape turn to her and she subsided again, lay in the sticky sheets, coiled herself up about a dull pain in her belly.

Quite suddenly she was in the midst of a dream. She was sitting in a room she did not recognise. It was an old bedroom, heavily furnished. She sat before a dressing table covered with luxurious perfumes, powders, tinctures. She opened a drawer to see a tumble of delicate, coloured undergarments. There was a box of bright jewellery which she danced upon her fingers. There was someone else in the room, standing by the window, watching her, smiling at her. He had given her all this. She was happy, childish, full-hearted. It was Ben. It was her father. It was First. She rose to run to him and embrace him with her gratitude, at which point she woke abruptly, gasped, struggled from the bed.

He was standing in the doorway, watching her. She felt as if he had witnessed her dream, was about to take his place within it.

316

'I was dreaming,' she said.

'I thought you were.'

'May I . . . go to the bathroom, please?'

She washed and dressed, conscious all the time of his waiting for her. The dream made her feel guilty, as if she had betrayed herself to him. She was afraid of him again. When she was ready, she came and sat before him, settling herself for him. He watched and waited for her to speak.

'Do you think dreams have meanings?' he asked at last.

She thought about this.

'Yes,' she said, 'but I don't think you can understand them, not in words. I think they are messages in a language that only the soul can understand.'

He nodded judiciously.

'Do you dream?' she asked.

'I sleep very little, brief catnaps. I have no time to sleep. But . . . but yes, I do dream. Not often in pictures, more in feelings. I have intense feelings, Rachel. I am interested in dreams. When the will is turned off, perhaps the truth is revealed.'

'Do you never dream about the past?'

'I have no past, Rachel.'

'That is . . . obviously untrue.'

Again the smile.

'You deceive yourself, Leader,' she said, using the title again insolently. 'You had a childhood, parents, friends, maybe even lovers too. What are you ashamed of?'

He considered this, dropped his eyes for a moment, then reached into his desk and, after a moment's rustling, drew out a folder. He opened it, glanced through its pages; then, holding it open, he offered it to her.

It was a sheaf of security reports on a family called Tollman, sad details from lost decades. On the first page

317

was a summary of the reports that followed: Kenneth Tollman, accounts clerk . . . died in a mental institution; Gwen Tollman, wife . . . died of cancer; Paul Tollman, police informant in the Central Region . . . shot; Susan Tollman, later Wilson . . . confined to Area Seven Neutralising Complex, died; Richard Tollman, left home at sixteen . . . no further trace, presumed dead. She flicked through the reports and, within their cold, official language, she caught the images of sad lives lost within the turmoil of the times, of victims of a world inimical to weakness and human pain. It took her a while before the significance of this file became clear to her.

'I had that compiled many years ago. I have never shown it to anyone.'

'Richard Tollman. That's your name?'

'No. I am Leader First. Richard Tollman was what those pathetic people chose to call me. I was not their child. That they bore me and nurtured me after a fashion for the first few years of my life, is incidental. I was not theirs. I knew this as soon as I knew anything. They hated me soon, and they were right to. I took as little from them as I could, and left as soon as I was certain of not being dragged back. There, Rachel. It is no mystery. I have no shame. As for friends, Anthony Standing is the only man I have called friend, and he is dead. As for lovers, no: none; never.'

'I pity you.'

'That is because you do not understand. I am more than human, not less. Sexuality, as even your Christian teachers knew, is a dilution of human strength and purity. It is a biological necessity, and around that necessity whole structures of debilitating fantasy have been constructed. I am above that necessity; it is the essence of my higher nature. I pity you, Rachel, I pity all of you in

318

your sexual pleasures because they have weakened you, made you a prey to dreams and hopes and illusions.'

'They are what keep us alive,' she said.

'Only half-alive, Rachel, only half-alive.'

She could no longer look at him. She dropped her face and felt the weight of herself pushing her down, felt the weight of his watching pushing her down, down below the surface where she could not breathe. She rose stooped under the weight and went without looking back into the bedroom, curled herself down on the bed, covered her face.

He did not rise immediately. Perhaps she slept for a moment. She came awake to hear him coming to the doorway, coming in and standing over her. She could hear his breathing, the creak of his shoes, a cracking of the joints in his fingers. In the darkness in which she had buried herself, an image of his masculinity came swimming into her mind, the parts of him she had activated with her fantasy once, when he had thrown her down and she had risen up, had made him for one moment real. She dreamed of doing that again, but she knew that if she opened her eyes, if she turned to him, the dream would be gone.

'Rachel,' he said, kindly, chiding her.

'Leave me alone.'

'Come on, Rachel. Don't give up now.' He knelt down by her, touched her side, the hard, exploring touch he had bestowed upon her before. 'You're so strange,' he said. 'You're like an animal, a frightened animal, brought in from the wild. I would like to open the cage and let you free. I would like to watch you running out through a meadow. Come on now. What would you like? Tell me. Tell me about your dreams.'

'Leave me alone. Please leave me alone. I want to . . . to pray.'

319

'To pray? Let me hear you pray, Rachel. What will you pray for?'

'For you.'

He laughed. A distant booming came, and the room shuddered.

'There's the voice of God,' he said.

She heard him rise and move away. She turned and opened her eyes, dragged herself off the bed, to the doorway, leant against the frame. The booming came again, closer. The sounds of splintering, smashing, conflagration, began to gather around them. He stood with his back to her, his head lifted as if he was interpreting the sounds, tuning himself to them.

'I'm afraid,' she said.

'Don't be afraid.'

'I want to be afraid.'

'You are weak.'

'Yes. Will you comfort me?'

He turned, curious, smiling.

'How can I comfort you, Rachel?'

'By holding me as I tremble. By feeling the fear in me. If you are really strong, you will do that.'

'Would you like me to give you something? To make it painless for you?'

'Why can't you understand? Why? For God's sake, it is so simple, so basic. If you are really a God, if you really are a man, you would understand. I don't want to die. I don't want to die. I want to be alive and I want you to know that I am alive, to be glad that I am alive. Is that so strange to you? In God's name, why is it so strange?'

At that moment, his God exploded very close. The whole mass of the building shifted, and the light went out. Rachel shrieked and found herself on the floor. She had struck her head, but she did not remember doing it, felt now only the lump of pain swelling at her temple and a continuous pounding that might have come from within or without.

'Help!' she yelled. 'Help me!'

She felt him lift her. He was strong and solid, as monumental as he had ever been. She needed his protection, needed his strength, for she needed someone, anyone, to cling on to; in the darkness he had become abstract. She clung to him, shuddering and gasping and clawing. He held her tightly, gripped her until she went still, then bore her through the darkness.

Suddenly she remembered what he was. He's going to kill me, she thought, waiting for it, the knife, the bullet, the lethal needle, the grip on her throat.

'Please. Please, don't kill me. Please . . .'

'Sssh.'

She felt herself being lowered. Her feet met the floor but sank under her.

'Be strong, Rachel.'

He lowered her back, and she found the bed behind her. He laid her out on the bed, straightened her legs and arms. She could hear him moving, purposeful about her, preparing her. The building vibrated and crackled.

She had wanted to die so often. There had been so many cancellations of her life that she had believed she had no meaning, that nothing mattered, that whatever was done to her would be of no significance. She had deceived herself. Now, in this place, at the hands of this man, she did not want to die. Her heart beat enormously within her. Her senses strained into the darkness. Her fear made her enormous, real in a way that she had never been before; no, not even when Catton's men were raping her daughter. She was nothing now, but she was still alive. Her life was all she had; it was the simple brute fact of her, after everything else had gone. She was more alive than he was, than he would ever be. There had to be some way, some way, in which she could assert her life against his death. The impossibility of this filled her with anger; her weakness now seemed a betrayal of life. Death and brutality and psychotic cruelty were more than she was, and it was an injustice at the heart of life, at the whole way the universe was made. She rose in her mind, and demanded of God why he had made it thus.

'Rachel?' The voice was soft, pressed on her face like fungus. 'Rachel? Pull up your skirt for me, Rachel. Quickly now.'

'Oh no,' she said. 'Oh no. Not that.'

'Do what I tell you, Rachel.'

'Kill me then.'

'You are going to live, Rachel.'

She wept, opened her mouth and let the sobbing out in great pulses.

'Have you done what I told you? Are you ready for me?'

It was death, one way or another; what did it matter? She gave in, pulled up her skirt, ripped the underpants and threw them aside, splayed her legs until they hurt, cried dumb, brutal tears.

She had no idea where he was. The voice had come from all around her as if from loudspeakers. When suddenly his hands gripped her thighs, a shock of reality went through her. She threw back her hands lest they should come into contact with him.

'You must bear my son,' he said, and as he did so began to prod himself at her, trying to find his way in, as incompetent as a masturbating boy.

She was not afraid any more, even though the guns

were close, even though what might have been voices, cries, footsteps could be heard close to their darkness. She was enormously weary, had come down now to a level she could comprehend. She could no more conceive his child than she could spontaneously will herself to explode; but that was not what this was about at all. He thought he was a god, but he was just another sad old pervert after all.

'This is absurd,' she said, reaching down and directing his penis, wincing as he wrenched into her and began to bump at her, grunting and growling. She lay inert and wanted only for it to be over; it was sordid and uncomfortable, but meaningless.

In her detachment, then, she began to have a physical awareness of him that was strange, quite different from her memory of him. She tried to connect the memory with the presence upon her and within her, but she could not. She could smell him, a dark, smoky reek of hardened sweat, human and simple. She became curious. She ran her hands over his head, the balding skull, the greased hair. She reached down and touched the loose meat of his buttocks. She had a clearer image of him now than she had ever had before.

He was beginning to pant with impotent violence. He had been gripping the sides of the bed, but now he put his hands on her shoulders, gripped tightly, painfully. She writhed and complained.

'Stop,' she said. Stop.'

He stopped, lay still upon her, gasping and helpless.

'Why are you resisting me?'

'This is stupid,' she said.

'Degenerate whore,' he said.

'That's no good,' she said, simply irritated at his simple inability to bring this off.

'Tell me,' he said.

'What?'

'Tell me what I must do.'

'I don't know . . . you have to believe in me. You have to . . . to give me something . . .'

'What? Tell me. What is it?'

'Kiss me.'

It was a dirty kiss, wet-mouthed, stale-breathed, and she shuddered, but then with resignation accepted it, opened her mouth to his, held his head, moistened her lips on his, softened and moved him with her tongue. He trembled within her and made something smile there. As I am, she thought, he is. There is no difference between us. There is nothing more for either of us but this moment, this tension between us. And the tension began to move, to melt, to become active.

He began to groan and roar deep in his throat, and outside, his roaring was taken up by the sound of tearing and smashing, the spasmodic surges of his loins by bursts of light that penetrated the darkness; and she opened her body at last for him, put her arms and legs about him, tucked him within her embrace, her body undulating in fluent waves of contraction and release. At times, a cold blast of awareness of what she was doing caught her, and she shuddered and churned with disgust, but behind this rose a swell of triumph. He twisted and jerked but she had the power now, held him tightly, translated every catch of his body into the process of their copulation; and in her consumption of him she was at last released, drifting back into her dream, wilfully, full of tenderness and gratitude for the man, whoever he was, whose head she clasped to her shoulder, bathing him in her tears, about whom she had locked her tired limbs, whom she welcomed within her dry, broken body at last, gladly,

gladly. The peace of God, of her God, came flooding through her.

It was not as he had imagined it at all. He had expected a triumph, a moment of exquisite physical pleasure. The circumstance was matchless. They had come to the point at last. When he had come to her, he had felt then a tenderness, a joy at her weakness, but also an impotence. At that moment he wanted to do something for her, anything she wanted. He wanted to give her life, set her free, release her.

Had she really thought he would kill her? Perhaps he might have killed her, but only if he had believed it to be an act of love. He wanted to perform an act of love with her. He understood then with urgent simplicity what had happened between Anthony and Muriel, and he forgave them with all his heart, admired them, envied them, imagined them in the pride of their lovemaking.

He lay down with her in the darkness, with the roar of destruction closing about them like a noose. It ought to have been perfect. He would give her his son to bear. Yes. That was the purpose. Everything was in place. Why then could he not translate his purpose into fulfilment? Why did he fail himself at that moment?

A nausea filled him. They were two old corpses copulating in a filthy ruin. When he pressed his body upon hers, when she took him into her, he felt loathsome. He knew his body so well, knew every motion of its physical desires and weaknesses. Why, when he applied himself to her, did he lose that sense of himself? What had she done to him? She had made him like this.

He set himself and concentrated entirely upon the gathering of semen within him. There was nothing else, only the push and push to bring that out. He did not think

325

he would manage it. His heart strove within him. He was clambering up a precipice, his body numb, losing grip. Every fraction of his strength was drawn in to that achievement, fighting against that fall.

And when he thought that he was going to fail, the anger rushed back into him. It was her fault. He wanted to hurt her then, to tear her open in his failure. This brought her into his cognisance again. He felt her touch upon him, her moving under him, steady, certain. She was at peace there: for all his fury and impotence, she was at peace. He could not understand it. It is weakness, he thought, it is degeneracy; she is enjoying this degradation; I have been right about women; but these thoughts came from an increasing distance. He felt the grip of her fingers in his flesh, the lifting of her belly, the kneading of her thighs. All his judgement was suspended. He felt himself fall, collapse, sink down into his awareness of her, let his weariness take possession of him, let her take possession of him; and as he did so, he realised that he was going to be successful. And when his ejaculation was achieved, he did not feel it as his. It seemed as if he had acquired her physical awareness, as if, as it happened, it was not part of him at all, but of her. It flooded from him, drawn from every part of him, from every organ, every secretion, every essence of himself, flooding into her. She had opened a valve within him, and he drained from it in a strong pulse that was not his pulse, was her pulse. She possessed and consumed him utterly. There must have been noise, terrible noise, all about them at that moment, but he lay in an absolute silence; and then oblivion, slipping away into nothing. There was nothing more to be done.

EPILOGUE

A man and a woman were engaged in the act of love. About them the world was ending in a tempest of violence; perhaps not everyone's world, but their world certainly; the world in which they had their meaning.

He made this world. He imposed himself upon it from a dark beginning until he brought everything within it into alignment with his own fantasy. He was a madman who made everything, everyone, conform to his insanity.

She was a subject of this world, a victim, therefore his victim, therefore the subject of his fantasies.

What was happening between them was not, therefore, an act of love in the literal sense, for he had imposed it upon her, not just at the moment he physically possessed her, but in the whole circumstance of her being with him, of her being who she was; she had no active part in it at all: neither, strictly, was it a rape, for she had been the subject of this man's fantasy for so long that she had no real independence of it, no will nor individuality to oppose him. It was the exercise of a monstrous egotism upon a blank receptacle of that egotism. It was the most dismal of human engagements imaginable: the act of love reduced not merely to a casual, violent release of over-charged masculinity, but to a final flourishing justi-fication for a generation of cruelty and murder, of masculine power enshrined as a final truth, of a lifelong love-affair with death.

Within her, as she received him, however, she found a last final strength to resist him. She did so by love, by accepting, in spite of everything, what he did to her as an act of love, and by communicating this to him.

The moment he became her lover, he was destroyed.

When he roused, they were there. He thought they would kill him at once, but they did not. He had little recollection of those moments. They dragged him out and struck him, but that was unimportant. He tried to ask where she was, but they did not answer, did not seem to understand what he said; at which he knew that she had escaped them. He laughed as they struck him. There was nothing that they could have done to him now. He had escaped them too, safe in the warm, receiving peace of her womb.

They have told me you are dead, Rachel, but I do not believe them. I can sense your life out there some-where, beating as strongly as ever. They are incapable of any kind of truth.

So. They have me here in a tiny white cell, airless,

windowless, just what I like. I refuse to answer their questions, refuse to enter into any dialogue with them at all. They have given me paper and pens. I know they will read what I write, cannot imagine that they will ever give this to you, but I know you are alive somewhere, and so I send this to you. I no longer care what obscene satisfactions they take from my words. You are out there somewhere, and I call to you. In the name of my son whom you bear in your womb, I call to you. I hope they have not been too cruel with you, and I hope when they read this, they will not ply you with further cruelty, but we are a long way beyond personal pain and personal hopes. I hope only that you can accept this as clearly as I do.

It surprises me still to be alive. They are obviously saving my hour of suffering for some grand occasion. I look forward to it keenly. Perhaps they are planning something especially macabre and protracted. I will welcome it. They have nothing with which to frighten me. Their inflictions will be my apotheosis. They are dwarves, cripples.

I am sorry that I came to the pleasure of women so late, but only when there was nothing else to be done was there time for it. It was the right thing to be doing at the last moment of my power. I feel as if I had saved it up for that moment, that it was a final flourish, a final assertion of my strength. I am grateful, very grateful, Rachel, for your offering of yourself to me. I knew, I always knew that you understood me and sympathised with me far more than you were ever able to admit to yourself, that you strove to find a way to bring what you had to offer to me. Your nobility and

331

integrity were perfect. If all women had been as you are, then we would have had no problem with women at all.

Guard our child with all your strength. Tend it and love it and tell it of its birthright. I have the image of you suckling our child. You are young again, a strong young woman with fine, full breasts, and I am the child who suckles, for I will be born again. You know that I will.

I am well and happy. Everything is as it should be. The destiny is working itself out. If they would give me just one thing that I wanted, which of course they would never do, it would be to see you again, to take you in my arms again, to comfort you and reassure you. I have come to love you, Rachel. You know that. I am proud of this. Be strong and free for me always.

They have stopped coming to see me. I am confined to solitude. They have taken the hint from my last letter to you, I expect. Perhaps I should write here the opposite of what I want so that they will, by counter-suggestion, dance to my bidding; but I will not use these precious pages, with the precious image of you before me, always before me, to construct a subterfuge. I have never lied, and will not do so.

I am truly glad to be left alone. There is a hatch in the door through which I am given a bowl of food in exchange for a pot of my exrement. They keep the light on constantly and, I am sure, watch me. Perhaps I am fascinating to them, like some alien creature, the monster First. I would like that. I expect, rather, there is someone racked with tedium, watching me hour after hour. I spend most of the time lying on my mattress in the quiet strength of my thoughts.

I have a large enough supply of paper to write you letter after letter. I will write more often. It is too long since my last. My mind is so full of things that I have to say, as it always was, that I will unburden myself to you, tell you everything, explain the truth with which I have been so prodigiously gifted, so that you will have it to pass on to my son.

I think you must be near the moment of birth now. I have no concern with time, but I feel that you are near that moment. I do not want to see you any more. This is not because my love for you is in any way diminished. The reverse is true. I want your freedom, and for them to bring you here, for you to come to me under their sufference, would be to tarnish your freedom. It would be sad to see you again. I have the memory of you strong and free, and I must not let anything soil that memory.

You must be absolutely free. You are alive in a clear space, with trees and fields near you, a humble place. You will have found a good man to look after you. When you give birth, you will be visited secretly by those of my brothers who have eluded their butcheries. They are not clever enough to have done more than deface the surface of the movement. You will bear my son, and you will be honoured for it.

I can hear them coming down the corridor. I assume they come at set times, but I have no watch. When they come, I always imagine that they will not just rattle at the hatch but will open the door, will have come for me at last, my executioners. I wait for that moment intently. The hope of it is the focus of my days now. I lie on my mattress and hear them coming, and my whole being gathers within me. All my energies muster and urge forwards to that moment. I tremble, and my eyes fill with tears. And after they have gone, I weep. My heart thunders within me. There are moments of loneliness then.

Perhaps they will leave me here forever. Perhaps they do not watch me. Perhaps I am really alone, forever. Perhaps I will be left to die. Perhaps they have understood my power. Perhaps they know that to kill me, to have any contact with me, will reach them in some way, will subject them to me. If that is the case, perhaps I have underestimated them.

The truth I share with you, Rachel, is eternal. Believe in me now as you did then, as I came to believe in you.

How long is it since I last wrote? It may only have been a few days. It feels like eternity. I dream of you constantly. Sometimes I even believe that you are here with me. I think that if I could truly submit myself to my imagination, if I could truly believe that you were here, you would be here, I could make you real. But I am cluttered with my flesh. It is becoming tedious and burdensome to me.

I am old and limp. I am foul. They have left me here to rot. My turds are black and my urine is milky, and it is a discomfort to pass either. It is not pain. Pain would be clean and clear. When I stoop over the receptacle, I do not feel I belong to myself any more. I feel as if clumsy instruments are hooked into me to draw my excrements out of me. I have lost all my hair, even the facial hair which I have been forced to grow comes out in handfuls. I do not see well. I have to peer down at the page now to know what I am writing. I live in a knot of tedious discomforts. There is a chafing sore on the inside of my thigh, red and open and spreading. Something comes in the night and sucks at me.

I long for you, Rachel, dream of you, but my body is clogged and awkward, will not let me go, will not let me be pure any more, physically pure. If I could be pure, I could bring you to life here. My mind is clear, a hard jewel, certain and indestructible, but my body betrays me, my clarity is a tightening knot within me.

Oh, I have so much to tell you, Rachel, and so little time. I lie on my mattress and the words swirl about my head. I find it difficult to come here and write. Often I have tried, but I cannot seem to stop the swirling. The words will not stay still long enough for me to fix them. They blur and dissolve, the words and the ideas. But I must do it. You must know.

Time is trickling out of me now. It is as if I have a leak that I cannot staunch. I am bleeding invisibly, internally perhaps. The vital force of me drains away day by day, hour by hour, moment by moment. Perhaps I have been here for years, perhaps I am now very old.

The food still appears, but I no longer hear them approaching. Perhaps they have carpeted the corridor to muffle their footsteps. Perhaps I am deaf. I live in a world of noise, of crackling and creaking, gurgling and scratching, but it might only be the noises of my own decay.

I try to remember what it was like. People and places were never important to me. I am a god. I am the source of all power, of all truth. Gods do not remember what was done, they only remember the burning of the emotions generated by what was done, the twisting pettiness of failure, the triumph of victory and fulfilment. I try to remember, to live all that again. At times I can still do it, at times I rise up as I was, as I am at the heart of me, under all the corruption to which they have condemned me. I am undefeatable still, to the last breath.

Oh, Rachel, Rachel. I have forgotten what you look like. I imagine you, but each time it is different, you are someone else. Sometimes you are male, sometimes female. Sometimes you are old, as old as I am, sometimes you are a child. Sometimes you are me as I was once, a long time ago, before I came here, before I knew who I was and set out on the destiny that brought me here. It is strange to imagine that, strange to imagine that there was a time, there might have been a time, when all this was not inevitable. I long for that time at the moments of my greatest weakness. It disgusts me that I should lapse into that. I become angry. I tremble and foam comes to my lips. My body shakes and strains. I want to shake it off, to be released into my truth again, but they have shut me off from myself here.

I am old now, Rachel. I am old. I am going to die soon. I never knew that it would be so dark. I never knew the darkness would be so big. I realise at last that I do not want to die. I am not afraid of death, but I do not want to die alone here. The darkness is rising like a tide about me. I made my religion out of my immaculacy, my solitude, life held tight until the moment of extinction, a bright burst of struggle, then nothing, and all was in that last bright burst, beyond which nothing mattered. They have cheated me of my death, have condemned me to this sick, slow smothering in my own mortality. I wanted at the last to be able to gather myself together and plunge into death, but I am old, have no strength for that. If only there was pain. I do not want to be old, Rachel, I do not want to die here.

I knew today that you were dead. It suddenly came to me, like the bandage taken off an amputation. I can't bear that. I can't bear it that my dreams of you, the hours and hours I have talked to you, written to you, lived with the warmth of you here, the only companion of my darkness, I can't bear it that all of that

337

was a lie. There is nothing now. Nothing. Nothing. I can think of nothing, imagine nothing. There is only the slow, sticky suck of my pulse, the gurgling of the breath that bubbles through the phlegm, the tightening of the knots of shrivelled bowel within me. I am afraid now. My fear keeps me alive, clutching at the last shudders of life within me. My life is disgusting. I do not eat. I do not see or hear. I lie in a blur of noise, rotting. I am a corpse, but I am not dead. I cannot die. I do not want to die. I am afraid to die. I wallow in my own corruption because only that is left to me.

I remember

I remember nothing. I

I remember a woman. It was dark. She was afraid. I comforted her.

I remember a woman. It was dark. I was afraid. She comforted me. She held me in her arms. She let me

I had done terrible things. I do not know what they were. She forgave me. You must find her. She will tell you. She will tell you that I am forgiven. When she held me, when she let me do that to her, it was forgiveness. She might have killed me. I deserved to be killed, but she took me into her. I crawled up into her and hid there, and she saved me. You must find her. You must bring her to me. There is not much time.

Who am I? What have I done? Why am I permitted to suffer in this way? I am a man, surely that. There was a woman once whom I loved, who took me in her arms, who took me into her body. In the name of that I am a man. What have I done that you have no mercy? Tell me who I am? Am I not, at least, to be forgiven?